Tale of the Fox

Loren S. Olsen

L.S. OLSEN

ISBN: 979-8-218-51133-3

First Edition

Cover design by Loren S. Olsen

lorensolsen.com

TABLE OF CONTENTS

N
E
S
W
Daiony Kingdom
Sanoul
Bamnai Forest
Hansu Region
Itson Region
Temyul
River
Nagaseo
Asandeo
Hot Springs
Pangul
Pit of
Keshin
Yento
Juhto

GLOSSARY

Asandeo Springs (ah-saun-day-oh): Natural hot springs in the Daion Kingdom

Bamnai Forest (bam-nye): A forest housing the Daion Kingdom

Divine Tails: A cult of humans who worship the Fox Demons

Fox Demons: Gumiho-inspired creatures that can call down lightning (red lightning) and can shapeshift into humans once they have obtained one thousand human souls

Fox Dens: The homes of the Fox Demons, scattered throughout the Bamnai Forest

Hansu (han-sue): Northeast region of Bamnai Forest

Heavenly Fox: Khana, the matriarch of the Fox Demons who resides in Sanoul

Hoji (ho-jee): Saint of the Fox Trappers

Inyeo-kan (in-yea-oh-con): A traditional Daion festival that translates to 'gift of kin'. Families gather to put together boxes of keepsakes that they then bury outside the village for future prosperity to find. It tells the story of a family, often holding portraits, personal items, or tools from their work

Itson (**it-sun**): Western region of the Bamnai Forest

Ji'sori (**jee-soar-e**): A rice-based beverage

Juhto (**ju-toe**): A village in the southeastern part of the Daion Kingdom where one of the Forsaken Sisters Guild is

Kimchi Stew: A stew made with fermented napa cabbage, green onions, tofu, pork belly, an anchovy broth, and spices served on a bed of rice

Kumisune (**coo-me-soon**): A Fox Demon that has collected one thousand human souls and has achieved their nine-tails. They are then able to shapeshift between their two forms

Mugunghwa Blossom: A pink and white flower

Nagaseo (**na-ga-say-oh**): Tetsu's home village in the eastern part of the Bamnai Forest

Pangul (**pan-ghoul**): A village in the southeastern part of the Daion Kingdom where Nari's first raid occurs

Pit of Keshin (**keh-shin**): An ancient sinkhole near Juhto where the Divine Tails hold prisoners and make sacrifices to the Heavenly Fox

Salaisna (**sal-aiz-nuh**): A traditional Daion festival that translates to 'day of the living dead'. The spirits of ancestors are said to return to walk the earth and the living gather for a festival. They often light lanterns with messages of hope and wishes

Sanoul (**saw-newl**): The Imperial City and home to the Heavenly Fox

Skulk (**s-kull-k**): A group of foxes

Temyul River (**tem-yewl**): The largest river in the kingdom that is just outside of Juhto

Wensi (**when-shee**): Daion currency

Yento (**yen-toe**): A village in the southwestern part of the Daion Kingdom where the Fox Trappers' camp is set up

Zither: String instruments

CHARACTER GUIDE

Mukami (moo-caw-me): The Silver Fox who stole lightning from the Dragons, Khana's mother

Suto (sue-toe): Mukami's mate and the tod that sired Khana

Nataru (nah-tah-rue): The Storm Dragon, wields lightning

Toshi (tosh-he): The Rain Dragon

Nari (nar-e): A Fox Demon turned human

Tetsu (tet-sue): A Fox Trapper

Chul: A member of Sook's skulk and Nari's Den brother

Sook (sue-k): Leader of Nari's skulk

Bojin (bo-gin): A member of the Divine Tails who works with Sook

Khana (caw-nuh): The Heavenly Fox

Yona: Tetsu's mother

Dal (doll): Tetsu's father

Iseul: Member of the Forsaken Sisters Guild in Juhto

Eun: Leader of the Forsaken Sisters Guild in Juhto

Kyung: Leader of the Fox Trappers

Ranmi (ron-me): Second-in-command of the Fox Trappers

Shik & Yul: Gather intel on the demons for the trappers
Sunhi (sun-hee): One of the benefactors of the Fox Trappers
Tamra: One of the benefactors of the Fox Trappers
Haku: One of the benefactors of the Fox Trappers
Zuma: Messenger for the Heavenly Fox

THE DRAGON'S CURSE

The Realm of Ethereal Light

MUKAMI THE SILVER FOX had always found beauty in destruction.

One such destructive force that the Dragons of the realm commanded was lightning. As a young kit, Mukami had watched as the Dragons danced among the copper clouds and azure heavens, their scales gleaming with light. Some conjured rain, others controlled the wind, and more kept the realm bright and beautiful. The foxes were resigned to a life in the Darkwoods, walking amongst the mortals who made their pilgrimages to the realm. With their sly smiles and ability to reap a soul with a single touch, the mortals feared the foxes and paid their devotion to the Dragons. Such was the Dragons' intent, even if the mortals didn't know that.

Mukami stood on the edge of a cliff, her paws set firmly on the ground. Nataru, the Storm Dragon, flowed across the sky. Her silver scales reflected the waning light as the sun descended beyond the horizon. It was like she was covered with a thousand tiny mirrors, as one mortal had sung about in an ode to the Dragon. Nataru huffed, her large nostrils flaring as steam escaped. The smooth scales on her chest began to glow as lightning sparked around her body. Dark clouds settled around her, growing dense as the lightning snaked its way through the clouds.

A raindrop struck Mukami's nose and a gust of wind pushed her from behind. She let out a startled cry as she tumbled over the edge of the cliff and sank her claws into the moss that covered its surface. The moss was not strong and the Silver Fox glared as Toshi, the Rain Dragon, flew overhead. His bright blue eyes beamed with joy and she pawed at one of his whiskers. Toshi turned his head sharply, his twisted white horns nearly knocking her from the cliffside. He simply laughed as he launched himself higher into the sky to fly next to Nataru.

Mukami slipped but another pair of paws clamped down on hers and heaved her up. She looked up at her mate, Suto, with a grateful smile once she was on solid ground again. He nuzzled her cheek and they sat side-by-side, their haunches touching as they glowered at the Dragons. While all other creatures of the realm roamed freely, the Dragons had a strict rule to stay airborne unless they were atop Mount Besu where their lair was. For if the foxes touched them, they could reap their souls and a soul like a Dragon's was much too powerful for one fox to bear. Or so they had been told.

"Is everyone ready?" Mukami asked as she scratched behind her ear.

Suto nodded. "The catapult we've acquired from the mortal realm is near the Den, hidden beneath the forest canopy. Once the Dragons see it, they'll know they're under attack."

"We only need to take down one Dragon," Mukami reminded him and set her sights on Nataru.

The foxes were going to steal her lightning.

Nataru's egg was covered with bright blue scales and had hints of white light shifting within. The foxes had taken the runt of her recent lay since it was small enough for them to carry and roll off of Mount Besu. Mukami pawed at the egg, nudging it across the moss-covered forest floor and toward the catapult. The plan was simple—rest the egg in the bucket and roll it out into an open meadow where the Dragons could see it. Once Nataru caught sight of her egg in danger, she was sure to come close enough for the foxes to touch her. One touch was all they needed to reap her soul and steal her lightning.

Suto lay near the entrance of the Den, grooming their only surviving kit, Khana. She was a beautiful vixen with alabaster fur and bore the markings of being the next Heavenly Fox—an honorary spiritual leader among the foxes. But still, it was difficult sometimes for Mukami to look at her. Two months ago, she had been out and about in the Darkwoods with her three kits, teaching them how to scavenge for berries and earthworms and hunt for voles. A storm had rolled in unexpectedly and Mukami thought that they would be safer waiting it out in a hollowed-out tree. The rain poured and thunder rumbled. Mukami had tucked her kits close and kept them fed. She had even dozed off for a few minutes but that was all cruel fate needed. A family of voles scampered by and the kits, eager to test their newfound hunting skills, wiggled their way free of Mukami's embrace. She had stirred to find them gone and could smell the stark energy in the air just before lightning struck a nearby tree. Its trunk split in two, spraying sharp shards of wood all around them. The kits' frightened howls still haunted her memory as the tree came down on all three. Mukami had to watch Aecha, Khana, and Jiho be crushed by the tree.

Only Khana had survived, albeit with two broken legs that were still healing. Mukami's jaw clenched tight and she growled deep in her throat. Nataru had flown right over them and Mukami had met her eye. She knew what had happened and didn't even care. Taking one egg wouldn't bring back Aecha and Jiho, Mukami knew, but Nataru deserved to see what it felt like to lose one she so loved.

Mukami straightened, her chest burning with hatred and rage as she barked to the surrounding foxes, "It's time! Bring the catapult to Shiwa Meadow."

The foxes, with the help of some mortals who had wide, shining eyes and a strange obsession with the foxes and death, rolled the catapult through the Darkwoods and to Shiwa Meadow. It was in Nataru's daily flight path and the mortals cranked the bucket back so it would be ready to set off. Mukami and Suto sat near the restraining rope as Khana wiggled on her back in a patch of dirt nearby. Her hindlegs were a tad crooked and she now walked with a slight limp but she was a lively kit.

Khana rolled onto her feet and strayed a bit further into the meadow, toward a patch of wildflowers. She plucked a dandelion with her teeth and brought it to Mukami, dropping the flower at her feet. "For you, Mama," Khana said with a gleeful smile. Mukami bowed her head slightly in recognition and picked the flower up between her teeth. She tucked it into the tuft of her chest and nuzzled Khana's forehead.

"Thank you, my light."

Her kit gleamed with the praise and ran off to collect more wildflowers. Mukami tilted her head back, her eyes narrowing as she searched the sky and waited for Nataru to appear. Suto stood next to her, quiet as well. It took an hour for Nataru to appear, her movement in the sky causing a slight breeze to rustle across the meadow. Her large, silver eyes scanned the area before she caught sight of the catapult in the meadow. The Dragon huffed and circled above, dropping slightly so she could speak with the foxes.

"What is the meaning of this?"

"Come down and I will explain," Mukami stated with a sly smile.

Nataru looked at the egg, squinting her large eye to see it better. The foxes waited patiently for the Dragon to make her decision—whether she would risk her life for her kin or not. Nataru dropped a little lower but did not land in the meadow. She hovered just above them, her serpentine body twisting as she circled above.

"How did you obtain my egg?" Nataru asked with a slight growl in her voice.

Mukami ignored the question and instead asked her own, "Do you remember what happened in the Darkwoods two months ago? When your lightning struck a tree that crushed my kits?"

Steam emerged from the Dragon's nostrils and her whiskers twitched. "It was an unfortunate event."

Mukami blinked, her lip curling back as hackles rose along her spine. She stepped closer to the restraining rope and settled a paw on the hook it was connected to. All she had to do was slip it free and the egg would launch into the Darkwoods.

Nataru dipped her head down. "What are you doing?"

"What does it look like?" Mukami retorted. "You took away two of my kits so I figured that it would only be fair if you lost one of yours."

The Dragon stared for a long moment, indecision making her brow wrinkle. Mukami knew what the eggs meant to the Dragons, as any kin meant to any parent. But for the Dragons, they only had one clutch in their lifetimes and each egg assured their continual reign of the realm. One egg, especially a runt, wasn't much but it was enough for Nataru to close her eyes, shake her head, and land in the meadow. Silence befell the foxes and the mortals as the ground rumbled at the impact. The Dragon snarled and reached forward to scoop the egg against her chest. Mukami released the rope before she could and leaped forward as Nataru stumbled in surprise. The foxes moved, swarming the Dragon as they all set their paws on her. Nataru let out a roar that nearly shattered their eardrums but Mukami laid her ears back and watched as the soul streamed from the Dragon's scales. It was pure light, warm and bright, that wrapped around Mukami and the other foxes like a dance. Nataru shuddered, her eyes flickering as her scales grew dark and the egg rolled beneath her back. The Dragon crushed it as she fell and sparks of lightning erupted from her body, striking each of the foxes in turn. Mukami was thrown halfway across the meadow, her body twitching as the electric charge zipped through her. She saw Khana hiding in the shrubs, safe but terrified.

Mukami's gaze drifted to find Suto lying flat on his back, all four paws in the air. Smoke wafted from his pure white fur and he blinked slowly, limbs twitching. Nataru growled as she lay on the ground, her body now curled around the crushed egg and the dead hatchling. A bitter laugh rumbled from Mukami's chest and it quickly turned into a hacking cough. She gasped for breath as she staggered to her feet. Her whole body burned with the immense power of light and energy within her now. Dark clouds gathered above as Nataru heaved her last few breaths. Mukami closed her eyes and lifted a paw toward the sky, trying to connect with the Dragon magic that flowed through her veins.

"Mama?" came Khana's small, frightened voice.

Mukami glanced down at her kit. Khana's eyes were wide, her ears flat and her tail tucked between her hind legs. She dipped her head down and nuzzled Khana's cheek. "It's okay, my light."

Khana looked at Nataru and her hatchling, her small body trembling slightly. "Are they...dead, Mama?"

"Yes, but they deserved it. Nataru took away Aecha and Jiho. The Dragons have mistreated us for centuries and they have underestimated the strength of our will to be free, to make a home for ourselves."

"But...we are home."

Mukami shook her head. "The Darkwoods are our prison, Khana, remember that. Now we have the power to change our fates."

A Dragon cry filled the air, so sharp and terrible it may as well have ruptured their eardrums. Mukami looked up and saw Toshi flying overhead. Rain splattered his scales and began to fall heavily as he circled Shiwa Meadow.

"How dare you!" He roared. "How dare you steal Nataru's soul! You spineless thieves lack honor."

Toshi let out another screech and this time, the ground trembled. The Dragons not only could control the elements and weather, but they could also cast judgment. They had created the Realm of Ethereal Light and the Realm of Eternal Darkness. The rain pounded Mukami's face and she scooped Khana close to her chest, bending her body over her kit to protect her. The ground continued to rock until it started to break open. Mukami gasped and grabbed Khana by the scruff of her neck. She ran from Shiwa Meadow and further into the Darkwoods, leaping through moss overhangings and over unruly roots. Khana whimpered softly and then let out a terrified howl as Toshi's rage caught up to them.

The Darkwoods disappeared as Mukami and Khana fell from the Realm of Ethereal Light to the Eternal Darkness.

A FIRE IS BORN

Seventeen Years Ago

SOOK CARRIED THE TINY, fiery orange kit into the Den, scooting across the dirt on her belly. Chul, one of the tods who was born last year, came to her side. He was curious but loyal and Sook knew he would make an excellent scout for their skulk. And a good playmate for her kit.

"How is she orange and you're not?" Chul asked, his dark eyes widening as he tilted his head.

Sook gently laid the kit on the dusty ground and sat, enclosing her in her paws. The little vixen was sleeping soundly and curled into herself, her fluffy tail tucked up between her hind legs. There was a blossom stuck in her thick fur, a lily from the temple grounds. Sook brushed the lily away and looked up at Chul. "A red fox sired her. One from Sanoul."

Chul gasped softly and dropped low to the ground, staring at the vixen. Movement behind her made her hackles rise slightly until she realized it was just another vixen bringing in another kit from the temple. Chul's focus shifted and he pounced over, his tail sweeping from side to side.

"Another vixen?" he asked with a hint of disappointment in his voice. He pawed at the dirt, his mouth pulling into a deep frown. "When are the souls going to be tods?"

"In due time, Chul, there will be more tods," Sook said with a light laugh. Her kit stirred then from her slumber, turning on her back as she yawned wide and stretched all four limbs out. She looked like her sir, which warmed Sook's chest with joy.

"Did you name her?"

"Gi," the other vixen said and looked at Sook, "and her?"

Sook blinked slowly, realizing that she hadn't even thought of a name yet. Her gaze drifted over the young vixen's features, her up-turned mouth and black-tipped ears. Her eyes slowly cracked open, so dark and beautiful that Sook imagined stars dancing across her vision. Then, the lily blossom caught her eye and a smile curved her mouth.

"I think I'll name her Nari."

Nari pranced around the Den, chasing a vole that had wandered in while the rest of the skulk was out in the forest. The rodent squeaked as she slapped a paw down on its tail and it panicked, rearing its head back to bite her. Nari let the rodent go but continued her chase, thinking this time it would be better if she caught it with her teeth. Chul and Gi barrelled out of another tunnel, followed by several other tods and vixens. When they saw the vole, it was no use for Nari to keep chasing it and she sat on her haunches, her shoulders falling as she pouted.

Chul came over and sat with her. He was an older tod, sired last year, but had stuck close to Nari's side the past several weeks.

"Why do you look so sad?" he asked. "Did you make friends with the vole?"

"No!" Nari yipped, shaking her head. She looked up at Chul, the dark fur around his eyes rising as he stared back at her. "I'm bored, though. When can we leave the Den?"

Instead of answering, he simply stood and wandered over to the entrance of the Den, glancing back at her to see if she would follow. Nari's heart leaped in her chest and she went after Chul. They shimmied out of the tunnel into the night and Nari's mouth parted slightly as she looked around. A warm breeze ruffled the bright orange and red leaves of the trees that surrounded their Den. The dead shrubs had been reinforced with a thicket of twigs to keep it inconspicuous as summer wore out into autumn. She looked up and up, falling on her back as the night sky greeted her with skeins of red energy weaving among the stars. Chul lay next to her on his back and lifted his paw toward the sky.

"One day, you'll be able to command lightning," he told her. "Me too, but I'm still working on it."

"What does the lightning do?" she asked softly, still mesmerized by the sight before her.

"It makes sure we keep our home."

And a home was all the foxes ever wanted, from the beginning of time to the end.

They stayed that way for a long while, watching the sky and stars rotate in the night. Though she had been sleeping all day in the Den, she grew weary now, listening to the song of the forest make its way to her ears. Nari closed her eyes and turned over, curling into herself as she sighed deeply. After a while, when she had nearly drifted off, Chul perked up. Nari squinted at him and rubbed her paw against her cheek. Chul's ears were rotating as he listened, his tail stiff.

Something flew over his head and embedded itself into a tree just behind them. Nari got up as Chul's ears flattened and hackles rose on his back. "Go back in the Den," he said quietly.

Nari hurried toward the entrance of the Den when she was picked up by the scruff of her neck. With a yelp, she kicked and twisted around. The creature that held her had dull, dark eyes and a scowl curling its mouth. It was hairless, save for a little bit atop its head and around its cheeks. She did not know what it was. Behind her, Chul let out a cry of pain and Nari squirmed once more, biting the creature's unusual paw as it lifted toward her face. The creature howled and dropped her. She landed and turned around, her eyes wide as she looked for Chul. The other kits were peeking out of the tunnel, quivering. Chul was climbing a tree, his claws sinking into the bark. Nari ran to join him but she was clumsy, she was not yet strong enough to hold her weight and fell.

Just as one of the creatures was about to grab her again, Sook and the rest of the skulk leaped into the small clearing, their teeth bared and backs arched. Nari tumbled into the thicket and laid low, watching as her tail tucked itself between her back legs. Sook growled as she pounced on one of the creatures, her canines sinking into the bare skin of its neck. A dark liquid poured from the creature and coated Sook's teeth. A small orb of light emerged from the creature and was absorbed into Sook's chest before she moved on to the next one. The creatures' screams filled the forest with terror but Nari felt a bit mesmerized watching her skulk leader's coat turn from milky white to red. It was a color normal foxes couldn't see, Sook had told her, so the demons had made it their own. They did have human souls after all.

Once the slaughter was over, Sook ordered that the bodies of the creatures be taken away from the Den. She looked around and caught sight of Nari in the thicket. As Sook came closer, Nari rushed out and hid beneath Sook. The redness on her fur smelled strongly of some metallic substance. It surrounded her and Sook pulled her forward.

"It's okay, Nari," she said. "You're safe. We're all safe now."

They had to move their Den after the first night of death and Sook had taught the kits that the creatures that attacked them were called humans. They were strong, they were big, and they were the enemy. The humans also held souls within them, that the demons were supposed to collect. Enough souls would grant them the chance to leave Earth and find a permanent home. Nari felt something burn deeply in her core, something that made her a bit sick in the stomach. When she told Sook, she had told Nari that that was contempt. That the humans were beneath the foxes and that it was their mission to remind them of that. To collect tithes for the Heavenly Fox in Sanoul. And so, Nari took that contempt and fed it, let it burn and grow within her until that was all she felt for the humans.

INYEO-KAN

TEN YEARS AGO

TETSU STOOD STILL AS his mother buttoned the cotton, high-necked tunic to the base of his chin. It felt a bit like it was suffocating him but he didn't complain. His mother had sewn his outfit for his first Inyeo-kan festival and he was too excited about the massive feast that would take place in Nagaseo's square to complain. Hopefully. If he could even swallow. Tetsu tried and was pleased that he still could.

"You look so handsome," his mother said as she stood, smoothing her hands over his shoulders.

He sniffed the air, his stomach grumbling as a waft of kimchi stew brewing outside caught his attention. Tetsu began to salivate and he raced toward the door, sliding it open as he stepped out. His mother followed, laughing as she joined him and took his hand in hers. His father stood in the courtyard, smoothing his hair back. He smiled as he saw them and took Tetsu's other hand.

"I'm hungry," Tetsu said and licked his lips. "When do we get to eat?"

"After the ceremony," his father told him, his voice soft and kind.

"Did you bring something for the box?"

Tetsu nodded and looked between them. "Mama said I can put our portraits in it so people know what we looked like."

"And the love we have for each other," his mother sighed. "Heaven knows there's not a lot of love left in the world today."

Tetsu guessed there wasn't much love in the world because of the fox demons. He scowled, his little nose scrunching up in disdain. He attended classes every other day with the other children in the village and most liked to whisper about what they heard from their parents. Fox demons were running rampant in the forest, thirsty for souls to steal. Their parents had told them that if they were bad, the demons would come to Nagaseo. Tetsu believed it, even though he'd never seen one of the demons before, so he tried to be as good as possible and not give his parents too much grief.

They left their homestead behind and walked together down a rocky, dirt path to the village square. The smell of kimchi stew, and fresh rice, got stronger as they got closer. Tetsu wiggled back and forth, squeezing his parents' hands to keep himself from breaking free and running for the feast. He was *so* hungry.

The village square became populated with families, dressed in their finest and their pockets full of things they'd like to put in a keepsake box. A few of the children ran around handing out hand-carved boxes to each father, who took it with grace. Tetsu's father bowed slightly at the waist and turned to him and his mother, smiling once more. They knelt on the ground and opened the box. His mother went first.

"I give to the future during this Inyeo-kan a swath of silk from my first hanbok." She reached into her pocket and removed the glittering, silver silk. Then her hands went to the black beads slung around her neck.

"Yona," his father interrupted with a gruff tone. "You cannot...put away your beads."

"They tell the story of who I am," she said softly.

Tetsu looked between his parents again as they shared a quiet look. After a moment, his mother removed the necklace and nestled it into the silk swath. Dal grunted and went next. He took a carving knife from his pocket and a luck charm that he had made for Tetsu. Gasping upon seeing it, Tetsu reached for the charm. He had wondered where it had gone.

"Papa, that's mine."

Dal looked down at the carving, that of a crow with two sets of wings. He had told Tetsu that the wings represented protection and freedom. The charm would shield anyone who held it against danger and it inspired hope that one day, the Daion kingdom would be free from the fox demons. Tetsu's bottom lip jutted out as he pouted and his father handed over the charm.

"You are right, I should not be the one to put it away." He dropped the charm into Tetsu's waiting palm and instead, removed a leather-bound journal and a ring from his finger. Tetsu clutched the charm close and sat back, watching his father drop the carving knife, the journal, and the ring in a little pouch into the box.

"I give to the future during this Inyeo-kan a tool that represents the work of my heart, a journal that is the physical manifestation of the inner workings of my mind, and a ring that has protected me thus far from lies and deceit."

Tetsu was next and he tucked the charm into his pocket, taking out the small portraits he had. "I give to the future during this Inyeo-kan portraits of our family," he said and set them in the box.

His mother leaned over and kissed his forehead. Tetsu smiled and asked, "Is it time to eat now?"

His parents chuckled. "Not yet," Dal stood, sweeping the box into his arms as he closed the lid. Yona helped Tetsu to his feet and they followed other families out of the village gates and into the forest. Tetsu tensed slightly as he looked around, sticking close to his mother's side. The trees loomed overhead, their canopy so thick it blotted out most of the reddish sky. He could hear birds chirping and insects buzzing all around. A stream ran steady somewhere to his left but he could not see the water, only hear it. They did not go far from the village but Tetsu could barely focus as his father buried the box.

A distant series of yips startled him then and everyone went still, staring into the forest. Dal stepped back and picked Tetsu up, putting his other arm around Yona. When nothing rummaged through the foliage toward them, they headed back to the village, their steps quick. Tetsu glanced over his father's shoulder and paled when he saw a whole slew of foxes appear from between the trees. They watched them with deep, dark eyes, their fur varying in color. He noticed most of them had more than one tail and his skin flushed with an abrupt burst of heat.

"Return," some strange voice murmured in his ear and he whipped his head around to look up at his father. But Dal was focused on reaching the village and did not seem to hear what Tetsu did. He looked back at the foxes and one with an array of tails flared out was staring right at him. *"Return to your kin."*

His mother stepped into his view, an uneasy expression on her face. She said nothing as her gaze roved over Tetsu's face and they surpassed the gates. They were promptly closed and armored citizens with swords fled to the walls of Nagaseo, climbing ladders to walk along the makeshift parapet. Though the foxes had soured the mood of the festival for a brief moment, Tetsu forgot all about them when he smelled the kimchi stew again. He was served a generous bowl and he dug in immediately, melting as the heat and sour and savory tastes touched his tongue. Zithers began to be played and dancing took place. Tetsu watched his parents twirl around, now relaxed and happy. He ate his stew and though his belly was quickly filling, he wondered if he could sneak another one.

At night, when the sun had gone and the eerie, red skeins of energy took up the sky, Tetsu lay in his mother's arms. She stroked his head and sang softly, her voice ethereal in the growing darkness.

"Young and bright may you grow, my love,
quick and sly may you be.
As the light that flows above, my love,
fills your heart with glee.
Kit-le-dee-la-lu-my love,
forever shall you be free."

IN THE BEGINNING

SIX YEARS AGO

HEAT. SEARING HEAT.

That was what Tetsu felt as he lay on the floor of his family's homestead. The bedroll beneath him felt too thin, the blanket covering his legs too heavy. His mother and father knelt on either side of him, faces blurred by the sweat dripping into his eyes. But he knew his mother was crying. He could hear her soft whimpers and hiccups, feel her tears splash on his bare shoulder. Tetsu closed his eyes and focused on the rhythm of his heartbeat.

It was slow. Painfully slow.

He was dying.

Yona brushed her fingers along Tetsu's forehead. His fever had intensified overnight. She turned and picked up a fresh cloth, dipping it in the bowl of cool water at her side. Ever since she acquired one thousand soul beads and was granted the ability to transform into a human, she had enjoyed this life with her husband and son. Dal, a humble woodcarver living in the Bamnai Forest who didn't worship the fox demons, was a breath of fresh air. Something new and exciting. Yona didn't have to keep secrets from him or feel like he submitted to her in fear. Dal simply loved her as she was.

She wrung out the cloth and gently laid it on Tetsu's head. With a fever this intense, there was only one way to save him. As Yona stood, the strings of soul beads wrapping about her waist and arms clunk together and she gestured for Dal to follow her out onto the porch. They stood beneath the awning, the night crisp with the scent of cherry blossoms and petrichor. A pleasant night for a horrifying reality.

Dal's dark eyes flickered and he crossed his arms, tilting his chin slightly. "Yona—"

"It's time," she interrupted and swallowed back her grief. Her fingers reached for the soul beads, and it drew Dal's attention. His brow creased and Yona glanced out into the courtyard, now dotted with lanterns. "Tetsu's twin souls are fighting one another, and I fear the fox may win. I cannot let my child be plagued by that kind of imprisonment. I must return to Sanoul. For his sake."

"Will you ever come back?"

Yona closed her eyes against the lantern light and pressed her palms against her legs. "I do not think I will in your lifetime, my love. It took me three hundred years to collect one thousand souls."

Dal shuffled closer and Yona could feel his hand briefly brush hers before he pulled her into an embrace. She stood in his arms and leaned into him, burying her face against his neck. When Tetsu was born, Yona told Dal that this night would come. That Tetsu's fox demon and human soul would silently battle for control. The taint of the demon and its mischievous ways was strong enough to trick Tetsu's mind.

Cause him to do things he normally wouldn't and fall sick.

He had snuck into the armory and discovered Dal's sword and former armor from his military days. Tetsu had not been careful and had sliced his abdomen, nearly impaling himself. Embarrassed, he kept the wound hidden until he grew faint and Yona discovered a festering infection. In his feverish state, Tetsu had mentioned a voice in his head that said it could ease his pain and suffering—if only he would submit to it. The fox demon would do anything for control.

Yona wrapped her arms around Dal, wishing that even when the world was falling apart, he would hold on to her. Remember her.

He said nothing as he drew back, and her arms fell to her sides. Yona returned to Tetsu alone and Dal pulled the paneled doors closed behind her.

Not but a few moments later, Dal heard Yona's voice, soft and light, as she sang Tetsu's lullaby to him. Her final goodbye.

"Young and bright may you grow, my love,

quick and sly may you be.

As the light that flows above, my love,

fills your heart with glee.

Kit-le-dee-la-lu-my love,

forever shall you be free."

Without me, Dal finished for her.

Tetsu felt different when he woke. Alive. Well. Imbibed with strength in every part of his being. He wanted to leap off the bedroll and out to the porch, run around the courtyard like the other children again. Until he realized only his father knelt at his side and held his hand limply in his. Dal, the always stoic, happy, and humble woodcarver, looked like a shell of himself. Dark circles plagued his eyes and his cheeks were gaunt.

How long had Tetsu been sick? Where was his mother?

Dal slowly began to shake his head before Tetsu could even ask. His father's voice was quiet and full of grief as he said, "Your mother has left us."

"But...why?"

"She had to," he said in a gruff manner. Dal took in a deep, shaky breath and pinched the bridge of his nose for a moment. His fingers were dry, his fingernail cracked from accidentally hitting it with a hammer. Dal gazed down at Tetsu, his features so similar to Yona's. He grit his teeth as he finished with, "The demons may win but show no fear, my boy. Never lay down and die when you are capable of so much more."

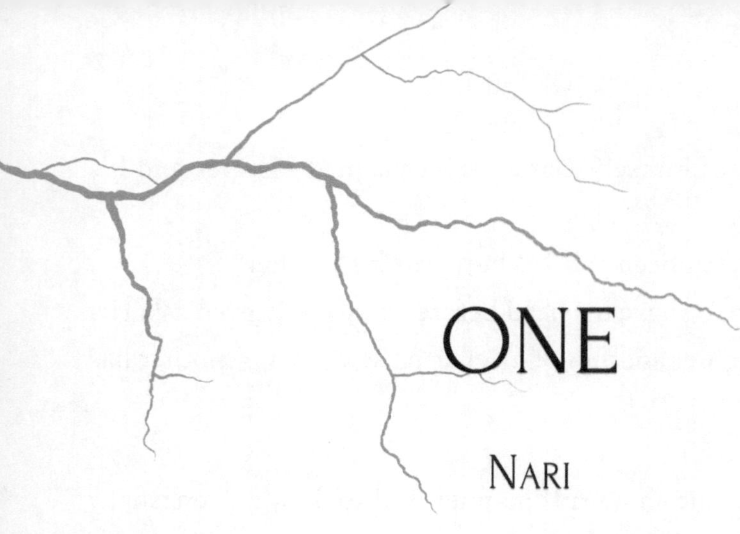

ONE

NARI

THE NIGHT CRACKLES WITH energy, lighting a path to the human village with streaks of crimson and deep rumbles of thunder. I run behind Chul, his three tails whipping against the air as he lunges forward. I follow behind, a bit timid, my tail nearly tucked between my back legs.

This is my first raid after months of training with Chul. I want to make him proud, he's my closest friend among the foxes and has agreed to let me shadow him, despite the risk. A young fox demon is often wild and reckless. I'm no different but I want to be a part of something and if that means collecting tithes from the humans, I'll do it.

As the autumn trees blaze by with each leap forward, my heart pounds in my chest. My paws strike the ground with a boom, adding to the cacophony of my fellow fox demons running alongside me. Chul glances back once, a canine slipping past his lip as he smiles. I'm keeping up with him though he claims to be the swiftest fox in all of Daion. I huff softly. Chul likes to gloat.

Our skulk soon comes upon the human village. At the sound of a soft whistle, we slow and spread out around the short wall that surrounds the village. I stay close to Chul, studying the architecture as we walk. The walls are made of cut stone and pasted together. Along the top are tiles of varying shades of brown, rather boring compared to what I imagine the roof tiles would look like at the palace in Sanoul—made of pretty jade. I imagine how they would shimmer in the daylight. One day, I'll go there. One day, I'll make Sanoul my home. It's the only place foxes are truly safe here.

Distracted by the wall, I blink and look around to find myself alone. The sky churns with clouds of crimson and lightning strikes just outside the village without warning. I startle, jumping back from the strike. I'm still not used to lightning—it took me some effort and many nights of training to finally command the bright red lightning.

In the village, an ear-splitting scream rings out as thunder follows, shaking the ground, and I find one of the gates. Chul is waiting there, his snout to the dirt as he walks back and forth. I don't know what he's searching for and stand aside instead, my head tilted at him.

Chul sniffs around for a moment more before going to the gate and standing up on his haunches. He pounds his paws against the thick wood but it doesn't budge. I feel my fur stand on end and in a flash, lightning strikes Chul.

I yelp, lifting my arm to protect my face before I look back at the gate. The wood is splintered and scorched, black smoke rising into the air, but it's open and...Chul is nowhere to be seen. I take a tentative step forward and a tuft of dark gray fur drifts right onto my snout. Chul's fur.

"Nari!" Chul hisses from the heavens.

I quickly drop to the ground and bury my face in my paws. "Oh, Chul."

"Nari! Get in here."

"I can't," I whisper. "You're in heaven."

A paw on my shoulder makes me jump and I glance up to find that Chul is alive, albeit a bit less furry on the top of his head. I leap up and tackle him to the ground, nuzzling my nose against his cheek.

"I thought you vaporized yourself!"

Chul grumbles as he pushes me off of him, "I stepped aside at the last moment but it grazed my head." He rolls to his feet and jerks his chin toward the gate. "Now come on."

I follow him along the wide path, where human homes stand on either side. They look foreboding with darkened, shuttered windows and black paint with white symbols on the outside. The humans are hiding inside, hoping our skulk will simply pass them over. Chul's tails sweep back and forth on the ground, picking up dust. Once the raid is over, he told me we would head to the Asandeo Springs to relax and clean up, which I'm excited about. The heat and steam will ease my tense muscles.

As we walk through the village, the air grows static with electricity once again. My ears perk to the sound of heavy breathing and the erratic heartbeats of the humans. I smell old woodsmoke and the remnants of a meat and cabbage meal as we pass a cookhouse. The other gates have been opened and Sook, our skulk's commander with eight tails, stands in the middle of the village square. All paths diverge here and I gather around Sook with all the other fox demons. Standing by Chul, I try to contain my excitement, but I can't wait to see Sook collect the first tithe.

Sook stands tall, shoulders broad and back arched. Her ears flicker and the light tufts sticking out from the tip look like they're dancing in the electric breeze.

"Humans, we are here to collect your tithes for Khana, the Heavenly

Fox. We know this village is not vacant. Come forward or we will have to take extreme measures." With that, Sook calls down lightning and it nearly incinerates the nearest building, sending a spray of shattered tile and wood everywhere. A series of screams erupt from inside and the smoking door is kicked open. Several children tumble out, followed by a man and a woman, as the home bursts into flames.

Sook leaps forward and snatches one of the children by the collar of his tunic. She drags him away, her snout wrinkling as she growls deep in her throat. The child's mother gasps and falls to her knees, tears soaking her cheeks as she begs Sook to be careful. The sight makes me a little uncomfortable and I shift on my feet, glancing out the corner of my eye at Chul. He only ruffles his back and stands up straighter. Humans seem to be much weaker than I thought. The child's father reaches into the sleeve of his tunic and a second later, a silver dagger flashes in his hand. He rushes forward, swinging his arm down in a sharp arc toward Sook.

But Sook rears back, pulling the child up, and all I see next is an eruption of red blood and the man's face turning pale. There's a breath of silence as a glowing white orb rises from the child's chest and Sook sets the child down. She reaches for the orb and it brightens for a moment before being absorbed into her paw.

The first tithe has been collected.

The other fox demons launch forward, knocking down doors and dragging the humans out into the cool night air. I stand there alone for a moment, unsure what to do as Sook collects the rest of the first family and when I look for Chul, he's disappeared.

Suddenly, something catches around my throat, a thin wire that slips beneath my fur and pulls tight against my skin. I let out a loud, high-pitched howl and twist, kicking my hind legs into the predator. The wire slackens a little and I take that as an opportunity to escape.

I lean my head back and slip free, darting toward the gate as my ears sit flush against my head. I shouldn't have come. I'm clearly not ready for this part of being a fox demon.

The gate draws near, a shining hope of escape, before masked humans jump out in front of me, their long swords drawn and ready for slaughter. They wear pure black tunics and trousers and would have blended into the night if the sky was not red with lightning. I screech to a halt, my tail tucked between my hinds as I try to think. But my mind is whirling and there's no guarantee that I can properly call down lightning. Sure, I've done it before at the Den, but Chul taught me I needed to be brave and have a clear mind to control it. Right now, I'm beyond terrified and I focus on the humans as they approach.

One of the humans pounces for me, lifting the sword high above his head. I dodge to the left just in time and take that momentum to jump up on the human and propel myself onto a nearby roof. I scramble for a tile to snag, slipping slightly and hanging halfway over the edge. The whoosh of the blade catches the air by my tail just as lightning is called down somewhere in the village. I pull myself up, hunkering low on the roof and trembling like I'm a young kit again.

Why did Chul run off without me? Maybe if I hop along the rooftops, I'll be able to find him. I pull myself up and leap over to the next roof. On the ground below, all I see is bloodshed and gore. My stomach turns whenever a downed fox comes into view with slashed necks or pierced bellies. This isn't how a raid is supposed to go. The humans aren't supposed to fight back. They're supposed to surrender.

I catch sight of Chul's three tails disappearing just beyond one of the other gates and when I reach the nearest roof, I jump over the wall and hit the ground. An uncomfortable feeling vibrates through my paws at the impact and I shake them out, glancing at the dark forest ahead. There's no clear path through it but as lightning flashes, I see

Chul ahead chasing a human into the forest.

I take off after him, thinking only of Chul.

One human, especially a fleeing one, doesn't seem too difficult to take care of. Kicking up clumps of dirt and dead leaves as I go, I draw nearer and nearer. Soon, we come to a clearing with dead leaves surrounding a large pond swamped with moss and lily pads. The human stops and flips around, a devious smile on his face.

His hair is loose and clings to his sweaty skin. My heartbeat quickens when I see what he wears, though. Dressed in all black save for the copper breastplate with a design like dragon scales, I know what he is in an instant.

A fox demon trapper.

I come to a stop just before the clearing and make a high-frequency sound only Chul can hear. His ears perk up but he doesn't look in my direction, lest he give me away to the trapper.

The trapper draws a long, curved sword from the sheath at his hip and the metal gleams in the light, engraved with human symbols I cannot read.

"You will be the one who dies, demon," the trapper spits and launches into an attack.

Chul easily deflects it and sinks his teeth into the trapper's calf. The trapper yowls and swings again, this time slicing Chul across his face. My heart lumps in my throat. I must do *something*. Taking a deep breath to fill my lungs, I emerge from my hiding place when the trapper has his back turned and before he can attack Chul again, I run and jump, slamming my paws into his back. He stumbles forward but whirls around, nearly taking my head clean off. Chul growls and grabs the trapper's arm, yanking him down to the ground.

The trapper kicks and flips over, hauling Chul's entire body across him and slamming him down. I can hear the impact of his skull hitting the ground, the sound crackling in my ears. I blink hard, my breath escaping me when Chul doesn't move. The trapper pulls Chul's mouth wide open, ready to thrust the blade up through Chul's skull but I leap again, knocking the trapper into the pond.

Water and moss splash high as the trapper falls and I dash to Chul's side. His eyes are half-lidded and blood-shot. I lean my ear down to his chest to find his heartbeat still thudding. He's alive, but I have to get him out of here before the trapper emerges from the pond.

A bright, white light catches my eye and I look at the water as it begins to glow and bubble. Is it…boiling? Cautiously, I take a step forward. The trapper is nowhere to be seen. I would have heard him splashing around if he had escaped.

Maybe he can't swim, which makes it easier, but thinking that sets my stomach on a roll. Without thinking, I dive into the water and find myself surrounded by hundreds of tiny spirit orbs. They glow a soft white, their shiny surfaces like the reflection of still water. The spirit orbs float up from the bottom of the pond, blooming from the trapper's chest like a flower. I swim down to him and see he's twitching slightly, his mouth hanging open. The sword is gone from his hand as he clutches his throat instead. I snatch the front of his tunic between my teeth, hauling him to the surface with a great deal of effort. The spirit orbs move as if they're afraid to touch me and I drag the trapper out of the water.

He doesn't move. I reach forward and poke his round cheek. No response. The light around us grows brighter and I glance back at the pond to see the spirit orbs rush toward me. I yelp and duck down as they bombard me, their light scorching my fur. A loud but quiet buzz numbs my bones as the orbs berate me repeatedly. I've only absorbed one spirit orb before, during training, and it felt nothing like this.

The orbs vanish within me and I huff, my snout stuck in the dirt. I breathe in a few earthy particles and then promptly sneeze. Reaching up to rub my snout, I feel no fur on the back of my paw.

I sit up and tilt my head in question, staring at the smooth, bare skin of my...whatever it is, it's not a paw anymore. The thing connected to my arm is flat with long digits that wiggle without me thinking about it. I glance at the trapper and realize that our paws—appendages—look the same. I look like...a *human?* My pulse quickens and I lean over the pond, shoving aside a lily pad to see my reflection.

Orange fur, the same color as my coat, sprouts from my head and just above my eyes...eyes that are wide and round but still completely black. My snout is tiny and my mouth bears an odd shape. I look so...bare, so human. With a gasp, I scramble away and reach for my chest as it tightens. Something clinks at the movement and I glance at my arms where hundreds of soul beads are looped around my skin. They are shiny, varying in shades of red and white. They're the spirit orbs I just absorbed, but...how am I human? Fox demons can only become human if they've collected one thousand souls.

I reach back for my tail to hug it close, but it's missing. I screech and dig my strange paws into the strange fur on my head.

"Nari?" a deep, wispy voice says.

I whip around and crawl over to Chul. He sits up slowly, his eyes narrowing on me.

"Chul! Are you okay?"

He flinches when I touch his paw and shakes his head. "Nari...you...you're *human.* But how could you—" he cuts himself off, his gaze drifting to the trapper. "You saved him?"

"I—I—" I gnaw on my lip. There's no good reason for saving the trapper. I just did it. I sit back on my haunches, glad that at least I still have four limbs, and hang my head in shame. "He's dead anyway. Drowned in the pond."

Chul is quiet for a moment before Sook's call shatters the silence. The raid is over and we have to return to the Den. Chul stands, wobbling on his feet, and I glance at him. "I suppose I need more training."

He shakes his head and then winces, lifting a paw to rub his temple. "Not as you are. You can't come back to the Den with us, Nari."

"What?"

"You're human now. To return to yourself, you have to bring the soul beads to the Heavenly Fox in Sanoul."

I scoot forward, grabbing the scruff of his neck. "Then let's go together."

Chul's ears perk up, though I can't hear the signal he does, and it makes my nostrils flare. "I can't," he says. "You need a human to show you the way and offer them up as a sacrifice to the Guardian at the Gate." His gaze drifts to the beads looped around my arms and waist, black pearls that shine under the reddish moonlight. "You have to hide those, too."

Water fills my eyes and I paw at my face, unsure where it's coming from. It must be the pond water dripping from my fur. "Don't leave me, Chul. I don't want to be human."

"I'm sorry, Nari," he whispers as he backs away slowly. Chul winces as he turns and limps away, vanishing into the night.

My heart grows heavy in my chest and I curl up on the ground, pushing the trapper onto his side. I stamp my feet against his back in anger and close my eyes. I never thought Sook's lessons about how to be a human would apply to me anytime soon but here I am, left alone in a body I already hate.

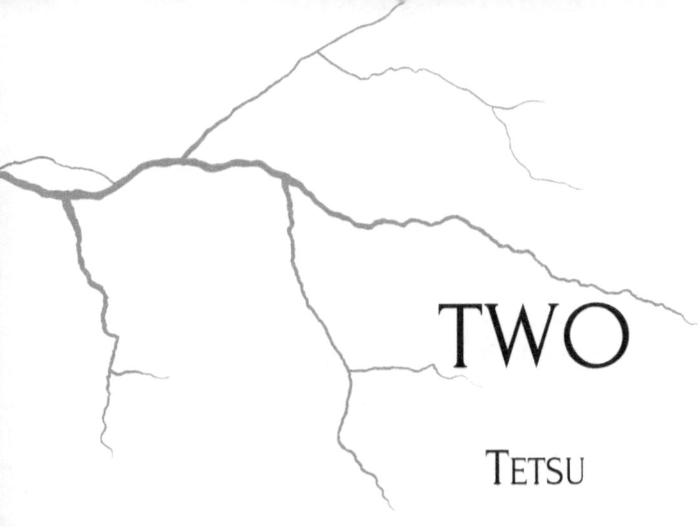

TWO

TETSU

I COUGH AND COUGH until my lungs burn and I gasp for fresh air. The bite wounds in my calf and arm pulse with pain and a headache hits me next. I groan softly, my body feeling like dead weight as it refuses to move.

I open my eyes and am startled to find that I'm not dead at the bottom of the pond. That pesky fox demon shoved me, and in my panic, I tried to grab the edge, but the sediment only crumbled in my hand. The wall of the pond was too slimy to climb up, even if I could swim. Hopeless, my thoughts turned to Mother and Father in Heaven.

After a few minutes, I'm able to wiggle my fingers and I gingerly flip over onto my back, my head rolling along. Something lies in a crumbled mess a few feet away from me. Exhaling slowly, I force strength into my limbs as I push myself upright, trembling terribly. I squint at the mess, expecting to find one of the fox demons dead, but instead, a girl is crying softly. She sniffles and whimpers, dragging her arm beneath her runny nose.

I sway as I crawl to my knees, the world tilting so much that I have to plant my palms on the ground, and my gaze wavers for a moment. Across the way, the girl squeaks and leaps up, her head whipping toward me. I stare once my focus returns and stiffen slightly as my eyebrows lift in surprise.

The girl has unruly, soft orange hair and big, dark eyes. Her arms are draped in beaded jewelry and she wears a very thin, ratty, and wet tunic. It sticks to her like a second skin and I quickly glance away, my cheeks heating with embarrassment.

"Did you—" I start but my voice feels raw and rough. I clear my throat and try again. "Did you save me?"

The girl blinks and scrambles away on all fours, looking awkward as she moves. Her wrist twists and she crashes into the ground, her face in the dirt. A laugh rumbles deep in my chest but then pain flares in its place and I wince. Slowly, I stagger to my feet, putting distance between myself and the pond. The girl is crying again, her shoulders shaking, and I cautiously approach her. She doesn't look like she's from any of the villages and I've never seen her before on my travels. Maybe she's one of the dispersed folk that live in the forest for whatever reason. Even though Fox Dens are littered throughout and well hidden, I can't imagine living out here.

I reach into my pocket and remove a few soggy Imperial notes, dropping them by the girl's feet. "Well, thank you for saving me."

Certainly, she can find her way to a village and buy herself some food or decent clothes. With an awkward nod, I pivot toward the village of Pangul and the girl scrambles over, tugging at the hem of my trousers as she asks, "Where's Sanoul?"

My shoulders tense at the question and I look down at her. Sanoul is the Imperial City where the Empress of Daion lived until the "Heavenly" Fox and her army of demons laid siege to the city. People were driven out or killed and the demons set up their Dens in the Forest.

Only Heaven knows why any person in their right mind would want to go to Sanoul now.

"Northwest," I tell her. "Why? Are you hoping to meet the Heavenly Fox herself?"

The girl's dark eyes wander over my apparel. "You're a fox trapper."

I grunt. "Yes, I am."

She rolls up onto her knees, crumbling the Imperial notes in her fingers. "I...I want to join you."

I snort and shake my head. "Go, take those notes."

"Ah, wait!" she gnaws on her knuckles as I sigh. "I...I don't know the way."

I glance south, where Pangul stands and between the thick trees rises plumes of black smoke. My mouth presses thin and I flex my hands in distress. Another village destroyed by the demons and more souls taken. I doubt anyone survived and if they did, they probably already escaped. I slip my fingers into my damp hair and slick it back. To the village of Juhto then, for supplies.

The girl is still kneeling when I turn to her once more. "Fine, I'll take you to Juhto. Come on."

As I walk forward, the girl follows on all fours and my brow furrows. *What in the world is wrong with her?*

"What are you doing?" I snap.

"What do you mean?"

"Why aren't you walking on your feet? You're crawling around like an animal."

"Feet..." the girl stops and I offer a hand to her. She stares at it and doesn't take it.

With another grunt, I grab her arm and pull her up. The girl wobbles, her knees knocking together as her legs bow. A terrified squeak escapes her as she exclaims, "Ah! I'm so high off the ground!" Then she promptly falls against my chest, her fingers digging into my shoulders.

"Are you an invalid?" I snarl before I can stop myself.

The girl doesn't seem to hear me so I scoop her up into my arms and opt to carry her through the forest. She remains still and stiff, her wrists folded over and her mouth agape in shock. Yes, she's an invalid for sure. If she is living out here in the forest, it makes sense. Although...how did she save me if she's too scared to even walk? Maybe she's an excellent swimmer or...something dangerous.

I consider plopping the girl on the ground and continuing to Juhto but as I look at her, she looks anything but dangerous. As far as I can see, there's no weapon on her and she looks fairly young, barely on the cusp of womanhood.

Juhto isn't too far from Pangul but after a few minutes, I have to set her down to rest. Leaning on the nearest trunk, I take in deep, steady breaths and rub my hand against my chest.

"It'd be great if you could walk on your own," I say. "You know, considering I was drowning half an hour ago."

She sits there, tearing apart a dead leaf with her fingers as she whispers, "I don't know how."

I push off the trunk and help the girl to her feet again, holding onto her slim, clammy hands. "Straighten your legs out and turn your feet forward," I instruct her.

The girl does, looking down at her legs. I take a tentative step back. "Lift one foot and then the other. Yes, like that. Follow my lead."

She wobbles as she walks but at least she's moving on her own. I loosen my grip after a few steps but she squeaks again in fright and holds on tight, looking up at me. Moonlight breaks through the crimson clouds above and illuminates her face. Her skin shimmers with freckles and sweat.

"Do you think you can keep up?" I ask as I let go of one hand and pull her forward.

The girl stumbles but catches herself. "M—maybe."

"We'll go slow."

We continue through the Bamnai Forest as I think about how I'm going to get supplies back to the camp. I was staying in Pangul for a night with Master Haku, waiting for a cart to become available but now going to Juhto, it's going to cost an arm and a leg to rent one. The trappers don't have any benefactors in Juhto to pay the price and the camp is too far to carry supplies to. So I'll take this girl to a Forsaken Sisters shelter and be done with her. Maybe there, they'll shape her up to be presentable in society, though it's not like there's much left to society anyway. The fox demons have taken over much of the kingdom while people have been forced into small villages, constantly being targeted for the demons to collect tithes.

The lightning-infested sky at night and clouds that give no rain during the day make life even more difficult. The fox demons have to be hunted down and trapped so, somehow, we can send them back to their realm. The Heavenly Fox would have to willingly open a portal but I don't think she'd do that when they could reign terror on Daion for the next century or so. I wasn't born yet when the invasion occurred but ever since the demons killed my father in a raid, I have vowed to kill every single one I see. Hopefully, someday, the trappers' forces will be great enough that we can take back Sanoul. For now, though, we just have to survive.

"What's your name?" the girl asks quietly.

"Tetsu of Nagaseo."

"Tetsu," she sounds out. "I'm Nari of...well, nowhere."

Nari.

I nod and we approach the gates of Juhto.

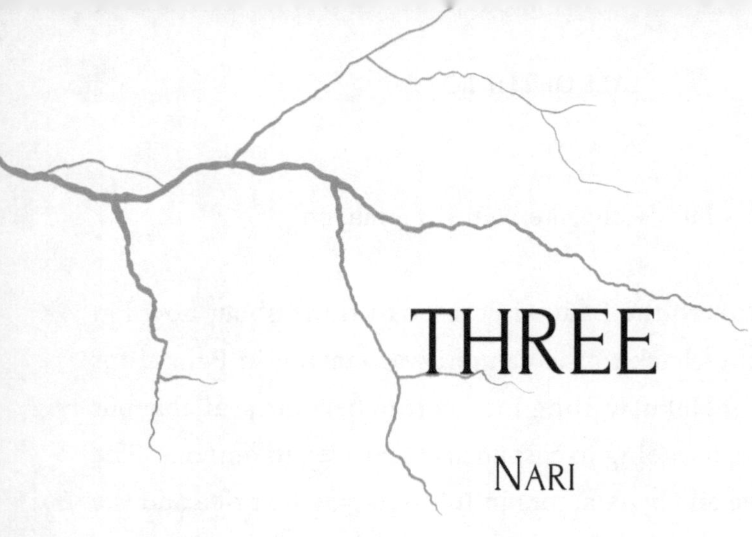

THREE

Nari

THIS HUMAN VILLAGE ISN'T much different than the other one, but my skin begins to crawl as we're let inside. I slide the beads off my arms and into the front pouch of the human garment I wear. Tetsu holds onto my strange paw as we walk through the village. There are a few stragglers out and about, but no one pays any attention to us. I still feel the tension building in my shoulders and back, wishing I was sitting in a hot spring right now but instead, I'm here. *If they only knew what I really am...*

Tetsu leads me to a crescent-shaped homestead with its own court-yard, surrounded by a stone wall. We pause outside the arched entrance and a guard materializes from the shadows, wearing an oddly shaped hat as he lays a hand on the hilt of his sword.

"State your business, sir."

"We're here to see Sister Eun. This girl has no home."

The guard glances at me, his expression remaining blank. I stare back and blink slowly until he nods and steps aside to let us through. Tetsu pushes me inside but doesn't follow. Quickly, I turn back to him.

Tetsu lifts a hand to his chest and tilts his chin down. "Farewell, Nari."

"Wait, what is this place?" I ask, panic flaring in my belly as I look around. I rush forward but the guard catches me around the waist and hauls me back.

"You'll be okay here, I promise," Tetsu says as he steps away. To the guard, he murmurs, "I fear she may be an invalid." And then he pivots and makes a brisk escape.

"Wait, no!" I cry and the guard grunts as he spins me around, leading me toward the homestead. I stumble up the steps and he knocks heavily at the wooden doors. My body trembles with confusion and anger. This obviously isn't anywhere close to Sanoul. Why did Tetsu leave me here?

A young woman wearing a gray and white robe embroidered with cranes opens the doors. Her eyebrows rise in surprise at the sight of me, but I find myself distracted by the woman's bald head. It's so shiny and smooth I almost reach out to touch it, just to see what it feels like.

The guard shoves me toward the woman. "A vagrant invalid for Sister Eun."

Invalid. I don't know what the word means, but I have a hunch it's not a kind one. The woman nods and takes my arm, pulling me inside. The doors shut and the woman glances at me, a light smile gracing her mouth.

"My name is Sister Iseul. Let's get you washed up and presentable for Sister Eun."

Iseul leads me down a corridor of paper-thin walls. They're painted with pink mugunghwa blossoms and four-pointed stars. Animals creep along the bottom in black paint, the strokes smooth and perfect. There are no foxes present.

"What is this place?" I ask as we come to a room with a large basin in the middle of it. A few girls carrying pails of water dump them into the basin. None of them look at me.

"This is the Forsaken Sisters Guild," Iseul says and turns toward a round stand in the corner. From it, she picks up a handheld device with bristles in a round shape that reminds me of guard hairs.

I duck right as Iseul reaches for the fur on my head with the device. She huffs, "Come now, don't be difficult. I'm just trying to brush your hair."

Brush? I have never heard of such a thing. And why does it need to happen to my fur—er, hair? It's perfectly fine. I run around the small space, trying to escape Iseul but she chases me and snags my fur in her fist. I yelp and growl low in my throat as I try to twist out of Iseul's grip. But the woman is strong.

"If you would stop fighting me, this would go a lot smoother. I'm just getting you prepared for a bath."

This is a bath? I'm used to rinsing in the river or the occasional hot spring whenever the skulk has a successful raid. Sniffing my underarms, my nose crinkles and I stop struggling, letting Iseul brush my fur—hair. It feels fine, though a little painful as she tugs on the tangles. I wince and fold my paws over the basin's edge as I close my eyes. I focus on the heady scent of the wood, rich and bright and earthy. It reminds me of the forest and the Fox Den. I rove through the Den in my mind then, its warm and moist air caking my fur with dewdrops. It was always rather dark but we foxes can see in the night; our eyes are made for hunting. And it never felt too cramped, as there were multiple chambers...

I whimper softly. I already miss Chul and my skulk. Right now, we would be tussling in the Den as if we were still kits, celebrating a successful raid with a feast and a dip in the hot springs.

I let the woman take off the thin garment covering my body and she guides me into the water. I sit there for a moment, legs flush against my chest as I shiver. The water isn't warm at all. My teeth chatter as Iseul dumps water over my head and body. Then, she takes a rough, cream-colored bar and scrubs it against my skin. I squirm and Iseul calls in another woman to hold me down.

"My heavens, your fingernails are nasty," Iseul says as she grabs my paw. *Fingernails...that must be what replaced my claws.* She tilts her head, shaking my paw. "At least you have dainty hands." *Hands, I have hands now.*

I store away the knowledge of what human parts are called and wince as she scrapes out the dirt beneath my fingernails. I still don't like the bar as she picks up my leg. It feels like my skin is being rubbed raw and I yowl as the torturous bath continues. When my skin is bright red and tingling, I'm lifted from the basin and wrapped in shaggy material that soaks up all the water. I snatch the former garment and remove the beads from the pouch before Iseul leads me to a different room. A large structure of wood sits squat in the corner with two paper-paneled doors on the front. The woman opens the doors and reveals an array of human clothes. Everything else has been so vibrant with human eyes but not these clothes.

Iseul chooses a white, knit smock that is shapeless and drapes it over my shoulders, buttoning it up at my ribcage. The fabric is heavy and warm, a comfort compared to the horrifying bath ordeal. Though it feels odd to wear human clothes, I've never seen a human without any. Since they don't have fur to cover their entire bodies, it makes sense they would need something else. It also has two pouches to hold my beads and thankfully, Iseul doesn't ask about them.

Then Iseul takes my hair and pulls it back tight and low, looping orange strands together until it's a rope that reaches the middle of my back.

"If Sister Eun accepts you, all this pretty hair of yours will have to go," Iseul tells me.

"Why?" I ask, swinging my head back and forth as the rope strikes me.

Iseul stills my head. "It's the way of the Sisters. Now you are presentable. Sister Eun will be at the shrine. Come along."

I follow, my bare feet slapping against the wooden floors.

FOUR

Tetsu

THE JUHTO MARKET IS bustling this morning as farmers from the west have arrived with their harvest. It's the last harvest of the year and since there's not much to go around, there's a limit. I browse the fruit and vegetable stands, taking a soggy piece of parchment from my pocket with the list of supplies that the camp needs. Mostly, we need food and arrows, but I don't know how I'm going to get enough food without Master Haku's monetary contribution.

With a sigh, I head toward the cart rental booth and the vendor gives me a wary look before her nose crinkles. "You reek," she says.

I grunt, ignoring the jab. "I need a cart to transport supplies to Yento. Kyung sent me."

The vendor adjusts the spectacles perched on the end of her nose and opens a leather-bound ledger, its hefty weight shaking the makeshift wooden booth for a moment. She runs her finger down the page before turning it over and tapping an empty line. "Uh-huh, as I suspected. Kyung's tab is almost full. I hope you brought enough money this time."

"We'll see." I set the list before her and she totals it up for me.

"That'll be 360 *wensi* for the cart rental alone and 230 for the supplies."

I cough into my sleeve, blinking hard as I stare at her. "What? That's a lot for a cart."

"For the things you need to haul, you'll need a cart."

I grab the list. "But there's just food and arrows--" I cut myself off as I see at the bottom, in the tiniest scrawl, that I need to pick up a shipment of new fox traps from the postmaster.

The vendor shrugs when I look up at her again. "Do you have the money or not?"

I remove the coin purse that Kyung gave me and dump the coins out on the booth. She counts them, quietly, and I glance toward the stables where a pair of mules are milling about, chewing on hay. If I don't return with the supplies, Kyung will be upset and we're already low on traps. The dispersed in the forest keep stealing them and reselling them. Maybe it'll come down to stealing a cart and mule...in the dead of night, when no one is around.

"Alright, you've got 308 *wensi*, which is nowhere close. Got any Imperial notes to make up the difference?"

I paw through my pockets only to remember that I gave the last of mine to Nari. I frown and curse softly. "No, sorry. Can't you just put it on Kyung's tab?"

The vendor tsks as she grabs an inkwell and dips a feathered quill in it. "Fine, but tell Kyung this is the last time. I thought the trappers had five benefactors with full purses."

"We're down to two now," I tell her.

She hums, writing down the price Kyung still has to pay. "I'll give you a medium-size cart for the traps and if you haven't heard, there's a new limit on how much food you can take. We're trying to ration out as much as we can here. Eventually, though, you'll have to get your supplies somewhere else."

"Thank you." I pick up the list and follow her to the stables, where she releases one mule and drops a harness on its head. The mule looks up at me with sad, droopy eyes and I pet its snout.

She straps the mule to a cart and directs it out onto the street. I climb up into the perch and thank the vendor once again. She waves me off, returning to her booth. I take the reins in my hands and set off for the postmaster first.

The fox trapper camp comes into view once I crest one of the long-since scorched hills and I direct the mule-driven cart down into the low valley. Yento used to be a thriving village where merchants passed through and brought all their rare wares. It was the village where the largest flea market was set up during the summer. Mother and Father used to bring me here to find exquisite furniture from abandoned noble estates or fine silk and cloth for clothes.

Now the camp sits in the middle of ruins with a makeshift parapet built around the cleared central square. Our tents look minuscule and less inviting compared to what used to stand in Yento. In the center, I see everyone gathered around the bonfire, swapping stories as they eat breakfast. My stomach grumbles at the scent of roasted deer and quail eggs with sweet peas and carrots.

I head directly for Kyung's tent, leaving the supply cart to be unloaded by the others. Inside, Kyung has a detailed and updated map of the forest spread out on the slim, oak table in the center. He leans over it, his scarred hands tracing old trade routes that the fox demons now use to get around the forest. The tent flap closes behind me with a thud and it catches Kyung's attention. He turns his head slightly, his blind eye sweeping toward me as the scar on his face stretches with the movement.

"Pangul has fallen," I say. "The fox demons hit it last night for tithes. Master Haku is dead."

Kyung grunts. Haku was a former nobleman with a hefty purse that supplied us with whatever we needed but now, he's the third of five that's been killed in a demon raid. They must know, somehow, who our benefactors are and where they live.

"We need to get Lady Tamra and Lady Sunhi somewhere safe then."

"I can do it, sir."

Kyung shakes his head and turns around, folding his arms across his chest. "No, I have another task for you, Tetsu. We've received word that there will be a fox-spawning ritual at the Itson Temple in two weeks. I'd like you to travel there and observe. Khana will be there herself, but you must not, under any circumstances, engage with her. Observe the ritual and report back."

The Itson region is deep in the forest and the thought of going there makes my skin crawl. No people live anywhere near it since it's infested with Fox Dens. I swallow hard and ask, "What about Shik and Yul? Why not send them?"

"They're busy with a different assignment. I've already asked Kang, Heira, and Aesoo to accompany you. The four of you will observe from each angle of the temple."

"Who's going to get Lady Tamra and Lady Sunhi then?"

Kyung waves his hand, dismissing me. "I'll head a rescue mission."

I nod and leave.

The other three trappers are at the supply tent, gathering dry food and strapping spare daggers to themselves, hidden beneath their clothes. We don't speak as Aesoo comes around with four dappled horses, handing the reins over to each of us. I fill my saddle bag with a compass, a map, and an extra set of clothes. I roll up a bedroll and strap it to the horse's rump. My stomach growls again so I sneak a handful of pine nuts into my mouth before mounting.

I'd rather stay at camp and rest for another day or two but we should begin our journey to the temple now. We don't know what kind of situations or people we'll run into. Besides, it's the beginning of the day, when foxes are sleeping. So without any fanfare, we leave camp on horseback. Though we're far from the nearest Fox Den, sweat coats my skin and I keep a hand on the hilt of my sword, ready to draw it at a moment's notice.

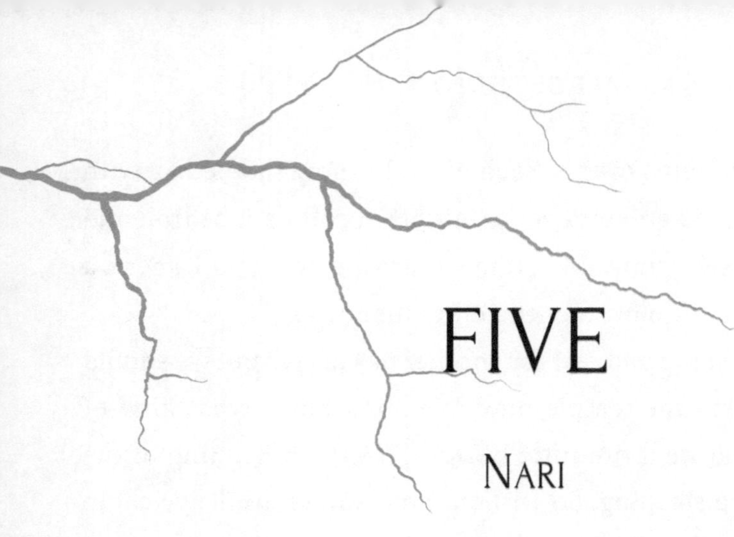

FIVE

Nari

SISTER EUN IS KNEELING at the shrine behind the homestead when Iseul and I arrive. She is speaking softly and occasionally bends at the waist, resting her head on the stone floor. I scratch my round-shaped ear and yawn. The sun is up and the warmth is making me sleepy. But there's no Den nearby for me to rest in, no darkness to swallow me whole and lull me to sleep.

A pristine garden with white sand, iridescent stone paths, and lush, green vegetation surrounds us. There's a small creek that runs throughout and on the other side of us stands an open-air structure, shaded from the sun. I turn from Iseul and walk toward the structure, my mind growing hazy as wave after wave of sleepiness hits me.

But Iseul snatches my arm and hauls me back. "Stay here," she whispers brashly against my ear.

"But I'm *tired*," I complain, not bothering to keep my voice down.

Sister Eun's shoulders stiffen and after a moment, she stands to greet us. The hair that hangs from her head is pure black and shines in the light as she steps away from the shrine. Her face is painted with red dots beneath her eyes and along her nose, a few red slashes look like whiskers on her cheeks. The robe that hangs from her slender shoulders is black with white cranes and swirling details along the hems and at the neckline. She doesn't look like Iseul or the other women I've encountered here. And she's not elderly as I expected. In fact, she looks like we could be the same age.

"And who might you be?" Sister Eun asks, her voice soft like a babbling stream.

"Nari."

"A girl from the forest," Iseul says.

Sister Eun nods as her mouth presses thin. She drifts toward us, her robe making her move like a phantom, and Iseul releases my arm. I stand still, my shoulders pulling together as my ears perk. I have the urge to flee as the strange woman walks around me before reaching for my hair. I jerk away and a low growl escapes me. Heat flares across my face and I blink, internally chastising myself. I'm not supposed to act like a fox but it's my nature; my form now, however, is human. Sister Eun steps back, her brows knitting in confusion.

"You're an odd one, aren't you?"

I blink slowly again, feeling myself grow sluggish. My gaze shifts to the sun-blessed structure.

I almost hiss at Iseul when she swats my hand. "Sister Eun is speaking to you."

My nose twitches as I look at Sister Eun again, cradling my hand against my chest. I don't like Iseul one bit. First, she tortured me with a bath and now she won't let me wander off into the garden and sleep.

"Why were you in the forest? What village were you born in?"

I shrug. "I don't know."

Iseul shades her mouth with her hand and drops her voice, even though I can still hear her. "The man that brought her said she was an invalid."

"Actually, he said I *may* be an invalid, whatever that means."

Eun and Iseul share a look. The former holds her hands out to me and beckons me forward. "Come kneel at the shrine with me, Nari."

I hesitate, knowing I shouldn't be wasting my time here with these human antics but how...am I supposed to escape the homestead? I can't walk out the way I came, the guards would stop me. The walls are too high to climb and I don't even know how to use these human hands. But the structure, I could easily leap over the wall from its roof. I lay my hands on top of Sister Eun's. I'll play along until they leave me alone and then I'll make my escape.

The shrine is stuffy, even though it's open to the air, but hundreds of little fires have been set, melting a stick. It also smells like the forest and I tap my hands against the ground, happy with the scent. We kneel before ancient scrolls written in the human language, which I can't read, and jade and ivory statues of different creatures. No foxes, though.

"Let us pray to the gods concerning your fate, Nari."

I look at Sister Eun and copy her pose, pressing my hands together and tucking my elbows against my sides. Sister Eun begins speaking in a strange language, her eyes closed, and when she goes down to touch the ground with her forehead, so do I.

After five face-plants and what feels like forever, Sister Eun falls quiet and sits there with her hands on her knees, her head tilted upward. She inhales, deep and slow, the smoke from the fires dancing around her nostrils. When she releases a breath, the smoke scatters and it reminds me of dragon breath. I want to bare my canines at the sight.

In the realm of mystical creatures, where my fox demon spirit was formed, dragons rule the skies. They come in many shapes and forms but are all bearers of the weather. The foxes are considered inferior, ordered to enforce faith and strike fear into the hearts of those who worship the dragons. Then the foxes stole the dragons' lightning in hopes of gaining a place among the upper caste, but we were banished to Eternal Darkness, a void-like existence where nothing but darkness and silence exists. Slowly, the fox demons disappeared and became a memory to the humans that once worshiped them. But the Heavenly Fox, Khana, saved our kin and will bring all the fox demon spirits into the world until there are none left in the Eternal Darkness.

I often wonder if the dragons know what Khana is doing. But it has been over four hundred years since the fox demons began their exodus from the Darkness. So maybe the dragons don't know, or they simply don't care enough about the humans to interfere.

"I see great things for your future, Nari," Sister Eun says softly and touches my shoulder.

I flinch and berate myself again, forcing myself to relax. I nod, offering what I hope is a warm, tame smile. If the great thing is that I'll be a fox again then it is, indeed, great.

"Now, Iseul will get you settled and prepared for the initiation ceremony tonight."

My mouth pinches at that, disappointment numbing me, but I nod again and offer an awkward bow to Sister Eun as I stand. I'll be long gone before they can make me a Sister. As Iseul turns and beckons me to follow her, I detour toward the structure that had first caught my eye.

Iseul's fingernails catch on my skin as she tries to snatch my arm, but I slip free and dart toward the structure, feeling odd moving at a quicker pace on two limbs. Beneath it, the coolness of the shade hits me in an instant and a wave of sleepiness washes over me again. I shake myself and swing around one of the posts, using my new hands to grip the tiles and pull myself up. I kick my feet as I scramble onto the slanted roof.

"Get down from there immediately!" Iseul hisses, trying her best to keep her voice down as she scolds me.

I ignore her and clutch the tiles, leaning forward so I don't tumble backward into the water below. The tiles feel rough beneath my hands, crafted with shades of red and brown sand. I reach the pinnacle of the structure and grip the spread wings of the dragon statue that stands on top. I pull myself to my feet and scan the wall beyond the homestead.

It's a bit further than I had hoped but I should be able to make it if I leap far enough. I glance down at my bare feet and wiggle my toes. "Don't fail me now," I whisper and hurl myself off the roof.

"Nari!" Iseul screeches, drawing the attention of the other Sisters wandering the gardens.

As I hit the tiles adorning the wall, my chest burns at the impact, but I grasp a few and hold on. The tiles dig into my stomach and I wince as my arms and hands begin to burn. Pulling myself up and on top of the wall, I crouch there for a moment to catch my breath.

Iseul stands beneath the structure, her expression furious as her skin flushes bright red. "Guards! Catch her!"

My gaze wanders to Sister Eun, who stands by the shrine, hands tucked into the draping sleeves of her robe. She stares at me, her head slightly tilted. At least someone isn't protesting my escape. An arrow whistles near my ear and I drop low on the tiles, my nose scrunching up into a snarl. I slide back and drop to the ground on the other side.

Landing with a thud, I stand, turn, and run into the forest.

SIX

TETSU

WE CHECK TRAPS AS we ride through the forest and into the Itson Region. I drop down from my horse and stride toward a cage just off the old trade route. The once clear dirt road is now overrun with weeds and fox prints. I push through the overgrown brush and pokey branches as I approach the trap and the pungent smell of death makes me gag. I pull my sleeve down over my hand and clamp it over my nose.

A dead fox demon lies in the cage, its body spread out and the poisoned bait dangling from its teeth. Its eyes are bloody and its fur is matted with mud and leaves. Flies buzz and maggots gnaw on a festering wound in the demon's side. My stomach rolls as bile lurches up my throat and I turn away, looking up past the canopy to the sky above. I don't know why it's never gotten easier, why I haven't adapted to the sight. This is what I do for a living now. This is what I kill.

Still, it's gruesome and unfortunately, I have to clean it up. I gulp in fresh air before turning to the downed demon and pull a pair of gloves onto my hands. I roll up my sleeves and hold my breath as I open the cage and pull the body out. I drag it toward the road and set it in the dirt, collecting dry twigs to set around its body. My horse huffs and stamps its hoove against the ground, turning in a circle as it flicks its tail. The flies move toward it, thinking they can find their next meal.

I take a piece of flint and steel, striking it until a flame sparks and set the demon's body on fire. The flames singe the fur and consume the maggots until they shrivel up. I leave the thing to burn as I head back to the cage and reset it with new bait. With a fox dead that long in a cage, it would deter any other foxes from getting close but I don't hear any water nearby to clean it and I'd rather move on.

"Tetsu, are you watching this burn?" Aesoo asks from the road.

"Yes, just finishing up with the trap," I say and push to my feet.

I return to the road with her and we stand together, watching ash rise as the fox demon is incinerated.

SEVEN

NARI

TETSU IS ACCOMPANIED BY three other fox trappers when I find him. They're traveling on horseback, packs strapped to their saddles. Staying low and quiet, I follow behind as we head west, deeper into the forest. I can't imagine why humans would want to travel this far. There's only Fox Dens and the Itson Temple. Still, I have to keep my guard up now that I'm human, too.

Tetsu and the other trappers decide to sleep during the day and move at night, which makes it easier for me to keep up with them. Though, I do miss my night vision. I've tripped over too many roots and have run into too many spiderwebs already. I'm also ravenous, so before any of them wake, I sneak near their horses and slip a few pieces of dried fruit or meat from their saddle bags. None of them have complained so I assume I am welcome to their food.

By the fourth night, we've passed several Fox Dens and evaded even more skulks lurking about. They don't attack the trappers, thankfully, because I need Tetsu alive and well to take me to Sanoul. However, I'm not sure how I'll approach him. I didn't expect to find him with others and I wish I had demanded he take me to Sanoul when we first met.

As the trappers rest, I sit down a fair distance away, panting slightly as I wipe away the sticky wetness on my skin. Being a human is so much work and I don't like it. I have to find somewhere I can't be spotted to answer the call of nature. Bugs seem to feast on my flesh every time I'm not paying attention to swat them away, and this wetness that encases my body...it's horrible and I smell. I haven't been this far west before; my Den is in the northeastern part of Daion and I know where every freshwater spring is located.

My shoulders slump as I think back on the night I was transformed into this disgusting body. I still feel a bit betrayed by Chul, leaving me to fend for myself. I know he can't help me, but I miss him every day. Quietly, I wrap my arms around my legs and hug them close to my chest. Mewling softly, I stroke my cheek with the back of my hand. I've been so focused on staying out of sight that I haven't let myself feel the loneliness surrounding me. Chul didn't even seem that concerned...maybe I am more his friend than he is mine. Maybe I clung too close too soon and he was glad to be rid of me.

The thought pains me to my very soul and I let my head fall back, my mouth open, ready to let out a cry. Until I hear a branch snap in two and I whip around, fingers digging into the soil as I squint into the dark behind me. A shadow in the shape of a large, ominous human moves and separates into three. I let out a high-pitched squeal as the largest lunges for me and the weight knocks me on my back. I exhale without meaning to, all the air being pushed from me as I sink into a bed of orange and yellow leaves. A filthy hand finds my mouth and I scream against it with my last breath.

"Stop squirming or we'll feed you to the foxes," a man hisses against my ear.

I squirm even more so, though my body is slowly going numb from the weight and the man shifts, finally getting off me. I breathe in and then gag, his skin smells like rotten flesh. I shove his hand off my mouth and scramble away. Another human hauls me to my feet and I dangle in the air for a moment, almost slipping free of the clothes Iseul gave me.

"She's pretty. A tiny, delicate thing. I think Gahra will like her a lot." The woman holding me says.

Gahra? Who is that?

The man grunts and reaches up to caress my face. "Yeah, it's too bad we can't try the product out first."

I snap my jaws at his fingers and he pulls back sharply. Another man laughs, but it's not cheery. It's slow and deep, making the entire earth rumble beneath our feet. The red clouds clear above and a shaft of moonlight illuminates part of the man's face. He has claw marks on one cheek and a patch over a missing eye. It seems that he's had his fair share of run-ins with the foxes.

He steps forward as the woman sets me on the ground and offers his hand. "Come along now, we're not here to harm you."

I glance at his hand and then his face before I pivot and run. The strangers crash through the forest as they chase after me but I'm a fox by nature, I was born to run. Not so much on human legs, however, and before I know it, I stumble upon Tetsu and the other humans. I stub my toes on an unsuspecting rock and trip, nearly sliding right into the small fire they've set up.

Tetsu leaps to his feet, eyes wide as he asks, "Nari?"

The strangers emerge from the forest and I hear the shining *schink* of swords being drawn. "Weapons down, the girl is ours."

I flip over on my back, wincing at the pain rising in my foot. The female trapper steps in front of me, her sword drawn. "What do you want with her?"

"That's none of your business," the sly, one-eyed man says.

Another trapper clears his throat and speaks up. "Regardless of what is and isn't our business, we know you three are nothing but filthy bandits. Leave now and your lives will be spared."

The large man with the rotten-smelling hands lets out a loud laugh. I feel someone touch my arm and I jerk away only to find Tetsu there, his brow furrowed. He helps me to my feet and I cling to his arm before he can let me go. Dropping his mouth near my ear, a few strands of his hair swing into my eyes and I blink uncomfortably.

"What in Hoji's name are you doing here?" he asks, his voice rife with panic. "I left you with the Forsaken Sisters a few days ago...have you been following us?"

I look up at him and my fingers dig into his arm as I whisper, "Take me to Sanoul."

"This again?" he snorts. "Why do you need to go there?"

Before I can think of a lie, a sword comes sailing toward our stomachs and Tetsu pulls me back, unsheathing his sword. He can't grip it properly with only one hand and so shakes me off. I quickly move behind him, grasping his tunic as his sword clashes with the one-eyed man's.

"Let me go," he grunts as he rushes forward and I stumble along.

"I don't—what am I supposed to do?" I counter.

"Run." Tetsu gasps as the blade grazes his arm, splitting his sleeve open. "Run and I'll find you, Nari."

"What about you?"

"I'll be fine."

"Pft," the one-eyed man huffs and he catches my eye over Tetsu's shoulder. "Don't wander too far, pretty."

I shove away from Tetsu and duck beneath the swinging arms of the large bandit before darting into the forest once more. My legs ache and burn with the exertion, but this is life or death and I hope that Tetsu doesn't die. If I were myself, I would call down lightning and obliterate the bandits. But instead, I scramble up a tree and perch among the branches, watching the fight from above.

My useless hands become engraved with the pattern of the bark and I hold on, feeling breathless.

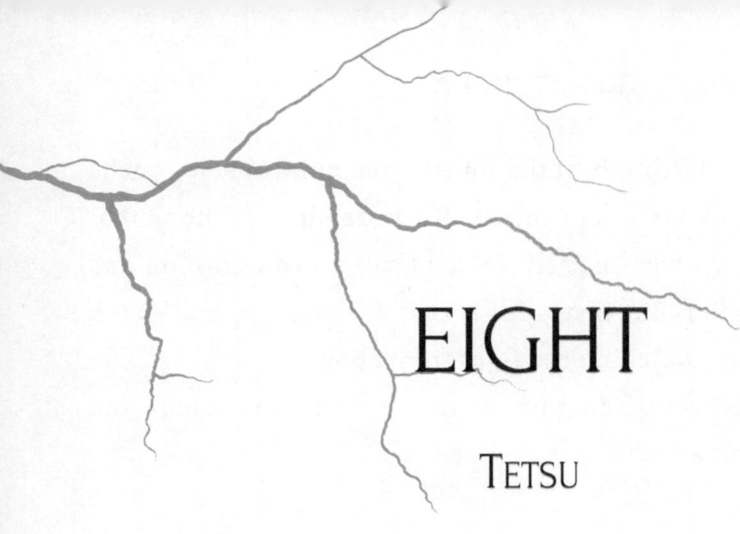

EIGHT

TETSU

I CAN'T BELIEVE NARI has followed me all the way from Juhto. What in Hoji's name possessed her to follow us deeper into the forest where fox demons thrive? I don't like being here, even with other trappers to keep me company, but we're heading deeper and deeper into enemy territory and her odd obsession with Sanoul makes me nervous. Maybe the girl just wants to see the once glorious imperial city for herself. She would have to see it from a distance, though, because I will go nowhere near the gate. That would be asking for death itself to pat me on the shoulder and take me away.

The enemy's sword swings up in an arc toward my head, nearly taking my ear off. I duck and thrust upward, just missing impaling the man with one eye by a hair. I've never been that great with swords. If Mother had come back, maybe she would have taught me better.

Mother.

A deep-seated and rare emotion jolts through me like I've been stabbed again. Sorrow pours from the deepest depths of my soul and floods my veins. Tears brim in my eyes and I let out a yell that cracks on the wind. My vision grows red and blurred.

I miss her every day but then why would I miss her when she left me at a critical time? On my very deathbed.

But she was also my confidante, the one who helped me believe in myself. I saw her as a goddess, but now she's nestled in my heart as a memory. IFather died the next year, killed in a raid by fox demons, and Mother never came back. She was a fierce fighter and I figured she could handle herself against a demon.

I fight with all my strength, sweat beading on my skin and a painful, burning sensation rippling through my muscles. But as quickly as the rage had come, it dissipates and a rush of nausea hits me. I stumble back, the sword slipping from my fingers and clattering on the ground. The world tilts as my stomach is tossed into a somersault. My cheeks puff out as bile rises in my throat and I fall flat on my bum.

Then, a voice creeps forth from the crevices of my mind.

It's soft and mischievous, swirling around my head and dancing from ear to ear. *"Let me take over so you can rest, Tetsu."*

"Take...over..." I say aloud, the words feeling heavy in my mouth.

The hilt of a sword strikes my head and I fall to my side, darkness crowding my vision as the voice lets out a frustrated cry before it falls silent.

I crack my eyes open to see the ground swaying below me. I'm tossed over the shoulder of a giant and my rope-bound hands swing back and forth, the rope straining against my wrists. I catch sight of another pair of hands and crank my head, though the movement sets off a raging headache. Through my hazy vision, I see Nari's orange hair streaming down to cover her face and arms. There are leaves and tiny twigs tangled in her hair.

The forest around me is unfamiliar but still dense and soon, the sharp scent of woodsmoke stings my nostrils. I crinkle my nose, feeling a sneeze coming on when Nari and I are promptly dropped on the ground. I groan as I strike the dirt, kicking up dust that makes me sneeze. Nari makes no sound and I see that her eyes are squeezed shut, her bottom lip trembling.

I try to scoot closer to her but the giant grabs me by the ankle and drags me toward the fire. The bandit woman sits on a fallen log covered in moss, sharpening a dagger with a smooth stone. The blade shines in the firelight as she turns it, revealing the jagged edge that will be excruciating to take out.

"Oh, he's got a pretty face, too, with those dark eyes and long lashes. Gahra likes the girls in the house, though. We could still sell him off as a slave."

My heart leaps into my throat. *Gahra.* I've heard that name before—and the reputation that precedes it. Gahra is known by many names: the Bandit Queen, the Scarlet Hand, and the Mistress of Bamnai Forest. Her organization is like the Forsaken Sisters but instead of giving the girls a better life, she exploits them to the mildly wealthy, the abusive, and the sick-minded—for money. The girls who go to her brothels never make it more than six months. It's a death sentence.

If Nari hadn't followed us, she wouldn't be in this kind of danger.

I have to get us both out of here.

But the woman has other plans as she puts the edge of the dagger into the fire, letting it heat until it's an angry, orange color.

"Let's brand him first. Flip him over and take that dirty tunic off. We'll see just how well his skin holds against the heat."

NINE

Nari

I LIE ON THE ground, paralyzed with fear. I hear the bandits talking about Tetsu, but I don't register what they're saying. The sky is churning with bright red clouds and dazzling lightning. How I wish, so badly, that I could call it down and save us. But even if I could, Tetsu would then know what I am and his duty as a fox trapper wouldn't let me get away.

Who knew being a human would garner so much danger? As a fox, I hardly had anything to worry about. Then again, I stayed at the Den as a kit and played close by in the forest until I was old enough to join the raid so...I'm naive to think such. Of course, the world beyond my home and comfort is dangerous. I just feel more comfortable facing it in a body I know.

A sharp yelp makes my ears perk and I struggle to sit up, my pulse pounding. I blink and see Tetsu on the other side of the fire, the bandit woman kneeling next to him with a cruel smile twisting her mouth. She presses a red-hot dagger against Tetsu's bare back, just between his shoulder blades. I gasp and rock forward, my bound hands hitting the ground as I scurry on all fours.

The large, foul-smelling bandit catches me and I rear back, sinking my teeth into his fleshy forearm. He curses and drops me. I kick off the ground and thump against Tetsu, landing on his back. He hisses and then groans. I slip to the side but spread my arms over his body.

"Stop it," I demand, though my voice is small and nothing worth listening to.

The woman's brow lifts. "Oh? Have we found a pair of lovers? How tragically perfect." Her hand snakes forward and I wince as the dagger hovers near my throat. It singes some of my hair that falls forward, leaving a nasty smell in the air. "If you're already experienced, you can get right to work and if you ever fall out of line, this boy of yours will be punished."

"He's not my lover," I retort, my nose wrinkling at the word. Humans have odd phrases for those they pair and mate with. "But I won't let you hurt him any further."

The woman chuckles and drops the dagger from my throat. "I'd like to see you try."

Without warning, she backhands me and I fly away from Tetsu, landing so hard on my back that it knocks the air from my lungs. I gasp and dig my fingers into the soil, unable to move.

The one-eyed man shifts into view, looking down at me with a disappointed shake of his head. I wait for the shock to pass through my body and take in deep, measured breaths. Human bodies are so fragile, it's pathetic.

I slowly get to my feet and clutch my chest, my body beginning to tremble as my fox spirit comes alive in me. If they want a fight, I'll give them a fight. When the one-eyed man turns his back on me, I pounce, dropping my bound hands over his head and around his neck. I pull back, bending my knees as I toss him right into the nearest tree, where his head meets the trunk and snaps back. He goes down easily. I duck beneath the sweeping arms of the foul bandit and ram my knee into his groin. He lets out a loud howl and stumbles back, eyes watery from the impact. I pull my arms back and strike his nose at an upward angle with my palms. The man shrieks.

My ears catch the motion of something whistling toward me and I lean out of the way as a small dagger flies past my head and lodges itself into a tree. I whirl on my feet and run toward the bandit woman, leaping over Tetsu as I kick her right in the stomach and now she's the one flying. She hits the ground with a thud and her fingers slip against her trousers, searching for another weapon. I take the dagger she was using on Tetsu, cut us both free in one swipe, and sprint for her, lifting my arm high and then bringing it down fast as I stab her through the thigh. Her flesh cauterizes itself, a puff of smoke escaping, as her scream echoes through the forest.

Tetsu is sitting up now and blinking, his eyebrows raised in surprise. I haul him to his feet and then we run.

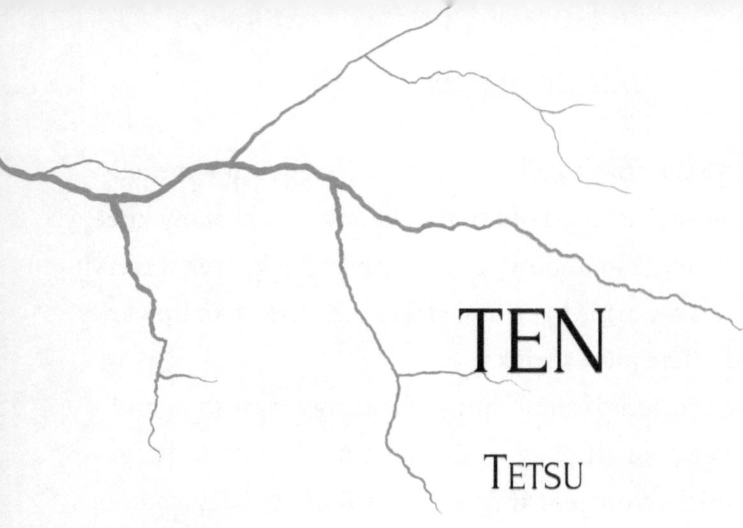

TEN

Tetsu

MY HEART TREMBLES IN my chest as we run and it's not because I'm out of breath. Nari's fighting skills came out of nowhere and I wonder why she didn't fight when we were first attacked by the bandits. Maybe she was afraid. Now, she squeezes my hand as we weave through the forest, her fingers clutching mine tightly.

At least my sword isn't smacking against my thigh and leaving a nasty bruise, I think with a grunt. The bandits confiscated it at their camp. I'm not that great with a sword, but it was a gift from Kyung when he finally let me join the fox trappers.

My muscles start to burn and my back aches from the brand so after a while, I tug Nari to a stop, dropping her hand. My skin is slick with sweat and I bend over, setting my hands on my knees as I take in shallow breaths. Nari hops from foot to foot, somehow still able to move.

"Are you even tired?" I ask.

"Huh? No, why would I be?"

"Because we've been running." I straighten and look at her. Nari's hair is tangled and wild, her dark eyes wide and her cheeks flushed. Somehow, she has managed to run in the calf-length smock she's wearing without tripping once.

"I like to run," she says and grabs my hand again, "now come on, we have to keep moving."

I stumble after her, glancing back the way we came. "Honestly, I don't think those bandits are going to be close behind."

"I doubt their minds have changed about selling us."

"That's...that's not what I meant."

We run until the night fades away and the sun rises between the thin trunks, the sunshine the only thing chasing us now. Finally, we come to a clearing and I sit heavily on a fallen log. I can feel the scratchy, dew-dropped surface through the seat of my trousers but I don't care. My legs are sore and I smell rank. I stretch my legs out, wiggling my toes in my boots.

Nari sits next to me and balances her elbows on her knees, cupping her cheeks. Her brow knits together as her bottom lip juts out. "Surely, I thought the bandits would have caught up to us by now."

"Do you want them to?" I snap, lifting the hem of my tunic to dab my forehead.

"No, but I just—" Nari cuts herself off and I glance at her.

She stares at me, well, not my face. Her gaze is focused on my exposed stomach and her mouth gapes open. I look down before I quickly drop my tunic and smooth it out. More often than not, I forget about the massive scar on my stomach.

"What happened?" she asks and gasps, pressing her fingers against her mouth. "That's not from the bandits, is it?"

What's with her fixation on the bandits?

"Obviously not, I'd be dead now if it was."

"What do you mean? Do hu—don't you have regenerative powers?"

Ah, I almost forgot why I left her at the Forsaken Sisters. This girl is delusional.

"No...we're mortal, why would we have regenerative powers?"

"Salamanders do and they're mortal," she points out.

I dismiss the fact with a wave of my hand. "So that's one animal. Not people, though." I slowly push to my feet, even though I don't want to move again for a thousand years, and stretch my arms out. "I guess we have to keep moving, right?"

Nari doesn't seem to hear me and I lean forward, snapping my fingers in her face. She startles and stands as well, nodding.

She doesn't take off running so we stroll through the forest now, which is a relief. I tilt my head up and try to search past the canopy for the direction of the sun. The light disappeared as we sat talking, but I still have to observe the ritual at the Itson Temple, even though I no longer have any supplies or weapons. This far into the forest, we're probably closer to the temple than the camp.

"Why does your face look like that?"

I drop my chin and lift an eyebrow. "Look like what?"

"Like you're confused."

"I'm focused. Trying to figure out which direction we're heading in."

"That's easy." Nari drops to the ground and presses her ear to the dirt and leaves. Then she turns her head and does the same with the other ear. Slowly, she rises and sits back on her legs, her shoulders hunching forward. "I can't hear anything."

An invalid for sure.

I reach out and awkwardly pat her head. "That's alright, I'm sure we'll figure it out."

Nari swats my hand away and hisses. I blink and step away, my lip curling. Why does she act like an animal sometimes? Maybe she grew up among them and was a feral child. It would explain her behavior.

She walks ahead of me from then on, arms crossed as she wanders back and forth, making a zig-zag path for me to follow. I sigh quietly to myself. There's no Forsaken Sisters shelter nearby to drop her off. Besides, she'll probably escape and ask me to take her to Sanoul once more.

An hour later, Nari stops near a large tree and scrambles up the trunk like a squirrel.

"What are you doing?" I ask.

She plops down on the smooth top of the trunk and dangles her feet over the side. Nari sticks her hands in her tangled hair as her eyes fall closed and she leans back on several sturdy branches.

"I'm tired."

Well, I suppose sleeping in a tree is a better idea than on the ground. It's the middle of the day so no demons are awake, but there are other predators in the forest. So I climb the tree and nestle into the nook alongside Nari. She falls asleep quickly, her fingers twitching slightly until her chest rises and falls in a quiet rhythm. I close my eyes. What a strange girl she is.

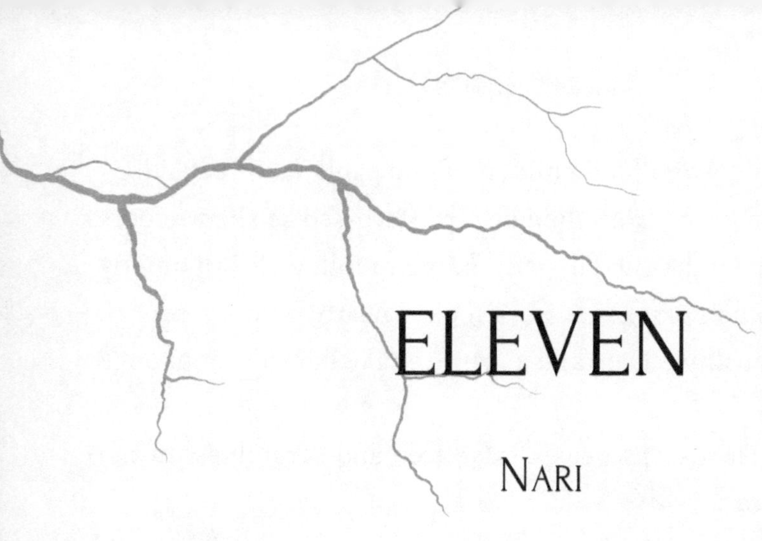

ELEVEN

Nari

I FEEL LOST WITHOUT my innate sense of direction. As Tetsu climbs higher into the tree to somehow see where we're going, I tick off the lack of abilities humans have on my fingers. No lightning, no regeneration, no internal compass, no night vision, and lackluster hearing. Why would anyone want to remain in these bodies?

Sanoul. I need to change back into my fox form soon.

As I'm about to voice my concern to Tetsu, I hear him scrambling back down to our little nest where we rested for the day. He crouches next to me and holds onto a branch, his dark eyes scanning the forest beyond before he drops his voice and tells me, "We're near the fox demon spawning temple."

My heart leaps for joy but then I smother it and let my brow furrow instead. "That's not good."

"Actually, it's perfect." Tetsu pauses, looking over my face before he goes on. "This is where I and the other trappers were going. We received word that there was to be a spawning ritual soon and we were supposed to observe it. I don't know if we've missed it though."

I shrug. "I wouldn't know anything about fox spawning."

"Right, right." He scratches his whiskerless chin and points behind his back. "We'll head there once the sun is down. But I need you to be absolutely quiet, Nari, do you think you can do that?"

"Yes."

His eyebrow lifts. "You won't go running into the arms of the Heavenly Fox, right?"

My stomach twists and my nose twitches as I curl my fingers around my smock. "Of course not. That's asking for death."

"Good." Tetsu sits, letting his legs fall over the side and I can tell he wants to say more.

"What is it?"

"Don't take this the wrong way but...were you raised by animals?"

Why would anyone take that the wrong way? I think to myself. *Wait, maybe that's a bad thing in human terms.*

Softly, I hum to myself, wondering how I should answer.

Tetsu continues, "I mean, you act like an animal sometimes. You didn't know how to walk when we first met. But you speak decently so...I was just wondering."

"Is it bad to live with animals?"

"Depends on the animal. If you lived with the fox demons, for instance, I don't think I could trust you."

I shake my head. "The foxes would never let a human live among them."

"Well, yeah. It makes sense." His eyes narrow. "We're archenemies."

"I didn't live with foxes. I lived with...wild dogs."

"Your entire life?"

I nod.

"And no...family has ever come to claim you?"

"Never."

Tetsu's expression grows distant and dusk descends on the forest, casting the green foliage in a golden glow.

"What about your family?" I ask after a breath of silence. "Are they the trappers?"

He grunts, sliding off the tree and scrambling to the ground. "Let's get moving. I don't want to miss the spawning itself."

It happens around midnight, I want to say. We have plenty of time until then. But I follow Tetsu and we pick our way toward the temple. I've only been to this particular temple once, as a newborn kit. I don't remember much of the night but the sky was vibrant and red and full of stars. It was beautiful, a manifestation of the Heavenly Fox's power.

When we reach the temple grounds, we hunker low behind a fallen pillar. There's no tree coverage over the temple so we have a clear view of the sky and the gnawing darkness that comes into the world. I sit next to Tetsu and take even breaths as hundreds of foxes emerge from the forest in all directions.

Most of them have more than one tail and carry a limp, fox kit body in their mouths. The temple itself is huge and made of smooth stone with pillars dotting the perimeter. The courtyard is long, round, and carved in the middle with the symbol of the foxes—a crescent moon on its back with two stones at the top and three raindrop-shaped markings flaring out from the bottom of the moon. The symbol will hold the soul beads as the Heavenly Fox opens the portal to the Eternal Darkness and spawns more foxes.

I'm beyond thrilled to see the spawning event take place, as I've only ever heard about it when talking to Chul or my skulk. Then it dawns on me—the Heavenly Fox will be here...she can take my beads and turn me back. I almost let a giddy titter escape me as excitement overwhelms me before I rein myself in. It's so difficult to let my fox nature go until I can get turned back.

As the foxes lay the kit bodies in a circle around the symbol, an ethereal, white light glows from the statue of the Heavenly Fox. It stands beneath a hollow structure shaped like an egg. The front is open and hangs over the statue while the back is closed and covered in moss and vines, keeping the statue safe from the elements. I stare, unblinking, as Khana materializes from the light in front of the statue.

While the other foxes bow low to the ground as she walks toward the symbol, I resist the urge to jump and run to her. But my eyes still brim with liquid and I make sure I don't look at Tetsu. He's very still and quiet anyway, but I see his hands curl against the pillar, knuckles white.

The Heavenly Fox's fur is a soft white, luminous and flowing as she walks with her chin held high. She has nine-tails and soul beads strung around her neck and ankles. The crescent symbol is black on her fur, resting at her forehead along with a jewel-studded crown. Even from here, I can see her eyes glowing silver. So glorious. I feel unfit to even be witnessing her divinity.

When she reaches the symbol, she sits back on her haunches and lets out a melodic bay that reverberates through my bones. She is much larger than the other foxes, nearly a giant, and they join in the call. My throat itches to join but I remain quiet.

Then she lifts her paw and the sounds stop. Khana removes the string of soul beads from her neck and ankles. They slip off the string and into the outline of the symbol, filling it. There's at least several hundred of them and I know, from Chul's stories, that she doesn't spawn a thousand foxes at once. There's another temple near the northern part of Daion where she will go next. Besides, it takes a fox a long while to collect soul beads and the batch she has now could only be from one.

She rises to stand on her hind legs and lifts her forepaws. Her footpads begin to glow and the air shudders right in front of her, just over the symbol. The red sky grows deeper, the color bloody and dark, and a sparking, white portal grows until it's large enough for a fox spirit to pass through. The sight is miraculous and wetness stains my cheeks. I want to be one of the foxes ready to take a newborn kit back to the Den. I want to be a fox again.

TWELVE

Tetsu

MY HANDS ARE CLAMMY and aching as I grip the pillar. I feel breathless watching Khana open the portal. She's much larger than I anticipated, standing about twelve hands tall. The other foxes are twice as small. Even if I wanted to, I wouldn't be able to defeat her by myself. It would take more people and skill than what the trappers already have and I feel my chest deflate as hope escapes. I didn't realize just how many foxes inhabited Daion and how powerful the Heavenly Fox is herself.

Khana sits back on her haunches and summons forth dark spirits from the portal. They swirl around her glowing body, taking the form of foxes as their legs and snouts lengthen, their bodies becoming slim and their tails long. I don't know where the fox demons come from or why they decided to infest our realm long ago. No one has ever sat down and asked a demon those questions. But they're certainly not from the Celestial Realm, where the good spirits reside. They must be from purgatory—a prison they're not meant to escape.

As I watch the spirits fly around the temple and dive into the seemingly dead fox kits, heat flares from the scar on my stomach. I wince, setting a hand there, and nearly yelp as I gasp quietly. My stomach feels like it's on fire and I lean back, rolling up my tunic to take a look.

Next to me, Nari whispers, "What's happening to you?"

I ignore her and stare at my skin, which is now glowing a reddish-orange. A strange light is being emitted along the crease of the scar, pulsing as it moves back and forth. The heat spreads through my body and beads of sweat rise on my skin, dripping into my eyes. I lean back on the pillar, biting my lip to keep from groaning as I look at the ritual again. I need to witness it so I can report back to Kyung.

Nari's fingers flit over my stomach but she burns herself and lets out a hiss. I glance at her, lifting a finger to my mouth. We need to be quiet or we'll die.

"Feeling a little warm, are we?" the voice says abruptly, mocking me.

I ignore it too.

Once all the spirits have fled from the portal, it closes with a whoosh and the kits rise, wobbling on their pudgy, short legs. The adult foxes stand and nudge the kits forward, toward the strange symbol and the Heavenly Fox. One by one, the kits sit in the belly of the crescent moon and Khana takes a bead and breaks it. A human soul shrieks as it emerges, face gaunt and ghostly until it's sucked into the jewel of her crown and silenced. Then she steps toward the kits, bows her forehead to theirs and the jewel glows at the touch of their fur.

Father told me long ago that fox demons were given a human soul that made them mortal. It also gave them the ability to speak with us and, when they collected several souls, it helped them shapeshift. But Father also said it was a rare occurrence for a fox demon to become human since collecting souls takes a long, long time.

I bunch my tunic in my fist and press it against my stomach, trying to quell the pain as I nestle my chin on the pillar. *"That's how I should have come into this world but it was stolen from me. Now I'm trapped."*

We watch each kit receive its soul and disappear into the forest on the back of one of the adult foxes. None come our way and soon, the pain turns into a cold, numbing feeling as the night winds down. When the other foxes have all dispersed, only the Heavenly Fox remains.

Before I push myself to my feet, another fox slinks to Khana's side. Their snouts twitch as their mouths open and close, soft chittering sounds passing between them. Nari shifts, crunching leaves next to me as she rises to her feet. She clasps her hands together, her head tilted as her eyes glaze over. I reach up as she sets a foot on the pillar. She swats my hand away but I get ahold of her and pull her back down to the ground, protecting her head with my arm.

Nari yelps in surprise and I stiffen, my breath escaping me as the chittering stops. Slowly, I glance over my shoulder and see the two fox demons staring directly at me.

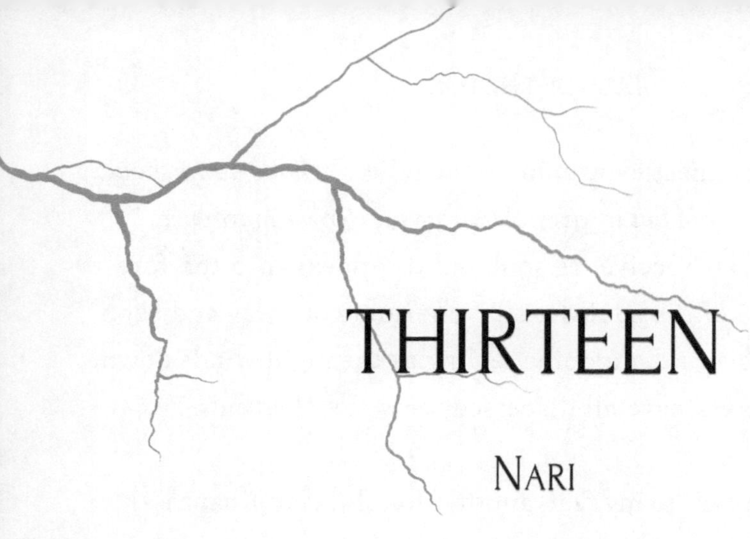

THIRTEEN

Nari

I try to shove Tetsu off me, but he holds me down and his hot breath hits my ear as he whispers fiercely, "*Be quiet. You're blowing our cover.*"

"Get off me!" I protest, not caring how loud I'm being. I need to speak with the Heavenly Fox.

Tetsu rolls off me but yanks me to my feet and I feel my shoulder pop at the force. I whimper and look back at the temple. Khana is gone, but another fox remains and runs toward us. Tetsu curses again and drags me after him.

"Run, Nari!"

I reach a hand out, wishing to tell the fox who I am but now that I can't exchange my soul beads tonight, I still need Tetsu to take me to Sanoul so I keep my mouth shut and I run with him.

"What were you thinking?" he chides. "You're going to get us killed!"

I don't reply and instead, my jaw tightens, teeth grinding. Behind us, I hear the fox's feet striking the earth as she chases us. If she catches us, I may have no choice but to hurt her, which I don't want to do.

Tetsu and I nearly ram into a tree that appears out of nowhere, but we split and clash on the other side. Shoulder to shoulder, his hand grappling mine. I feel static charge the air and look up past the canopy. Energy flows in veins against the sky, sparking and ready to strike. Quickly, I release Tetsu and stop, turning toward the fox.

She leaps into view and skids to a halt, dropping low as a growl curls her lips.

"Nari!" Tetsu cries.

Slowly, I get down on my knees and bow myself to the ground, laying my hands flat. I maintain eye contact with the fox and after a moment, she straightens. Her gaze shifts from me to Tetsu and her tails stiffen as she stares at him.

I hear Tetsu's soft footsteps behind me as he creeps forward and reaches down to grasp my arm. The fox doesn't move and I shake him off.

"Stop it."

The fox's ears twitch and she steps back, dipping her head. Then she turns and flees into the forest, disappearing from our sight. I let out a sigh of relief and stand, brushing my hands over my smock. It's far dirtier than it was a few days ago and suddenly, I wish for a bath. Hopefully, there's a spring nearby.

Tetsu spins me toward him and grips my arms, his face a little too close to mine that his features blur slightly.

"You're absolutely insane, you know that?" he tells me.

"I'm not insane, I was showing her submission so she wouldn't attack us."

For a moment, Tetsu is quiet and a cool breeze sweeps through the forest, ruffling our hair. I feel my skin flush as his gaze softens and shutters, eyes roving over my face. I quickly step back and turn on my heel.

"Let's find a spring to wash up in. I think we've rolled around in the dirt enough."

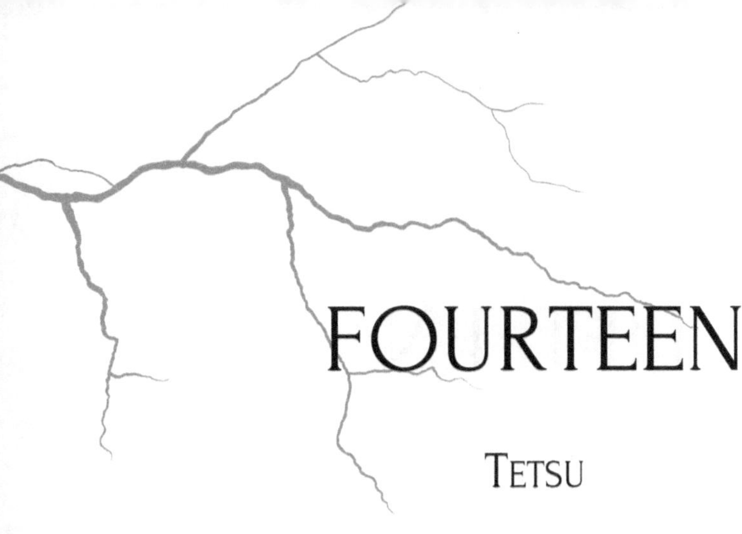

FOURTEEN

TETSU

I WANT TO SCOLD myself for the thoughts swirling through my head. She's strange and out of her mind and yet, a quick thinker and a warrior. I rub my cheek as my skin grows hot with a blush. This girl is like no one I've ever met and not only does the demon leaving us alone confuse me, but now, more than ever, so does Nari.

Glancing at her, I feel my pulse quicken for a moment. She's a mess, with leaves and small twigs stuck in her hair. Her smock is grimy, smudged with dirt, and torn at the hem. I know I look just as disastrous. The last few days have been wild and even though I didn't expect to ever see Nari again, I'm glad she's here now...so I'm not alone in the Bamnai Forest with demons at every turn.

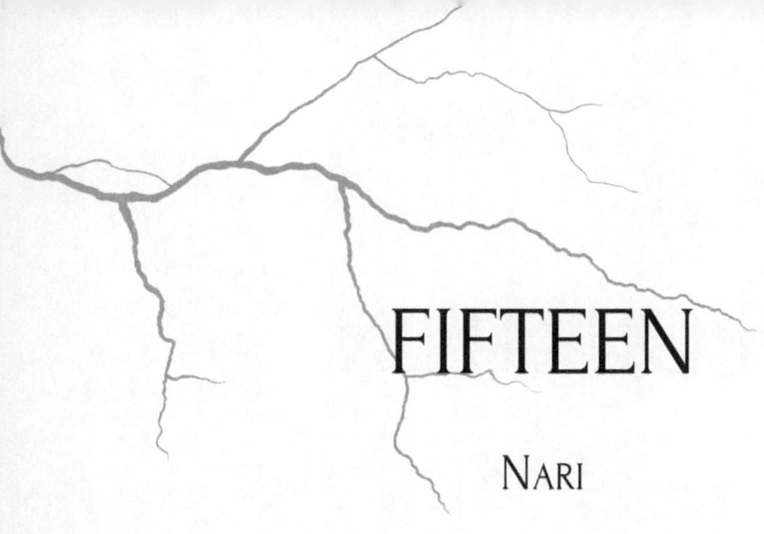

FIFTEEN

Nari

I GNAW ON MY lip as we walk through the forest and dawn approaches. Tetsu was looking at me strangely and I don't know what came over him. I almost revealed my true nature to him, but I'm desperate. Besides, once we reach Sanoul, I'll probably never see Tetsu again or if I do, it'll be during a raid.

Regardless, I must stay human enough for now.

"I hear something," Tetsu says at my side and stops, turning around.

I listen too and hear the faint sound of bubbling water. We move off our path to the left and pick our way through briars and hanging moss. The natural spring we come upon is a bit small but big enough that Tetsu and I can keep our distance. The steam is heavy as it swirls around us and I dip my toe in to test the water.

"Ow!" I draw my foot back and my toe beams bright red.

"It looks like it's boiling," Tetsu says and shakes his head. "I don't think it's a good idea to cook ourselves."

"There must be more nearby, right?" I tiptoe around the spring and listen for water.

The further we go, the darker it gets as the trees crowd in around us, but we manage to find another spring. This one is deeper and bigger, with a reasonable amount of steam. I test it and slip my whole foot inside. It's pleasantly warm and not scalding hot.

"This one works."

When Tetsu doesn't say anything, I glance at him to see him staring at the water. It appears black with a shallow shore ringed around the edge.

"It looks deep."

I turn to him and take his hand, his gaze shifts toward me. "I can hold on to you if you like."

"While we're bathing?" Tetsu's face flushes until he's the same color as the sky.

I know I'm missing something here. So I ask, "What's wrong with bathing together? I did it with the dogs all the time."

"Well, it's…it's different. We're…you're you and I'm me and…" he releases my hand and steps away, covering his face. "It's just weird, okay?

"But why?"

Tetsu shakes his head. "I'll wait till we get back to the trapper's camp."

I place my hands on my hips and huff, "We don't even know where we are or where we're going. And you stink."

"So what?" he sits down, pulling his knees against his chest, his back to me.

With a sigh, I step forward and crouch beside him, my hands on the ground. "I know you're afraid of the water, Tetsu. If you like, I can teach you how to tread it."

"You won't be…pressed up against me, will you?"

"No, I can just hold your hand."

Slowly, he nods. "Okay."

I help him to his feet and we move to the edge of the pool again. Into the water I go, tugging him along until he stops me.

"What are you doing?"

"Getting in the water."

"But your clothes...it'll weigh you down."

I look down at the smock I'm wearing. I always considered my fur to be comparable to human clothing but then I remember the horrendous bath at the Forsaken Sisters. I chuckle awkwardly and bounce out of the water.

"Oh yeah, I forgot about that."

Peeling off my smock, I hear Tetsu shriek and he turns away. "I'm just...I'll go to the other side and get in."

"Why?"

He hurries over without saying anything and is mostly obscured by the steam. I drop my smock and hop in the water, splashing Tetsu as I dunk beneath. He yelps and once I surface, he's already up to his waist in the water. The scar on his stomach looks livid as it touches the water, flushing with color.

I hold out my hand and Tetsu gingerly takes it, keeping his arm straight and stiff so I'm as far away as possible. He also stares intently into my eyes and never looks beneath the surface.

"Just flutter your feet back and forth," I instruct him as I guide him off the shore.

Tetsu gasps when the sand falls away and he's left with nothing to stand on.

"Flutter your feet," I tell him again.

"I'm doing that."

I dunk my head in the water but it's too dark to see and Tetsu curses. "Don't look!"

"I'm trying to see your feet, dummy."

"You don't need to. See, I'm staying above the water."

His chin soon meets the surface and he tilts his head up, eyes wide and terrified. "Sweep your arm too," I say. "Like this."

I show him and Tetsu splashes widely, tossing water right into my face. I sputter and blink, my eyes stinging with the heat and I whisk away the stray droplets.

"Slower, you don't need to be so frantic."

"Why did I agree to do this?"

I shrug. "I don't know. Just focus on moving and you'll be okay."

His eyes fall closed and he tries to even his breathing out. I yawn and smack my lips. After this, I'm climbing a tree and falling asleep. Later, when we wake, we can figure out where we're going since Tetsu has to report back to the trappers. A thought brews in my mind. The trappers ought to know the way to Sanoul and if they want to take down the Heavenly Fox, they may strike there soon. Though it makes my stomach coil, I know what I have to do—join the fox trappers. It goes against everything I am, but I must do all I can to get to Sanoul.

"Ah, Nari!" Tetsu suddenly rasps and scrambles for me. He grabs me and his weight catches me off guard. We begin to sink.

"What are you doing?" I ask, trying to free my arms from his crushing embrace.

"I felt something touch my foot."

As my toes flex, I feel something slimy slide along my ankle and calf. I pull my leg right up...and into Tetsu. He groans as his face pinches in pain.

"Oops, sorry."

"This is horrible, I'm getting out."

I give him a gentle shove toward the shore, but he still flaps around as he scrambles to get out. The steam covers him as I swim the opposite way. On the shore, I grab my smock and dunk it in the water. The grime washes off with a few dunks and I scrub it with my hands. I squeeze the extra water out and then drape the damp smock over my shoulders and knot it at my waist. It gets cold quickly and I shudder, rubbing my hands on my arms as I search for Tetsu.

He emerges from the other side of the spring with his head hung, his tunic and trousers also damp. His mahogany hair curls against his forehead and around his ears. Something stirs in my belly--a warm, fluttering feeling. I know exactly what it is and I swallow hard, pivoting away from Tetsu. There's no way a fox should ever develop feelings for a human.

Never.

SIXTEEN

TETSU

I SHIFT FOR THE thousandth time, wincing slightly as the sharp, spindly branches dig into my back and bones. Nari is fast asleep, curled up and snoring softly. Her hair falls over the edge of the trunk and flutters in the breeze. That same breeze makes my clothes cling to me and my skin cold to the touch.

Bathing in the spring was a disaster and when I grabbed her...*ugh*, I don't want to remember the feeling of her body against mine. My skin heats just thinking about it and I pull the collar of my coat up to cover myself. I didn't mean to grab her but something definitely touched my foot. Maybe it was just grass...in a hot spring.

As the day wears on, I climb higher in the tree, swaying gently on the limbs. I push aside fragile green leaves slowly taking on their autumnal coat of color and find myself on top of the forest. I squint, shielding my eyes against the sun as I search for the temple. A sliver of a pillar appears, glistening in the light and I'm glad to find we're far, far away now.

Carefully I spin myself around to look in the opposite direction for some sign of life. Tendrils of black smoke rise in the distance, an angry storm brewing just above. Pure white lightning strikes the ground, ruffling several trees in its wake. A peal of thunder rumbles across the forest next, cracking like a whip in my ears. I'm guessing the target of nature's storm is another village but that is natural. We can't do anything about it. The sky only churns with red clouds and lightning at night, when the real nightmare commences.

Regardless, the demons will pick their way through the village tonight and collect more souls to spawn their kits.

With a grunt, I shimmy back down to Nari and stare at her for a moment. I can't imagine how she managed to survive this long in the forest, even being raised among wild dogs. She must have run into the demons occasionally and bowing herself to the ground wouldn't fool a whole skulk.

When we reach Juhto, I'll take her back to the Forsaken Sisters and head to the trappers' camp.

I sigh and snap off a nearby branch, slipping a small throwing dagger from my pocket. It's not the right kind of knife for whittling but I'm too anxious to sleep and carving something out of nothing will keep my mind occupied for now.

SEVENTEEN

NARI

AFTER ANOTHER NIGHT OF walking through the forest, we make it back to the human villages at dawn. Tetsu immediately reaches for my arm and directs me to Juhto, where the Forsaken Sisters Guild resides, but I shake him off and run in the opposite direction.

"Hey—Nari, come back here."

"I'm not going to that guild!" I retort.

The humans walking along the roads between villages glance at us, brows raised. I tear through scratchy bushes and leap off rocks sticking halfway out of the ground. Thorns catch on my smock and tug relentlessly, but I pull harder and free myself.

Tetsu catches me around the waist as I stumble into a grove of trees and the momentum takes us down. We crash to the ground, my shoulder hitting his chest as he turns just in time for me to land on him.

"Ow," Tetsu groans.

I squirm in his arms, trying to pull them apart so I can free myself, but his grip only tightens, pressing into my stomach.

"Let me go, Tetsu."

"Why'd you run away from the Sisters?" he asks gruffly, his voice grating against my ears.

"Because they're strange and unkind."

"But it's free food and shelter for you. And clothes."

"I can find those things by myself."

When I realize he won't let me go, I collapse against his chest and let out a frustrated sigh. Tetsu doesn't stand, he just lies there, drawing in deep breaths and expelling them. I turn in Tetsu's arms so I'm facing him.

He stares at me, a blush creeping along his cheeks and ears. "What are you doing?"

"Looking you in the eye," I say.

"Turn back, it's weird."

"You're the one holding me hostage!"

"Shhh!" His eyes dart here and there, searching for any other sign of life. "You don't need to be so vocal. If people hear that, they'll think the wrong thing."

I smirk and tip my head back, breathing in as I prepare to let out a scream. But Tetsu's head comes up and his mouth covers mine so that when I unleash my scream, it's muffled. His eyes are wide and he's bright red. I jerk back and quickly drag my mouth on the shoulder of my smock, trying to get rid of the saliva that coats my lips.

"What was that?" I snarl.

Tetsu releases me and I tumble off him. I sit up and hunch over, rubbing my mouth again until my skin burns.

"You wouldn't pipe down," he says gruffly and rubs the back of his neck. "Just...go back to the Forsaken Sisters, Nari."

Then he runs off and I turn my head to watch where he goes.

I shake my head and say to myself, "I'm not going back there, dummy."

Once I feel ready, I stand and follow the path Tetsu left. He has slowed down to a walk but is still far enough away he won't be able to hear me. We traverse through the forest and across a meadow with permanent scorch marks on the ground. Tetsu leads me to the trapper camp, which looks to be among the ruins of a human village, and I hang back as he walks past the wooden planked walls. The camp beyond has a firepit in the middle and tents set up, the largest one just across from the firepit. A dozen humans meander about, one carrying a large pot that looks like it might break his back and soup sloshes over the sides.

Tetsu goes to the largest tent and slips inside, the flap slapping him. I sit on the ground and pluck blades of grass, twisting them together as I wait for him to reemerge. A few minutes later, he does, alongside a tall man with shoulder-length, black hair and a prominent scar through one eye.

I stand and approach the camp with a straight back, shoulders relaxed. Tetsu speaks with one of the trappers who was with him and the woman now has her arm in a makeshift sling and a nasty, yellowing bruise on her face. When his gaze finds me, his eyes widen and his mouth drops open. I stride into the camp and stop, setting my hands on my hips as the trappers turn to look and the conversation dies quickly.

The man with the scar pivots and his hand goes to the hilt of the sword at his side. "Miss, what brings you out this way?"

Tetsu is sneaking forward, eyes darting between me and the man. I feel my pulse quicken and my throat feels dammed up. *Say you want to join, Nari. Say you want to join this band of murderers.*

"She's, uh, clearly from the Forsaken Sisters," Tetsu states with a breathy chuckle as he gestures to me.

I shake my head. "No, I'm not. I want to join you."

The man's eyebrow lifts, stretching his scar so it beams white. "And what do you think you're joining?"

"The fox demon trappers, of course." I point to Tetsu. "I know him, we witnessed the spawning ritual together."

The man's head whips toward Tetsu, who shrinks away under his intense stare. "Really. I thought you said you were alone."

I take another step forward and clasp my hands together. "Well, he thinks me an invalid so maybe he felt like he was alone."

"You speak rather well for an invalid," another trapper murmurs.

I shrug.

The man comes toward me and though I feel my knees grow weak, I stand my ground. My head falls back as I look up at him and now I see that his eye with the scar is murky and gray. He's half-blind.

"What happened to your eye?" I ask before I can stop myself.

He leans down a little and his rank breath makes my nostrils seize. "Years ago, when I was a young man, I lived in a remote village on the Itson Cliffs. It was high enough that we thought those demons couldn't climb up and kill us. But we were wrong. They used their hellish magic to destroy the cliffs and the village collapsed, killing nearly everyone in the landslide. I was trapped beneath rubble, only part of my face exposed, and I watched as the demons roved over the bodies of my kin, taking their souls.

"A young demon with only one tail found me and thought it'd try to carve out my eye, torture me a little for fun. At least it was still too naive to take my soul but that didn't matter. I was trapped under the rubble for days until I realized no one would come find me so I had to save myself. As the only survivor, I fought my way through the forest and came here, establishing this clan of trappers. There was no mercy given that day and I will not grant mercy to those beasts."

He shuffles closer and I stiffen, feeling tension bundle tightly in my shoulders. "So, I must ask if you are willing to do the same. Joining this clan means life or death, miss, and merciless slaughter. We kill any demon we see. Can you do that?"

I swallow hard, my stomach in knots as I squeak, "Y—Yes."

"What was that?"

"Yes," I say a little louder, but my voice still trembles.

The man straightens, staring down his crooked nose at me. "What village do you hail from?"

"None. I'm a child of the forest. Raised by wild dogs."

"Hmm." He is quiet for a moment as he scans my face. "And no family has claimed you?"

"No."

"Then, if you're willing to learn how to fight, we can offer you a place here."

I nod. "Thank you."

"My name is Kyung. And you are?"

"Nari," I tell him.

He reaches for my shoulder and pulls me forward, turning as he raises his voice for the rest of the camp to hear. "Everyone, we've got a new initiate. This is Nari."

Grumbles are passed around and I can't make out what anyone says. But Tetsu comes up, his mouth pulled back in an uncomfortable half-smile as he says, "Kyung, I don't think it's a good idea for her to join us."

"Why not? It seems that you two are friends." Kyung retorts and smacks my shoulder.

I stumble into Tetsu, who quickly pushes me away. "I *really* think she should be taken to the Sisters Guild."

The man tsks and breezes past us. "So there's a girl your age here now, Tetsu, and you think she's cute. Don't drag me into your teenage drama."

Tetsu chokes and coughs into his elbow, whipping around as he stamps his foot. "I don't think she's cute!"

The rest of the camp snickers and Tetsu glances around before he sends me a glare and stomps away to another tent.

EIGHTEEN

TETSU

I TRIP OVER THE bedroll in my tent as I scramble to the wall and lean my ear on the tan canvas. Ranmi, Kyung's second-in-command and the camp's residential mother figure, speaks with Nari as they walk to the tent beside mine.

"Well, that was an entertaining spectacle to see. Nari, right?"

"Yes."

"I see you've gotten a smock from the Forsaken Sisters, were you there before?"

Their voices are muffled as they enter the tent and I strain to hear as Nari says, "Only for a little bit. I didn't like it much."

Ranmi lets out a husky laugh. "No girl in her right mind would willingly join the Forsaken Sisters." She pauses. I hear a trunk creak open and the lid thuds against the ground. "I've got trousers and blouses in here that I don't wear anymore. The trousers may be a bit long in the leg but we can roll them up and pin them if you like."

"I've never worn trousers before."

"Really?"

Nari doesn't reply so I imagine her shaking her head, her unruly orange locks shifting at the movement. Then Ranmi says, "I'll step out to let you get dressed. Just holler when you're done and I can help you make some adjustments."

"Thank you...what was your name?"

"Ranmi."

"Thank you, Ranmi."

"Of course."

As Ranmi's boots scuff the ground, I tiptoe to the back of the tent, where another flap that the other two trappers I share with have pinned. I rip it open and slip out. The rest of the trappers are gathered around the bonfire, waiting for breakfast to be served. The smell of chicken and cabbage drifts to my nose, making my stomach growl. I smack my stomach and dart to Nari's tent, tearing open the back flap.

Nari whips around, holding up the too large trousers around her waist, and her nose crinkles in disdain. She looks like she's wearing a giant's clothes and I refrain myself from chuckling.

She glares at me and keeps her voice low. "What do you want now?"

"You shouldn't be here," I whisper.

"Blah, blah, blah, I know that's what you think but you can't get rid of me now."

"What are you trying to get at?"

She rolls her eyes and goes to cross her arms when the trousers slip and she grabs them again, her knuckles white. "*Sanoul.*"

As if I could forget. I take a step forward and Nari stiffens, her gaze whipping over me as the corner of her lip twitches. "Do you realize how dangerous the imperial city is?"

She opens her mouth to protest before stopping herself and turning, calling, "Ranmi!"

I hurry out of the tent through the back and sink to the ground just outside, resting my head in my hands.

"Oh my," Ranmi laughs as she enters the tent a second later.

"I'm rather small," Nari says.

I zone out as they chat about idle things, my mind swirling with thoughts. Why am I so worried about Nari joining the trappers? Clearly, she can take care of herself considering the demonstration of her skills against the bandits. She would make a great asset to our community, in that regard.

Am I anxious because she's my age and I've been feeling flustered and confused ever since I met her? I exhale slowly and run my fingers through my hair, letting the strands fall against my forehead. If Mother was around, I'd ask her about these strange feelings. Or even Father, though he never talked much or expressed his feelings once Mother was gone.

No, no, it's definitely her fixation with Sanoul. That makes me incredibly uneasy. How can I even trust her when she's so obsessed with getting to the imperial city?

The flap snaps open and Nari comes out. She crouches before me and grabs my tunic, tugging me forward. My mouth falls agape as our faces nearly collide and I blush. Nari's black as midnight eyes bore into me, narrowing slightly.

"Why don't we pretend to be friends, Tetsu? I'm genuine about being a fox trapper," she pauses and swallows hard. "I mean, why should I waste my life in the Forsaken Sisters Guild when I could be doing something to change it? The more, the better, right?"

I glance away. "I suppose." Nari leans closer and I flinch, going in the opposite direction. "What are you doing?"

"Just accept that I'm in your life now, okay? It's not going to change, no matter what you try to do or say. So, can we be cordial about this moving forward?"

"I—" my gaze betrays me, flickering to her mouth for a split second. I quickly tilt my head back and stare at the clear blue sky through the tree canopy. "I suppose."

"Say yes, Tetsu."

"Fine, *yes*, I'll be cordial."

"Good." Nari squishes her finger against my nose and stands. From the firepit, the cook bellows, "Breakfast is up!"

NINETEEN

Nari

THE CHICKEN AND CABBAGE soup we're served with a slice of buttery bread makes my eyes widen and one taste sends me to the Realm of Ethereal Light. My legs bounce happily as I slurp the broth and tear into the chicken chunks. I haven't eaten since I became human. My belly bulges as I stuff myself and I feel increasingly drowsy. I want to curl up and sleep until nightfall.

I sit at the firepit with the other trappers, chin cradled in my palms as I close my eyes and take a snooze, until Ranmi nudges me awake. I push to my feet and follow her to a rack of weapons on the far side of the camp, yawning when her back is turned to me.

She sets her hands on her hips and juts her chin toward the weapons. "Are you good with any weapons?"

"Just my hands," I tell her.

Ranmi steps forward and grabs two small daggers from the wall. They have leather-bound grips and the blades are shallow, shaped like an elongated diamond. She demonstrates how to hold them first.

"These are lightweight and easy to use. Just imagine they're an extension of your hands." She holds the daggers and steps back, slicing at the space between us in quick, ruthless motions.

I shudder slightly. As a fox, the movement would cut up my face and neck. As a human, my chest and abdomen. Ranmi keeps her arms firm but fluid as she goes again, gripping the daggers. I watch and try to imitate the motions before she hands them to me. I wobble as I step back and copy her attack.

I'm sloppy and slow and bumbling around like a fool. The daggers feel strange in my hands and I much prefer a bare-handed method. Or lightning. My gaze drifts upward at the thought to the red-clouded sky churning above.

"You're stiff," Ranmi says, drawing my attention back to her. She steps around me and fixes my stance. "Think of yourself as water. Stalwart and powerful, but still able to glide and rush with ease."

I try to do as she says but sleepiness clouds my mind and Ranmi figures I might be better with a bow and arrow. We move to a shooting range, where I catch sight of Tetsu sitting in a tree, his arms crossed, head leaning on a thick branch. With his eyes closed, I figure he must be sleeping. My spirit stirs in my chest and a mischievous smile curls the corner of my mouth. He's a perfect target.

Ranmi fits me with a bracer on my right forearm and positions me behind a mark in the dirt. Though Tetsu is a fair distance away and to my left, she warns me not to hit him and to aim for the target pasted to a tree trunk directly in front of me. I nock an arrow and lift the bow, drawing the string back to my cheek. I glance at Tetsu again. Light shines through the canopy and highlights a stray lock of his hair fluttering against the branch.

I turn my torso slightly and release. Ranmi lets out a surprised sound as the arrow flies toward Tetsu and it catches that stray lock, pinning it to the branch. He jerks awake, his hair ripping and his eyes wide, and Ranmi snatches the bow from me. Out of the corner of my eye, I see her hand raise and lay flat, ready to chop at the slope of my neck. I duck and spin around, grabbing Ranmi's arm and pulling it back and up against her. She gasps and goes still, her hand forming into a fist.

Tetsu drops from the tree and runs toward us, his hair flopping and spilling into his eyes, which he angrily shoves back. "Did you shoot at me, Nari?" he barks.

"Not on purpose," I lie and blink at him.

Ranmi huffs. "I saw you turn at the last moment."

"I didn't kill you, did I?"

His mouth drops open and he lifts his hands, his voice rising. "That's not the point! You saved me from drowning only to get us caught by bandits, chased by a fox demon, and now you're trying to impale me!"

"Not quite. You did drown."

Tetsu stares at me, his dark eyes swimming with anger and strife. I let Ranmi go, shoving her away and say, "I told you I was better with my hands."

She reaches up and rubs her shoulder, her gaze wary. "Yes, you are. I guess I'll tell Kyung your strength is in hand-to-hand combat." She looks between us. "You two better work things out and *don't* kill each other." Ranmi lifts an eyebrow at me.

I tuck my hands behind my back. "I swear, I won't."

To Tetsu, she asks, "Can you handle yourself?"

"Yes," he says gruffly and crosses his arms again.

Now with his sleeveless tunic, the muscles in his arms are more defined against the dark fabric. I drag my gaze from analyzing him to his face as Ranmi hesitantly leaves us alone. I wait until we can't hear her clomping through the forest anymore before I let out a deep sigh.

"What are you sighing about? That you're absolutely insane?" Tetsu snaps.

My eyes narrow to slits but I stay where I am. I have a biting remark on my tongue but then an idea dawns on me. Tetsu may try to act all rough and tough but I've seen one consistent side of him in the last few days we've spent together. The not-so-skilled, awkward, blushing boy. Our back-and-forth banter and shenanigans remind me of playing with the other kits in the Den.

It was our way of being affectionate and strengthening the bond within the skulk. Of course, we'd snap to attention and wise up whenever Sook came around. I feel like Tetsu is a kit I should be a bit kinder to—especially seeing that I need him to be my true self again. And what better way to be kind than to play to his human nature?

I close my eyes and let my expression soften. Though I'm still too young to find a partner and bear a not-live kit body for the Heavenly Fox, I've seen vixens and tods flirt and play while in heat. All I have to do is gain his trust and not be so...deadly.

But it's in my nature.

Again, I sigh and look at him, letting my mouth fall into a slight pout. "I'm sorry for being so aggressive. It's just..." I trail off and swallow hard, forcing myself to stare at him until heat flushes my skin. "Among the wild dogs, we would play to show affection for one another and sometimes, it would get rough. I see that such a method doesn't translate well when I'm with other humans."

Tetsu grunts softly and reaches up to rub the back of his neck. He lifts his shoulders in a shrug and asks, "Why would you be doing that with me? I'm just a stranger."

"You're not so much anymore." I pause and let myself swing back and forth. "I mean, I don't know a lot about you, but I find that I—I—like you, Tetsu." I stammer out.

I feel my heart pound in my chest, even though it's a lie. I don't have a full grasp of human emotions just yet or what it even means to like someone.

When I look at him, he's gone completely still and is flushed red. Tetsu blinks several times and I wonder if he's simply stopped functioning. Tentatively, I shuffle forward. He leaps back, trips over his own feet, and falls.

A breath of silence passes before I burst out laughing. Tetsu's brow knits and he whines, "It's not funny, Nari!"

I cover my mouth, still giggling, and manage to say, "I can't help myself."

Tetsu stands and brushes the dust off his trousers as he steps toward me. I stare at him with large, dazzling eyes and he softens just a little.

"I didn't know what I was getting into when I met you, but it's sure been an adventure so far." Tetsu gnaws on his lip, drawing my attention there before I reprimand myself and my cheek twitches as I look into his eyes again. He clears a wide berth around me and I turn with him. "I understand where you're coming from but right now, it's just strange and honestly, I feel like you've gone from saving me to wanting to kill me. I know I'm not the brightest or best there is but we're supposed to be allies. All people are."

Tetsu stops and sticks out his hand. "Let us be allies then." I sniff before I slowly walk to him and he waves his hand. "Shake on it, this is me being cordial."

"Allies it is," I mutter and set my hand against his. Tetsu locks his fingers around mine and bows slightly at the waist. His hair slips forward and I wonder what it'd be like to groom and pull back into a topknot. At least it would keep the hair out of his face.

But instead, I bow back and then he releases my hand. I let him go back to camp and then turn away, plopping down to the ground.

Pulling my knees against my chest, I stare into the forest and let wisps of ideas churn through my brain.

Humans are more receptive to kindness than aggression. I can be kind. I was always kind to Chul.

Tetsu gets flustered if I show skin or am too close to him. I'll keep my distance and only get close as he allows it, to build him up to being comfortable and vulnerable around me. I will get to Sanoul one way or another.

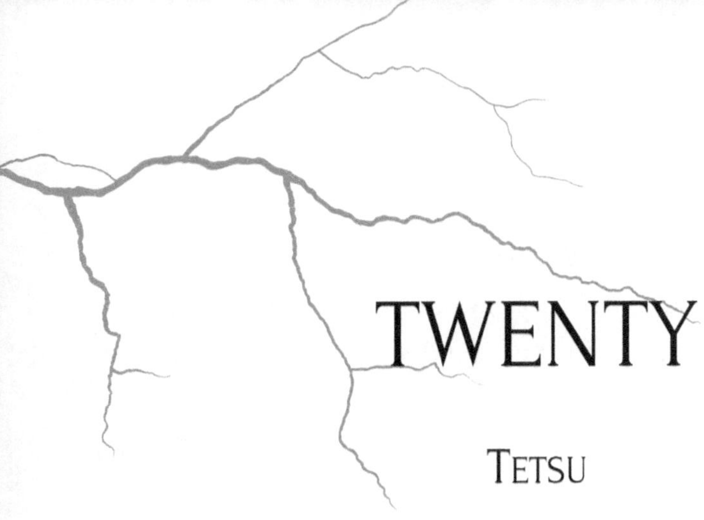

TWENTY

TETSU

NARI LIKES ME…

And I don't know how I feel about that.

Occasionally, I do enjoy our banter but that little stunt with the bow today was way too far. Is she sending a message? That if I don't stick to her terms, the arrow will be in my forehead next? I shudder and rub away the gooseflesh that pops up on my arms. She's truly something scary.

I head to Kyung's tent, where he sits on hand-woven mats with Ranmi. Their discussion comes to an abrupt halt as I enter and Kyung grunts, "Just the man I wanted to see. Ranmi was telling me about you and Nari."

"She's insane," I blurt out. "Why'd you even let her join us?"

"I thought you could learn a thing or two about lying to me, Tetsu. She seems like an honest girl."

He gestures for me to sit and I drop to the ground with a thud, tucking my legs beneath me. Kyung runs a hand through his shoulder-length hair, giving me a pointed look. "But that's not the only reason. I'm cautious. It's better to keep an eye on her here rather than have her lurking around the forest."

I blink in surprise. "Cautious? What for?"

Ranmi snorts. "Really, Tetsu? As you said yourself, the girl seems to be unstable. She may be one of us but that doesn't mean she's fully on our side."

I gnaw on my lip, thinking for a moment before asking, "Do you think she's a demon?"

Ranmi shakes her head. "She looks too young to have obtained one thousand souls."

"And we would have heard back from Shik and Yul if one of the demons turned into a human," Kyung adds.

I knot my fingers together and nod. Shik and Yul are the scouts who observe and know nearly everything about the fox demons. Well, enough to make us weary of them and understand their attack patterns. But at the raid of Pangul, I only saw one fox with eight tails, the one that killed Master Haku. She didn't transform so she didn't have one thousand soul beads yet.

"Regardless, her behavior is unacceptable, but," Kyung shares a glance with Ranmi and lets a smirk grace his mouth, "maybe the girl fancies you, Tetsu, and this may be the only way she knows how to show it."

With a sharp exhale through my nose, I cross my arms and retort, "Why does everyone think that because we're the same age, we ought to fancy one another? I think she's so clingy because it seems like I'm the first person she actually communicated with. When we first met, she didn't know how to walk on her own two feet. She said she was raised by wild dogs and I believe it."

"And what do wild dogs do when they're trying to capture another's attention?" Ranmi asks, hardly waiting for me to answer. "They tease and play. Nari clearly doesn't understand how human relationships work and is a bit aggressive, but I'll have to agree with Kyung. She likes you."

Though Nari just admitted it to my face, I'm still skeptical.

"I'm banning her from the weapons rack until she can learn to be civil, but Tetsu, just be patient with her. Maybe you can be friends."

"I'll be her ally, that's all. There's no reason to make friends in the world we live in."

Kyung's good eye twitches and he nods. "I'm assigning you to keep an eye on her and report anything you find concerning."

I snort. "Everything she does is concerning."

"You know what I mean." Kyung dismisses me with a wave of his hand and I stand, leaving the tent.

Outside, I glance around the camp and see Nari strutting through the place like she owns it. As I watch her, a wave of sleepiness washes over me and I'm even more upset now that I'd been rudely interrupted during a nice nap. I have to get back on schedule of sleeping during the night but for now, I'll snooze while the sun is up.

I slip into my tent and drop on my bedroll, my mouth falling open as my eyes flutter closed.

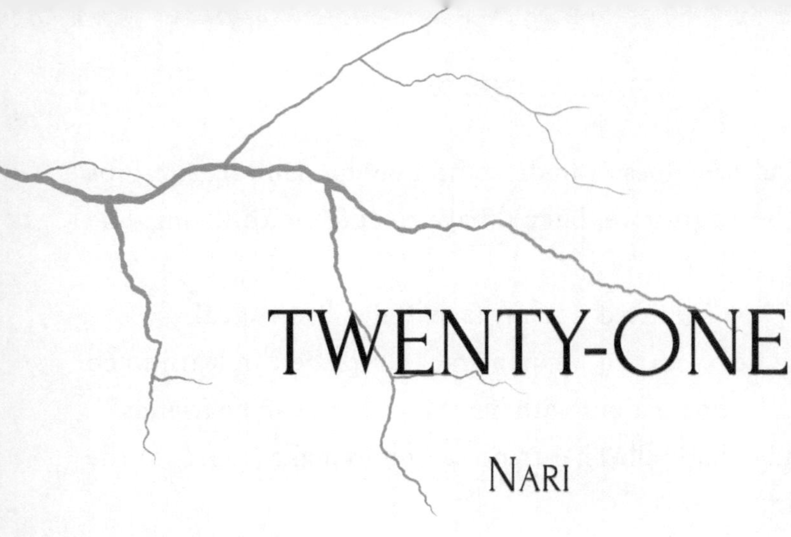

TWENTY-ONE

NARI

"YOU HAVE TO BE kind," Ranmi tells me as I sit across from her and Kyung in his tent.

I know shooting at Tetsu today was a bad idea, but I couldn't help myself. So I simply nod.

"Say you will," Kyung orders.

My nostrils flare slightly at the command but I comply. "I will be kinder to Tetsu."

"And not shoot arrows at him."

"And not shoot arrows at him," I repeat.

The two share a glance and a smirk. Ranmi leans forward, balancing her chin in the palm of her hand. "Now, we know you didn't grow up among people but you're going to have to take it up a notch in learning. If you want Tetsu to like you, I don't think aggression is his cup of tea."

How can you put aggression in tea? I want to ask.

"He's...softer than he may appear or act like," Kyung says, swirling his hand in the air. "So be gentle. Smile, flutter those eyelashes, and soon enough, you'll have him falling in love with you."

I blink slowly. *Love?*

They chuckle and then shoo me from the tent. I feel less reprimand-ed and more confused but I suppose I can try being kind. I tap my chin as I walk to my tent, though, wondering about aggressive tea. It must be a human thing.

TWENTY-TWO

CHUL

CHUL AND SOOK OBSERVED the trapper camp from a distance. He turned his head to and fro, his neck popping at the movement and he winced. He had been resting in the Den for the last two weeks after the incident with the fox trapper and Nari. And even though he and Sook should have been sleeping, this was the time when humans were awake.

Nari. His gaze zeroed in on her as she strode through the camp, her shoulders back and chin high with confidence. Chul's brow lifted. Since when had she changed from the playful, naive vixen he knew in the Den to acting like she had been human her entire life?

Next to him, Sook let out a low growl and tipped her head toward the main tent in the middle of the camp. Chul growled too, hackles rising on his back as he saw the trapper he'd chased after standing outside. The boy was tall and lanky, his sleeveless tunic and trousers black, his boots scuffed up. His eyes followed Nari and Chul felt heat burn in his chest. The sky above charged with electricity. It made his stomach turn just seeing Nari as a human but now, she was among the enemy and Chul couldn't do anything to keep her safe, lest he expose her true nature.

Sook pawed at his shoulder and said in a soft voice, "Calm down, they're not going to hurt her."

Chul shook himself and settled back as the boy retreated into another tent. Nari turned and walked in the other direction. Her expression was pinched, her brow furrowed as she paced. Apparently, she was bored and lost in thought.

"That boy was the one she saved from the pond."

Sook stared at Nari, studying her. "He looked familiar, like another human in one of our raids a few years ago. Did you happen to hear his name?"

"No."

"Hmm." Sook was quiet for a moment before she settled down on the ground and Chul did the same. They were hidden now in foliage and he soon felt himself drifting off, though his body refused to fall asleep completely as they were not safe so near to the trapper camp.

Finally, Sook spoke again, "Before you were spawned, there was a vixen named Yona who had collected one thousand souls and turned into a human. She and I were kits together but we didn't get along. When Yona turned, she left the Den and chose a human to take to the Guardian at the Gate. As you know, we're supposed to bring the soul beads to the Heavenly Fox as soon as possible.

"But it took Yona years before she came back to the Den as a fox. She didn't stay long and left to serve in Sanoul, but I always wondered why she had waited so long to turn back." Sook paused and glanced at Chul, her black eyes reflective in the light. "I think Yona must have fallen in love with a human and had a child. You said you smelled a familiar scent on the trapper, right?"

Chul bobbed his head. "It was a dark and sharp scent, that's why I followed him. I thought he might have turned but was from a different skulk."

"I don't have proof that Yona delivered the souls to Khana so this is only speculation, but if she didn't, she may have granted it to that boy. If he is a child she bore in the time she was human. So, when Nari touched him, she took the souls Yona had left behind. That's the only way a young vixen like her could have turned. She couldn't have collected one thousand all by herself."

One thousand human souls stored in one body? How was that even possible? And why would Yona do such a thing instead of deliver them to Sanoul? It was the only reasonable explanation for Nari turning, if Sook's speculations were true.

"I think she's chosen the boy to take her to Sanoul," he told Sook. "That must be why she's staying with the trappers."

"We'll have to keep an eye on her and make sure she goes."

"I'll take up the task," he offered.

Sook stood and started walking toward the Den. When he didn't follow, she asked, "Are you coming with?"

"Later. I want to make sure Nari is okay."

"She looks fine to me."

Chul grunted. He knew better.

TWENTY-THREE

SOOK

SOOK WAS ABSOLUTELY SILENT as she picked her way through the forest and to Bojin's cabin. She was careful in where she stepped and ducked beneath stray branches and walked on mossy patches. Humans were walking along the old trade routes, going from village to village. During the daytime, she noticed the humans would whistle and laugh and be far more relaxed than they were at night when the foxes were awake.

No matter. She wasn't here to raid any of the nearby villages and walked further into the forest. As Bojin's dilapidated cabin came into view, Sook prowled low to the ground in case any other humans were lingering nearby. Bojin's cabin sprouted moss and vines and had an ugly tree growing from the middle. It was held together by graying planks of wood, the gaps between them growing wider with age. Bojin himself sat outside, completely still and covered in rags. The human sported a ring of hair around his chin and beneath his nose. The beard was so long it almost covered his rotund belly.

Sook let out a soft bark to alert him of her presence. Bojin slowly straightened and inhaled deeply, his eyes opening. He was a strange human but a great help, nonetheless, and had not tried to kill her. Though he provided her with information about the villages, it seemed as if Bojin had not set foot in one in years. He was an outcast, a firm supporter of the foxes.

Bojin slid onto his knees as she approached, barking again. He bowed himself to the ground, his filthy hands caked in grime. Sook stood aside, her snout twitching at his rank scent and he lifted his head, looking at her with wide eyes. Bojin's bulbous nose was smudged with dirt.

"Have you heard of a human named Yona?" she asked him, her fox voice translating into human speech by way of the spirit that resided in her.

Bojin pushed himself up and stroked the end of his beard. "Yona? The name sounds familiar."

Sook hadn't seen what she looked like as a human so she couldn't offer that detail to Bojin but she did know when she turned. "She would have been here around twenty years ago. I need to know if she had a child."

"Hmm," Bojin's eyes squinted as he thought for a long, long while. Sook sat on her haunches and absently pawed at the dead leaves and patchy grass that covered the ground before her. Finally, he gasped and snapped his fingers. "Twenty years ago, you say?"

She nodded.

"I do recall seeing a particularly beautiful woman wandering the trade routes at night. She walked on all fours when I first saw her and I thought it was weird. Before I could ever approach, a woodcarver from one of the villages found her. I remember that he thought she was possessed. The woman snarled and scratched and told him her name. He figured she was just feral, not possessed."

"What did he do with her?"

"He swept her up and carried her to the nearest village." Bojin lifted his broad shoulders in a shrug. "From then on, I only saw her walking like a normal person and dressed in simple tunics. She seemed easily assimilated."

"Did she bear any child?"

Bojin went quiet again, rapping his fingers against his knee. "I vaguely recall seeing her with what looked to be a rounded-out stomach once, a few years later. But she was covered head-to-toe in a thick, fur coat since it was winter. The village was raided soon after and that was the last I saw of her near this part of the forest. I imagine they went northeast to Nagaseo."

"That's helpful, Bojin, thank you."

He nodded. "Why are you looking for a human anyway?"

Sook didn't answer and instead asked, "Can you write? Do you have parchment and ink here?"

It was a long shot, she knew, but if this woman was really Yona and had bore the human boy, Sook needed to get him to take Nari to Sanoul. Though Sook had never told Nari she was technically her mother and had birthed her kit body, she still cared for the young vixen. Nari was part of their skulk and she knew how much she and Chul had grown close over their time in the Den. It was seventeen years ago, in human terms, when she first laid eyes on the little kit with soft orange fur and an overly large head. Sook had watched her open her ink-black eyes in the spawning ritual and fallen in love.

Bojin grunted as he pushed to his feet and bumbled into the cabin. Sook heard him shuffling around and could see him through the gaps. She had never been inside, in case he attempted to ambush her, and didn't care to see what he lived like. He returned with a piece of torn parchment and a small bottle of ink, a magpie quill tucked into his beard. He looked at her expectantly.

"I need you to write a letter. Pretend you are a parent writing to your child."

"A letter? For who?"

"A human boy."

Bojin sat and she could tell he wanted to ask more but Sook began to dictate what it should say.

"My child, I write to you with grief in my heart. As you know, your mother was taken and hasn't returned yet. The truth is, she chose to leave." She paused as Bojin wrote, redipped the quill, and then continued, "The demons that infest our lands have brainwashed her and she is now their prisoner in Sanoul. Your mother loves you dearly, never think otherwise. She left to protect you and when you are older, I hope you can rescue her. Go to Sanoul, but don't go alone."

Bojin mouthed the words as he finished and looked up at her. "What should I sign it as?"

Sook shrugged and took a wild guess. "As 'your beloved father'? I don't know if this boy will be receptive to the letter but I must try."

"Signed, your beloved father." Bojin held the parchment up and read it over before he stood and clipped it to a line strung with his other patchy clothes.

From where she sat, Sook could see the ink staining the parchment but she couldn't read it.

"It'll have to dry," he told her.

"Scorch it too so it looks like it was found in a fire. I'll be back tonight," she said and turned, running off into the forest before he could reply.

TWENTY-FOUR

Nari

NIGHTTIME MEANS THAT WHILE the trappers are sleeping, I find myself wandering outside of the camp. Though I'll keep my distance from Tetsu, I know he'll be awake now and I don't want to confront him. I feel awkward and not so hopeful about what the future holds. I've already made Ranmi wary of me and she ran off and told Kyung. So if the trappers kick me out, or worse, force me back to the Forsaken Sisters, I don't know what I'll do.

As I walk the perimeter of the parapet, I hear the rustle of branches and crunch of leaves just beyond my reach. I stop and turn, squinting to see in the dark. A set of eyes reflect the silver of moonlight above and I step forward.

Chul emerges, albeit slowly, from the bushes he's hiding among and I bite the inside of my cheek to keep from squealing in delight. Instead, I drop down to my knees and grab him, tugging him into my arms.

"Chul, you're okay," I whisper, my voice muffled as I stuff my face against his black fur. He stinks but I don't care. At least for a second longer.

"Yes, I'm alive, thanks to you," he replies. I release him and Chul glances at the entrance to the trapper camp, which is only twenty paces away. "We should head out further. I don't want any of the trappers to hear or see us."

I drop my hands to the ground and start following him on all fours. But it's uncomfortable because my limbs are not the same length anymore so I straighten and wipe my hands on my trousers. Chul leads me away from the camp to a secluded grove where I see Sook waiting. Her eight tails gently thump the ground and her dark silver fur looks perfectly groomed. Sook has always been put together, even during raids her fur doesn't get messed up.

I feel so strange standing above them so I kneel before Sook and Chul. That's when I notice a piece of parchment beneath Sook's paw, neatly folded up. Sook's mouth spreads in a smile, her canines hanging over her bottom lip.

"Nari, I'm so happy to see you. You look quite different as a human."

I shrug and wiggle my arms. "It's not great but here I am. I'm trying to get to Sanoul, I promise."

"I know. That's why you're at this trapper camp, right? The boy with the dark hair, you've chosen him to escort you?"

"Tetsu? Yes, but he's so stubborn," my shoulders drop and I huff. "We were out by the Itson Temple and could have turned north instead of coming back here. I don't know why I didn't just drag him along."

Sook nods and sets a paw on my hand. The pads feel rough on my human skin but I don't say anything.

"Speaking of the boy...Tetsu, you said?"

"Yes."

"Speaking of Tetsu then, I have a letter for him. One I retrieved from an abandoned home on our recent raid. It's from his father."

"Oh?" My brow lifts in curiosity. "Do you...want me to deliver it?"

Again, Sook nods. I counter with, "Wait, how do you know it's from his father? We can't read the human language."

Chul and Sook share a glance, their whiskers twitching before she says, "I fabricated the letter *but,* if Tetsu reads it and decides to take action, he'll be heading to Sanoul soon."

"What does it say?"

"That his mother is there, taken by the foxes." Sook clears her throat. "If Tetsu believes the letter and confirms what I suspect about him...I don't know if he'll be suitable for the Guardian at the Gate."

"Why?"

"He may be half-fox, Nari. *But,* I am not entirely sure."

My eyes widen at the possibility and I want to ask more but we hear someone crashing through the forest. I snatch the letter from Sook and she and Chul scatter, leaving me alone in the grove. I lie on the ground, the letter clutched in my fingers, and squeeze my eyes shut. The footfalls patter off and I hear heavy breathing.

I open my eyes to slits and see a lanky figure obscured by the shadows of the trees. Chest rising and falling sharply.

"I felt...I heard the demons," Tetsu rasps.

Slowly, I sit up and pretend to be absolutely terrified. The liquid fills my eyes again of their own accord. "Th—they d—dragged me away. I could—couldn't scream."

Tetsu strides toward me and crouches, reaching up to cup my cheek. His brow is pinched but his eyes are soft and open. "You're okay, Nari, I've got you."

He straightens and looks around, pulling a short dagger from the belt slung around his hips. "Which direction did they go?"

"I don't—I don't know," I sob, hunching over my knees as my body shudders.

"Nari, it's okay," Tetsu sighs and sits on the ground with me, pulling me into his arms. I lean on his chest and hear the thunk of his heart beneath my ear. He shifts slightly and reaches up for the letter. "What's this?"

My mouth opens and closes like a fish as he unfolds the letter. Tetsu reads it quickly, his skin paling at what it says. I see his jaw clench tight and his head whips up, eyes narrowing on me. I scramble away but he grabs my tunic and yanks me back. The tip of his nose nearly touches mine in a fox kiss and his rapid breath is hot on my skin.

"Where did you get this letter from? Who is it for?" he snarls.

"The demons…" I trail off, letting my shoulders hunch and brow furrow in fright. "They gave it to me and left."

Tetsu stares at me, confusion and anger churning in his gaze. He releases my tunic and lifts the letter, turning it toward me. "Read what it says."

I look at the parchment and my nose twitches. The inked symbols just look like random marks to me and I feel an embarrassed blush creep onto my cheeks. I pull back, resting a hand on my throat as I croak, "I can't read."

"Are you sure?" he asks skeptically. "Just try."

"Um, it says…the demons want something? I don't know, Tetsu."

He turns the letter back and reads it again. "It appears to be a letter for me, though I don't know who penned it. Those demons can't write with a quill. But…and you wouldn't know anything about my family."

"It's about your family?"

Tetsu nods once and then his nostrils flare. He pushes to his feet and offers me a hand. I take it and stand next to him, my knees knocking together. I can really be a frightened, helpless vixen when I need to be.

As he sets an arm around my shoulders and leads me back to the camp, he says softly, "When I was eleven, my mother left my father and me. The next year, he was killed in a raid and I joined the trappers. My father never told me where she went and I always assumed she just abandoned us. If that was the case then…but this letter says she was captured by the demons and taken to Sanoul."

"Why did she leave in the first place?" I ask.

Tetsu's nose crinkles and his lip curls. "I don't know. Maybe she didn't love me as much as I thought."

We reach the camp and he helps me inside before abandoning me for his tent. I go to my own, where Ranmi sleeps soundly on her bedroll, her light-colored hair spilling over her bare shoulder and thin pillow. I drop down to my bedroll and comb my fingers through my hair, gnawing nervously on my lip. I hope that Sook and Chul's plan will work but I feel doubt sitting heavy in my chest. Would Tetsu try to find someone who he thinks doesn't love him? Foxes and humans may be different but we have one thing in common: we don't look for love where it can't be given.

TWENTY-FIVE

TETSU

THE RING. I NEED the ring.

I quietly search through the keepsake box I hid just outside my tent. It holds miniature portraits of my parents and one of us together when I was a baby. There's a small carving knife, the handle worn down by Father's use, along with a carving of a crow with two sets of wings. Father carved it as a luck charm and I believed that it protected me when the demons raided Nagaseo and took Father's life. That long night beneath the scorched ruins of our homestead had me clutching the charm close until I was strong enough to free myself. I dug up the keepsake box from my first Inyeo-kan and put the charm inside. It serves better as a memory now that I am older and wiser.

I brush aside a swath of silk from Mother's favorite hanbok and a necklace of black beads she always wore. Father's leather-bound journal is tied with a worn cord and I take it out. Attached to the end of the cord is a little pouch and inside, a ring Father wore on his right hand.

I shake the ring into my palm and stare at its black glass finish, cut perfectly smooth with diamond-like shapes. Father didn't fear the fox demons and he simply wanted to live his life well. He believed in greater things and had obtained this ring from a mythical jeweler who claimed that if worn and passed over any thing or person, would reveal its true nature. It means that I can see whether there's a lie in the letter; if I choose to believe in the ring's power.

I remove the letter from my pocket and open it again. Slowly, I slip the ring on my finger and move my hand over the letter, expecting the characters to rearrange themselves to reveal the truth.

But they don't.

I try again, my heart pounding in my chest as I analyze the characters closely for even the slightest movement. The word 'prisoner' flickers for a brief second. Or, at least I think it does. I'm concentrating so hard that my eyes start to cross and water. With a shake of my head, I set the parchment down and rub my temples.

Regardless of what Father believed, I'm not sure the ring even works. I glance at it. It does look suitable on my finger so I might as well wear it and maybe it will come in handy. I replace the other keepsakes in the hand-carved, wooden box and bury it once more, shoveling handfuls of dirt and packing it down with my palms.

I crawl back into my tent and twirl the ring around my finger, wondering if that flicker was real or not.

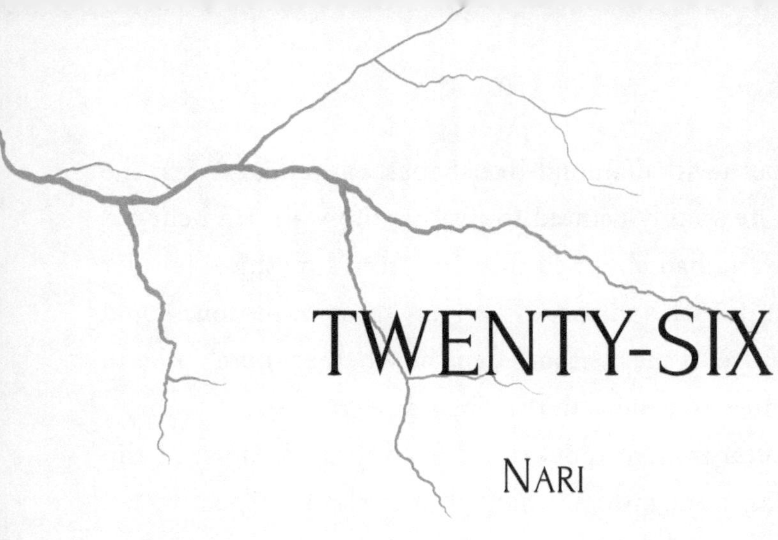

TWENTY-SIX

Nari

RANMI WAKES ME WITH a touch on my shoulder and I squint at her, wanting to burrow beneath the thin blanket that covers me. Its threads are coming loose and it smells like hay but it blocks the light outside during the day. It imitates the Den and brings me a sense of comfort.

"What is it?" I mutter, yawning wide and letting my legs stretch out until my ankles pop.

"Are you going to sleep all day?" she counters with a lifted brow and doesn't wait for me to answer. "There's a festival in Juhto a couple of us are going to. I was wondering if you'd like to join. We have to leave soon to get there before noon."

"A festival?" I ask as I sit up. My hair falls in tangled waves around my head, brushing against my cheeks. "What's that?"

Ranmi sighs, "You really are a girl of the forest, huh. It's an event where people get together and have food, make lanterns, and run around in animal masks. The festival is for Salaisna, or Day of the Living Dead."

My brow furrows at the name. "What does that mean?"

Ranmi shakes her head and pulls me up. I stumble over the blanket and she lets me go only to toss my trousers and a bright red blouse at me with a thick white sash. I barely catch them in time.

"If I explain everything, the day will be over before I'm even done. You'll have fun." Before Ranmi leaves the tent, the corner of her mouth lifts as she says, "Tetsu is coming."

I blink at her. Then I realize what she means and I feel my skin heat. "Oh."

If this festival is supposed to be fun then I'll take that chance to grow closer to Tetsu, if he doesn't try to hide from me. Ranmi steps out and I dress, albeit slowly as sleepiness still nips at me. The blouse is too large and has wide sleeves that hang over my hands. I comb my fingers through my hair, wincing as I untangle it. There's so much maintenance that goes into taking care of a human body, it's exhausting.

I struggle to tie the sash around my waist until Ranmi pokes her head in to see what's taking me so long. I point to the sash. "Do I have to wear this?"

"It will keep your blouse closed so yes," she tells me and beckons me forward. I turn as she ties it tight then I join her outside with the other trappers.

They're all wearing various colors of long-length tunics with wide sleeves but Tetsu wears black, his usual color. His gaze glides over me for a brief moment before he looks away and folds his arms. I swear I see his face start to turn red before he strides ahead, leading the way to Juhto. As we leave the camp behind, I can't help but notice that everyone else's clothes fit them well and I feel swamped in mine. I lift my arms and flap the sleeves, my mouth forming an 'o' to make a bird sound before I stop myself. Ranmi laughs anyway.

"You're an odd one, Nari."

I quickly drop my arms and blush.

My gaze drifts to Tetsu up ahead, walking by himself at a brisk pace. I slip around the other trappers and hurry to catch up. The blouse weighs heavy on my shoulders and the material knocks against the back of my thighs. It's more like a smock than a blouse and I tuck my obnoxiously long-sleeved arms behind my back as I walk next to Tetsu, my legs working to keep up with him.

"Hi."

"Hello," he intones and I see his shoulders tense as they rise a bit toward his head. "What do you want?"

"Nothing, I'm just walking."

"I see that. At least you've learned to walk on your own."

My nose twitches at the jab and I want to retort with my own jab but, as I've learned, humans don't take well to aggressive teasing. I let out a quiet breath, dampening my fox spirit, and instead say, "Ranmi told me this was the day of the living dead. It sounds rather morbid, don't you think?"

"It's a tradition," he quips.

"But...what *is* it?"

Tetsu groans and lifts his hands to his face, rubbing his temples. I catch sight of a black ring around his finger and it catches the light with each movement. A minuscule beam hits me in the eye and I squint, scowling.

"Why are you making that face?"

I lift my hand to block the beam. "Your ring."

Tetsu drops his arms and vigorously tugs his sleeves over his hands. He grumbles something under his breath and I swallow hard, feeling like a failure. What am I supposed to do to make this boy not afraid or weirded out by me? I wish I had more time before I was turned into a human. With years to study the humans, I would know how to act like them. But I was only exposed to humans two times, one during my test where I absorbed a soul, and the other during my first raid, which ended in this disaster. The rest of the time, as a young kit, I stayed close to the Den. We hunted, we played, and we stayed far, far away from the humans, as Sook told us to.

I set my hand on my cheek and mewl softly, mourning my life before. When things made sense.

"What is it?" Tetsu asks, his voice softening for a moment before he clears his throat. "I mean, I can tell you about Salaisna."

I nod, not trusting my mouth to say anything. If I just listen, maybe he'll be kind.

Tetsu's head lifts and he looks off in the distance, letting his arms swing naturally at his sides. "It's called the day of the living dead because we believe that on this day, our ancestors return to walk the earth for a little while. We gather together for the festival and eat food and light lanterns with messages to our ancestors in hopes that by the time night falls, they'll send a message back."

"What kind of messages?" I ask.

"It could be for anything. Most people ask for advice or wisdom. I...haven't gone to the festival in a couple of years so I probably won't make a lantern."

I gnaw on my lip, wondering if I should mention the letter but Tetsu beats me to it. "Yes, I know it'd be wise to ask about the letter. But, if I'm being honest, I don't even know if I believe my father's spirit would come back. Why would any?" His head drops, his jaw clenching as his brow furrows. "I'm sure Heaven is much better than being here with these demons."

An afterlife with no foxes? It sounds awful.

But I nod, hoping my expression displays something akin to Tetsu's.

Eventually, we fall quiet until we come upon Juhto and I tense up, glancing in the direction of the Forsaken Sisters' homestead as we enter through the open gates. I find myself shifting toward Tetsu and grabbing his arm.

"You won't drag me to the Forsaken Sisters, right?"

He glances toward the homestead and chuckles lightly. "No. Not today, at least." He lifts an eyebrow at me. "As long as you behave yourself then we're good."

"We're good," I say. "I'm just not used to interacting this way with others."

"Well, there's plenty of time for you to learn. And since you're one of us now, we're honor-bound to help you."

"Honor bound?"

"Yeah." Tetsu looks down at my hands wrapped around his arm and then into my eyes again. "It means that we're obligated to look out for each other."

"Hey, you two make a cute couple! Would you like to participate in this year's Heart Quest?"

Both Tetsu and I jump as our heads whip toward a smiling woman holding two large bags of heart-shaped bread. She wears an apron and her hair is done up in a tight bun, pulling her skin back. I linger on the bread and feel myself begin to salivate. It looks delicious, golden brown and dusted with herbs and butter. I bet it smells just as delicious.

"Uh, we're not a couple," Tetsu says and I look around for the other trappers to find they've dispersed. I see Ranmi disappear among a crowd gathering in the middle of the village.

"Oh, ho, ho, it's not just for couples." The woman shoves a bag toward us and I reach out to take it, licking my lips. Tetsu swats my hand down. My lip curls, ready to hiss at him.

"We're not interested."

"I am," I say and release him, stepping toward the woman. "Does it involve eating that bread?"

She turns to me and leans forward a little, dangling the bread in my face. "Depends on whether you want to be the predator or the prey?"

"Which one gets to eat it?"

"The predator."

"I'll be that then."

"*Nari.*" Tetsu grunts.

I turn to him. "What?"

The woman clicks her tongue. "You need a partner if you want to participate."

I gasp and tug on Tetsu's tunic. "I need a partner, Tetsu!"

"Shh," his eyes wander, a line creasing between his brows. "Calm down." To the woman, he asks with a sigh, "How much do you want?"

"I've decided to be generous today and you don't need to pay a fee to participate. It is a festival, after all, and we're here to have fun."

His mouth pinches slightly and I recognize it as his skeptical look. Then he sighs again, this time louder and with his whole body. "Fine, we'll participate. I guess I'll be the prey."

The woman's grin widens and she spins on her heel. "Come along then. We'll get you fitted with a predator mask, miss."

I bounce along, my hair smacking against my shoulders and back as I follow the woman to an obscure booth down a shaded alleyway. "I get to wear a mask? I like this already."

Tetsu tugs on the back of my blouse when I get too close to the woman and keeps a hold of it when we stop at her booth. She shimmies around to the other side and lifts a sheet with only a single mask left. A fox mask.

I stop bouncing as I stare at it, my eyes going wide. It's the most beautiful thing I've ever seen and I reach out to touch it, running a finger along the smooth, alabaster surface with a faux textured pattern. The details of the face are done in black paint with red dots, lines, and the fox symbol on the forehead. There are two strings of faux soul beads beneath the ear and the eyes...the eyes are swimming with various shades of red. My pulse quickens. It sure looks demonic.

"Nobody else wanted to be a fox so this is all I have," the woman says unapologetically.

Tetsu pulls on my blouse. "Then I think we'll have to pass.""No!" I retort and grab the mask. "I'll wear it. It's okay."

"Nari—"

"Excellent!" the woman gestures for me to turn around and I do, lifting the fox mask to my face as she adjusts the strap over my head and hair. I even out my breathing as the mask fits snugly to my skin and to my surprise, the eyes are see-through, though they do cast a reddish film over everything. I look up at Tetsu and see his mouth is pulled downward. He turns to the woman and I do too as she tells us about the Heart Quest.

"As prey, sir, you'll be tasked with guarding the bread while your miss here hunts you down. You can go into the forest beyond and when she catches you, you can come back here to claim your prize."

I gasp. "There's a prize? What is it?"

The woman chuckles lightly as she hands Tetsu a loaf. I sniff, trying to get a whiff of it but the mask blocks my senses. "You'll have to see when you come back. Now go."

Tetsu doesn't move and stares at the bread in his hands. I lightly shove his shoulder. "Go and hide."

He gives me a pained look, gnaws on his lip, and then turns, walking away. I glance at the woman again and ask her, "How long should I wait before I run after him?"

She lifts a hand to her chin, observing Tetsu. "Considering how slow he's moving, I'd give him a minute or two."

"Okay, okay, tell me when he's out of sight and don't tell me where he's going."

"I know." A smile curves her lips. "He seems a bit stiff. Maybe try and loosen him up a little later, alright?" She winks at me and I don't know what she means but I'm too excited to care.

I close my eyes and imagine tearing apart the bread in my fingers and stuffing my nose in its buttery, flaky goodness. We've had bread at the camp for supper a few times but it's always been rolls, not a full loaf. Still tasty, though.

"Okay, he's gone now."

My heart leaps in my chest and I pivot, running down the alley. I look around as I burst into the space before the gates, my arms lifted and hands clawed. A few humans look at me, judgment lifting their brows, and I drop my hands. *Don't be feral, don't be feral.* Calmly, I walk past the gate and look around the forest. I don't see him and I know he'll be meandering somewhere, wishing this was over sooner rather than later.

Back in Juhto, I squint toward the crowd, who are chatting and dancing and holding up thin rectangles above their heads made of an off-white, opaque material. I look for Tetsu's topknot but...there's a sea of them. I move toward the crowd and start to weave my way through, growing uncomfortable as the sun breaks through the clouds above and makes me feel damp beneath my arms and my upper back. I open my mouth to pant and shove through, breaking out on the other side.

I double over my knees and pull the blouse away from my skin, trying to get some cool air in there but it doesn't work. The material is too thick and it's too big. I consider taking the blouse off but I don't see any other humans without it. Then, an idea clicks as my fingers slip against the sash. I scurry down another alley where no one can see me and shed my blouse, dropping it to the ground. I take the sash and tie it around my chest. It feels weird to cover myself up but humans don't gallivant around naked. I miss my fur covering my entire body.

I pull the long bits of the sash forward and try to tie it until I give up and tuck it in tight. When I look up, I see a familiar form walking out of the gates that face east and I kick off the ground, running for Tetsu.

"Ha, I see you!" I shout.

He startles, glances back at me, and then takes off running into the forest. I follow behind, leaping over thick roots and ducking beneath stray branches that threaten to shred my clothes. Tetsu may have longer legs but I love running and as I draw nearer, I hop on a rock and use the momentum to pounce on him. We tumble to the ground and Tetsu grunts as I land right on top, his face hitting the dirt. But at least his arms have saved the bread from meeting the ground, stick straight and lifted just a little above his head.

"I caught you," I laugh and snatch the bread from his fingers, lifting the fox mask.

Tetsu rolls and I fall off, but quickly straighten and sit next to him with my legs beneath me. I take a bite of the bread and rock back and forth happily as it melts in my mouth. When Tetsu sits up, he rests his arm on his propped knee and glances me over. His face promptly turns bright red.

"Wha—what happened to your clothes?"

"I'm wearing them," I say with a full mouth, my voice muffled by the hunks of bread.

"Your hanbok," he looks away, scratching his chin.

"The blouse? It was too hot and heavy. I repurposed the sash."

"I can see that." He groans and removes his own tunic, tossing the black material at me. "Just cover up, you look dumb."

I roll my eyes and drop it back on his leg. "That doesn't matter, I caught you and I got the bread. Do you want some?"

Tetsu takes the tunic back and replaces it over his shoulders but doesn't slip his arms through. I find my gaze drifting over his nicely shaped arms and the sliver of his chest that is exposed from his undershirt. He shakes his head firmly and buries his face in his hands.

"No. I, uh, I guess I'll go back to the village."

Awkwardly and without his hands, he stands and starts walking forward...only to ram right into a tree. I burst out laughing and the sound echoes around us, high-pitched and loud.

"Quiet, Nari!" he hisses, whirling on me as he drops his hands.

I roll to my feet and lift the bread above my head, cheering, "I got the bread, I got the bread!" I shift it toward him. "Are you sure you don't want some? Because you know I'm going to eat it all."

Tetsu's nostrils flare as he looks at the bread and then steps forward, breaking off a hunk of it. He looks angry as he eats it and then his expression smooths out and his eyes widen. "This is the best bread I've ever tasted."

"Yes, yes it is."

He shuffles closer and picks off another piece. Before I know it, there's less bread and less space between us. I tilt my head back, looking up at him and Tetsu meets my eyes. His blush returns full force and mine does as well. I feel something stirring in me, a feeling I've never felt before, and I move closer. He blinks and his breath grows a little heavy but he doesn't step away.

"This was fun," I whisper.

"It was," Tetsu admits.

Slowly, I reach up to touch his face and he swallows hard, his gaze shifting to my fingers. I have the overwhelming urge to bring his face down to mine and nuzzle his nose. A form of affection among foxes, usually reserved between mates. Is this how I can gain his trust to take me to Sanoul? The thought, though all I want, makes me feel a bit sick to my stomach. I curl my fingers and gently knock my knuckles against his jaw. I step back and laugh awkwardly.

"Race you back to the village?"

Tetsu is quiet for a moment and I can tell he's thinking, probably processing what just happened. He shakes his head. "I'll walk."

"Oh, okay."

I turn and take off, conflicted with what I'm feeling. I don't want to manipulate Tetsu, that doesn't seem right, but am I manipulating him when these feelings, whatever they are, feel real?

TWENTY-SEVEN

TETSU

NARI IS WAITING FOR me just outside the alley, her cheeks flushed pink from running. She leans on the stone wall of a shoemaker shop and my gaze flickers over her for a brief moment, my skin heating. Nari makes me feel...different and I don't know if it's good or bad. She's fierce and annoying and naive...but also confident and cute. Very cute with her large, dark eyes and unruly orange hair. Her freckles look like stars and her tiny, upturned nose reminds me of a canine. She's short too, the top of her head just barely scraping my breastbone.

Thankfully, she found her discarded hanbok and has tied the sash, rather horribly, around her waist again. When she notices me staring, she straightens and though her face lights up, it quickly crumbles into a bout of uncertainty. Still, she smiles as I approach her.

"That took you longer than I expected."

"We were out pretty far," I say.

"Not really," she counters.

I grunt and gesture with my shoulder toward the alley. "Should we see what we won?"

Nari turns and walks, bouncing on her heels. "I hope it's more bread."

The woman at the booth perks up when she sees us and grins. "I see you've not a morsel of bread on you so I assume you caught him."

"That I did," Nari states enthusiastically and casts a smug look at me.

"And it didn't even take that long," the woman says, glancing at the pocket watch in her hand. She squats and ruffles through what sounds like wooden crates beneath the table, the black sheet over it stirring at the movement.

"Why are you set up away from the rest of the festival?" I ask.

It's odd that she's all the way down here rather than in the main square with everyone else. My heart suddenly seizes in my chest. *What if she poisoned the bread?* I step forward and block Nari from moving further with my arm. I growl at the woman, "What game are you playing?"

She stands, holding a jade-colored box in her hands and blinks at me. "Whatever do you mean?"

"Yeah, whatever do you mean?" Nari echoes.

I ignore them both and retort, "Did you poison the bread? I didn't see anyone else around the village wearing masks and chasing each other. And why did you have a fox mask in the first place? You should have gotten rid of it long ago. Unless you're one of those demon worshipers."

The woman blinks again before her brow furrows and she says gruffly, "That's a heavy accusation. If you must know why I'm down here instead of in the square, it's because they've already chosen another baker to offer up food and sweets for the festival. I'm not making a profit, but I'd like people to try my lot so I created this little game years ago. The village council hasn't told me I couldn't do any of this and I'm not in anyone's way." She glances at the fox mask still stuck on Nari's head. "As for the mask, it's pretty, but I certainly do not worship those demons. They take too much from us as is, why should I let them take my faith?"

I study the woman's face, fluttering my hand at my side to see if the ring reacts to any lying. But it doesn't and I drop my arm. Nari bounces forward and removes the mask, setting it on the table. I glance at it, my lip curling at the crescent moon symbol and the stark red eyes of the demon.

The woman clears her throat and sets the jade box on the table, pushing the mask aside. "Now that we're clear, I have a prize for each of you."

Nari clasps her hands together, her eyes wide as the woman opens the box and reveals individually wrapped bags of candy. There are wobbly jelly balls, sweet rice cakes, cubes of honey cookies, and chocolate cream rolls sprinkled with caramelized sugar. I feel myself begin to salivate and happily take the candy, opening it to pop a jelly ball in my mouth.

"Well, that's it. Thanks for playing," the woman winks at us. "And if you ever want to try my other delicacies, my shop is that way and around the corner." She points in the opposite direction of the square.

"Thank you," I say.

"Thank you!" Nari squeals.

"My pleasure."

We walk toward the square, where everyone is making their own lantern for the exodus to the Temyul River just outside the village. Children with chubby cheeks and hands painted yellow run amuck, much to their parents' chagrin. I tuck my candy into my pocket and reach back to take Nari's arm. She's already munching on a rice cake and a single grain sits on the corner of her mouth. It takes all my strength not to flick it away.

"What are they doing?" Nari asks, her mouth full.

I glance at the booth where the lantern materials are being sold.

"Making lanterns to release over the Temyul River."

"Why are they yellow?"

"Because it represents hope."

"Hope for what?"

I shake my head and pull her toward the booth. A child is running the station, sitting on a high stool and pretending to be very professional in her silk hanbok and a practiced smile.

"Good day, sir," she says, straightening her back. "Would you like a lantern?"

"Yes, please," I tell her as Nari peeks out from behind me.

The girl gathers ornate patterned wax paper, glue, and a small spool of wire. She hands it to me and then turns her palm up. "That will be nine *wensi*."

My eyebrows lift in surprise. "That's expensive, don't you think?"

The girl shrugs. "I didn't set the price."

With a sigh, I remove my coin purse and drop nine *wensi* into her palm. I could have bought a small sack of rice, a bundle of scallions, and a packet of broth for nine *wensi* at the market.

The girl grins. "Enjoy!"

Then she hops off the stool and runs over to a young boy making his own lantern but having a tough time as it's not a cylinder but an abstract object. When he sees the *wensi*, though, his mouth falls open and they hop around with excitement, claiming they're rich now. My eyes narrow slightly. I feel like I just got scammed by children.

But Nari tugs on my arm, drawing my attention to her. "Come on, it looks like everyone else is almost done."

We find a space to sit down and I lean forward on one hand, taking the wax paper with the other to lay it flat on the ground.

"We have to glue these pieces together first and then build the structure," I say.

Nari sits on her legs, her head tilted as she rests her hands on her knees. She watches intensely as I glue and fold the paper. It's a little sloppy but I nudge the spool of wire toward her.

"Why don't you work on the skeleton? Just make a circle and then have two wires crossing each other like an x."

She takes the spool and picks at it with her fingers, her nose twitching until it comes loose. Dropping the spool, it unravels and rolls across the ground. Nari laughs while I sigh and gather it back up.

"You didn't say how big the circle needs to be."

"As big as this." I finish gluing the paper together and show Nari the top of it.

She measures it with her hand, from her middle finger to the base of her palm, and then sets it flat on the ground. I watch as she tries to craft a circle out of the wire but fails horribly. Suppressing a chuckle, I reach out to help her. The wire is thin and malleable, almost too much so that we have to be careful otherwise we'll ruin the shape.

The sun beats down on the nape of my neck and sweat dribbles from my armpits and down the crevice of my back. I take an unsuspecting whiff, hoping that I don't smell incredibly bad, even though I chose to wear black, as I always do.

Together, we finish the skeleton of the lantern and slip it inside the cylindrical structure. The square is emptying quickly as people take strips of cloth dipped in wax and stream out of the village toward the river. We hurry to catch up and Nari holds the lantern while I shed the top layer of my hanbok again, hanging it around my neck like a fresh kill.

"This is so exciting," Nari says softly, turning the lantern around in her hands. "And it's so pretty. What are we going to do with it now?"

"Light it and let it ascend into the sky," I tell her. Someone bumps into me as they hurry past and I stumble into Nari. She nearly falls at the impact but my hand shoots out to grab her waist, steadying her. We both stiffen and my breath escapes me as my pulse ticks in my head. We're jostled again and I curl my arm around her, pulling her against my side.

Nari says nothing, only clears her throat and holds the lantern close. I look down at the top of her head and realize my armpit is too close to her hair. I gnaw on my lip, panic rising in my belly. I feel so self-conscious being this close, but I don't want her to get knocked down and trampled by the crowd.

A soft humming sound pulls my attention to the front of the crowd and it grows louder as it trickles back to us. I hum along to the quiet hymn that belongs to a civilization long passed, before the fox demons commandeered the Daion Kingdom. The words of the hymn have been lost to time but the melody lives on, now as a common lullaby sung to babies or during festivities like this. The melody is slow and bright, each high note punctuated with a broad hum while the rest flows together.

I let the hymn transport me back to Nagaseo, the village I called home. My parents and I lived in a homestead with three other families who worked together to make a living. While Father was a woodcarver and had built the homestead from the ground up, Mother worked as a weaver and occasionally in the surrounding rice fields.

I often played in the courtyard with the other children, though Mother watched me like a hawk. If I got too rough, she'd call me home and make me roasted rice tea.

My chin drops as tears threaten to spill down my cheeks. I miss Mother, even though I shouldn't. If the letter is true, she didn't abandon me but if it isn't...did she leave *because* of me?

The sound of the rushing river berates my ears and I look forward as the crowd spreads along the bank. Above the river is a clear sky with faint skeins of red energy moving above the clouds. Even during the day, the demons still have an influence over the sky in certain places. I guide Nari to an open spot and we wait for someone to pass a lit candle to us so we can set the wax ablaze.

Nari glances at the people on our left, who have their eyes closed and are murmuring their wishes beneath their breaths. She leans into me and whispers, "What are they doing?"

"Making a wish to go with the lantern."

"Can I make one?"

"Sure."

She closes her eyes and thinks for a moment, a line forming between her brows. I do the same, wondering what I should wish for even though I don't really believe anything will come to fruition from this. My thoughts wander back to the letter, though, and I curl my fingers tightly against Nari's hip.

I'll wish for an answer. The next step. Is Mother *really* in Sanoul? If so, how am I going to get inside? I've never been anywhere near the imperial city before but Kyung told us it's protected by a behemoth that will devour humans if they get too close.

When Nari nudges me, I open my eyes and accept the candle I'm handed. She leans forward and ties the cloth dipped in wax around the base of the lantern.

"Did you make a wish?" she asks softly.

I nod and a subtle breeze passes along the bank, ruffling our clothes and hair. I tip the candle toward the cloth and it ignites. Nari rises to her knees and scoots toward the river, her hands inching toward the top of the lantern as the flame spreads. I pull down the long, large sleeves of her hanbok to her elbows so they don't catch on fire.

The humming grows until it crescendoes and I lean down to Nari's ear. "Now you let it go."

She shudders slightly and releases the lantern. It hovers, almost plummeting to the river, until the fire puffs hot air upwards and lifts it higher. Nari watches with wide, curious eyes and I watch her. I like this side of her, the wonder and excitement she exuberates. She certainly seems like a normal girl now, rather than one raised by wild dogs. But I suppose her childhood let her become the young woman she is now. A girl with talent and wonder alike.

A girl I happen to like a lot.

TWENTY-EIGHT

Bojin

BOJIN YAWNED AS THE faithless left the bank of the river. He'd been awake all afternoon following the vixen and her human sacrifice. Now, they remained behind, sitting on the cushy ground of the riverbank. Her head was tilted back and she continued to stare at the lanterns as they lifted higher and higher. Bojin looked up too. They would soon break the clouds and then be carried off or struck down by the energy flowing above.

He sat hunched against a thick trunk, scraping the grime from beneath his fingernails with a knife. As a member of the Divine Tails, he knew the way of the foxes didn't include regular human hygiene but he was bored. Sook had told him to wait until nightfall to deliver the next message and hopefully, this one would get the boy to go north and take the vixen with him.

The boy curled his arm around the young vixen then and she leaned into him, kicking off her thin slippers as she dunked her feet in the river. Bojin's eyebrow lifted. It seemed as if the boy, a fox trapper he had learned, had grown quite fond of the vixen. Of course, it wasn't uncommon for the foxes to lure humans into their beds to gain their trust and then sacrifice them to the Guardian at the Gate. Humans were foolish enough to only see beauty and never the danger. That was one reason he had joined the Divine Tails. The Kingdom of Daion had been cursed and was rife with sin, humanity straying from the worship of the ancestors and their animal counterparts.

So the fox demons were sent to punish them. Their judge and executioner and Bojin could not love nor fear them more. He was a devout worshiper but remained here in the southern part of the kingdom to spy for Sook and other skulks. He felt such was his calling.

As dusk rolled in and the vixen and the boy spoke in soft tones, Bojin quietly stood and ambled over to the river. He was far enough they couldn't hear him and covered by the trees and hanging moss of the forest. The parchment he'd written the message on was already neatly tied up and stored in a tin container. All he had to do was drop it in the water.

He waited a few more minutes as darkness closed in and the sky sparked red before letting the container fall from his fingers. It caught in the current and bobbed beneath the surface for a moment before it was carried on. Bojin dropped low to the ground and peered at the two as he waited.

The vixen perked up first and pointed. The boy swiftly stood and scooped the container up, glancing into the forest. Bojin stuffed a hand against his mouth as he tried not to snicker. He enjoyed fiddling with the humans and causing fear or uncertainty in them.

Slowly, the boy opened the container and unrolled the parchment. The vixen stood, staring up at him, and Bojin waited. If the boy didn't take the bait this time, he didn't know what else Sook would ask of him. Bojin wasn't above kidnapping. In fact, he hadn't done such in a few years now. He flexed his fingers and then rubbed them together, letting a breathy snicker escape him.

The boy crumbled the parchment in his hand and lifted the other to his hair. Bojin watched the vixen's lips move as she asked what the matter was. He said nothing and turned, stomping back toward the village. The vixen followed along, her gaze drifting to the forest.

When they were out of sight, Bojin stood and walked back to his cabin, where Sook was already waiting. She was licking her paw, her ears twitching until she heard him and turned.

"Is it done?"

"Yes. I don't know if he'll take the bait though."

"We shall see." Sook's black eyes narrowed slightly as she looked away from him. "If he doesn't, the skulk will have to take the matter into our own paws."

Bojin nodded and Sook darted off without a thank you. He sat outside his cabin, built a fire, and daydreamed about the juicy human hearts he'd once eaten on a visit to the north.

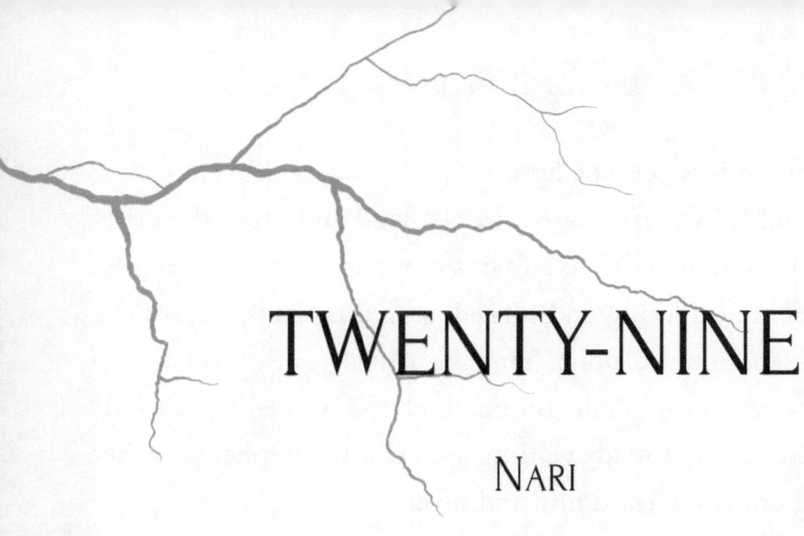

TWENTY-NINE

Nari

A METALLIC, MEATY SMELL assaults my nostrils and stirs me from my sleep. My eyes crack open and I slowly claw away the blanket from my face. My bedroll is wet and I scoot over, lifting my blanket as I sit up. The scent wafts forth and I gag when I see both dry and fresh blood soaking my bedroll.

I scream.

Ranmi bursts into the tent a second later, her eyes wide and a dagger drawn. "What is it?"

"I've been stabbed!" I cry as liquid streams from my eyes.

Skidding across the tent floor to me, Ranmi quickly pats me down and then her nose crinkles. "Oh...*oh*."

"Where is it coming from?" I ask desperately.

A pinch of pain hits me in the stomach and I startle, my hand flying there to feel the wound for myself.

"You haven't been stabbed," she says calmly.

"What do you mean I haven't been stabbed? I'm *bleeding!*"

"Yes, yes, I know. But...you've never had a menstrual cycle before?"

"Menst—I don't know what that is!"

The tent flap opens and Tetsu sticks his head in, dark circles beneath his eyes and his hair messy. One particular curl falls right between his eyes. "What's all the ruckus? I'm trying to sleep in the tent next door."

"I'm dying," I tell him and fall on my back, curling into myself.

Tetsu rushes forward and Ranmi bats him away with her arm. "It's nothing, Tetsu, just go back to your tent."

"Why is there blood everywhere?"

Ranmi gives him a pointed look and Tetsu's eyebrows lift. "Oh." He backs away, a blush tinting his cheeks as he rubs the back of his neck. "Uh, good luck with that, Nari. Bye."

He ducks out of the tent and I look at Ranmi, whispering, "What's happening to me?"

"It's your menstrual cycle."

"I don't know what that means." I groan.

She sighs and sits, tapping her fingers against the blanket. "It means that you can now bear children. Though, I don't know why it's come so late for you...how old are you?"

I shrug. *Bear children? Does she mean this is the estrous cycle? That I understand.*

"Why is there blood?" I ask and wince as my stomach rolls. "And pain."

"Since you did not get pregnant during your ovulating period, your body is shedding old lining and that's where the blood and pain come from. Your reproductive parts."

"I don't want to get pregnant though."

"Which is perfectly fine, of course, you don't have to any time soon. But this is what happens every month for women."

My jaw falls slack. "Every month?"

Ranmi nods. "Mhm," she sighs and leans her chin on her palm, "being a woman is just *great* sometimes."

I slowly sit up and stare down at my soiled clothes and bedroll. "I've made a mess."

"It's okay, I can help you clean up and get you some fresh clothes."

"I should probably bandage myself too."

"No, no, we don't use bandages. I'll show you what I use." Ranmi stands and holds her hands out to me. "Now come along. We can sneak out the back so nobody sees."

"So this only happens to women?"

"Yes."

"That's dumb."

Ranmi laughs. "It is, isn't it?"

I sit on the edge of the spring, eating my candy as she runs her fingers through my wet hair, detangling it. The heat and steam feel nice and I don't want to get out. I set the pouch on the bank and sink a little lower, letting the water graze my chin.

"How long does it last for?" I ask, my breath making the water ripple.

"It depends. Some only bleed for three days and others may bleed up to a whole week."

I stick my tongue out as I shake my head. "*Bleh.* Can I stay in the spring until then? I like it here."

She laughs again. "I wish, but no. You've still got to help around the camp. Work doesn't stop just because you're menstruating."

I put my arms out in front of me and let them rise to the surface. I never knew human women had to go through this every month. The more I learn, the more I want to be a fox again. Then, something dawns on me. If I'm in the equivalent of a fox estrous cycle...that means, what I've been feeling for Tetsu, has been caused by this. A sigh of relief deflates my chest. So it's just like me being in heat, finding him maddeningly adorable. And the feel of his hand on my hip, his arm around me...I shudder and wiggle my fingers in the water.

"What was that? Did you get cold?" Ranmi asks.

"Oh, it's nothing. Just thinking."

"Well, your hair is done. I have fresh cotton cloth strips you can use. Turn around and I'll show you."

I turn to her, disturbing the water, and watch. Ranmi takes the strips and lays them atop one another until they're as thick as my fingernail. Then she ties the ends and lifts the cloth toward me. It vaguely resembles undergarments, though oddly shaped.

"I also got you some black trousers in case the blood leaks through."

"Thank you," I say softly.

Ranmi nods and stands. "No problem. I'll be over there while you dress."

She leaves me be and I rest my arms on the bank of the spring for a moment. I think back to yesterday by the river when Tetsu and I saw that letter in the water. He wouldn't tell me what it said but I think it might be about his mother again. If he's half-fox and she was the fox, then it would make sense for her to be in Sanoul. I wonder now, though, if he'll really go there. It isn't a place for humans, especially if they want to live.

I shake myself from my thoughts and climb out of the spring, twirling around to dry myself a little. I don the awkward undergarment and then my trousers and a blouse. I squeeze the water out of my hair as I go find Ranmi and we head back to camp.

THIRTY

Tetsu

SANOUL.

The name of the imperial city has been ringing in my ears since Nari and I left the river behind. The strange letter was an answer to my wish but it feels like dark forces are at play. Whoever penned the letters knows too much about me and my family...and the struggles of my heart.

I announce myself before entering Kyung's tent, who promptly sighs and sets down his evening tea. I sit across from him and fold my arms on the short table.

"What is it now?" Kyung asks.

I rap my fingers against my arms and gnaw on the inside of my cheek before I say, "As fox trappers, I feel like we should take the fight to the demons...in Sanoul."

Kyung's eyebrow lifts and his blind eye takes on a dark shade of crimson as if it's filling with blood. "Why would we go there when our forces are miniscule, Tetsu?"

"Our group hasn't grown much in years, true, and I know not

everyone feels fit enough to join but are we just going to sit back and say we're trappers when we barely do that?"

"We've gone hunting before, as I'm sure you remember, and set up traps all over the forest. And while you were out at Itson Temple, we attacked a skulk. Killed seven demons."

"I didn't know that."

"Mhm." Kyung sighs. "Of course, seven isn't a significant chunk but we showed them our might and they retreated." He shrugs and leans back on the sturdy wall of the tent. "I'd call that a win."

I keep my mouth shut. The trappers haven't been actively fighting against the demons and I liked it because I've come to learn that I'm not very good with a sword...or fighting at all. But now...now I have a reason to go to Sanoul.

I set my hands on the table and push to my feet. "Well, sir, with your permission, I'd like to go on a surveillance mission to Sanoul."

Kyung looks at me like I've sprouted fluffy ears and nine tails. He scoffs, "You can't be serious, Tetsu. You're not ready for that kind of mission."

"Are you, sir?"

"I'm not the one thinking about going," he retorts, his jaw clenching. "Do you know what Sanoul will be like? You might as well surrender yourself to the demons and let them eat your heart."

"They don't eat hearts," I say, my brow knitting. "I think."

"What they do and don't eat doesn't matter. It'd be a death sentence, Tetsu, you're not going."

"But my mother—" the words slip out before I can stop myself and my chest rises and falls with a quick breath. I step back and lift my hands in defeat. "Okay, I won't go. I just thought we could try taking the demons down a notch."

I duck toward the entrance of the tent but pause when Kyung says,

"Don't you see that it's a hopeless cause? There are too many demons and not enough humans. We were never going to win this war, Tetsu. Daion was never going to be ours again."

I pivot on my heel, my mouth feeling dry. "If it's hopeless then what are we even doing?"

Kyung shakes his head and sips his tea. "Fighting to live another day. That's it. In the end, the demons will take us all. I'd like to delay that fate for as many as I can."

The state that humanity has come to is a sad one indeed. I leave the tent and stride across the camp. I'm not going to Sanoul to end the torment of the demons, but I didn't realize just how much of a lost cause humanity is now. It's obvious but something no one wants to admit. Not when the demons attack and decimate entire villages. Not when hundreds can simply be spawned at once.

Stopping along the wall of the camp, I slip to the ground and rummage my fingers through my hair. Kyung is right, going to Sanoul will be a death sentence. But what if I don't go inside? Maybe I can hang back and observe it from afar then devise a plan from there. I don't want to go alone, though.

I leap to my feet and race for Nari's tent. She's talking with some of the other trappers and I clear my throat. The chatter stops and the flaps open as Nari pokes her head out.

"I need to talk to you," I say and take her hand, dragging her out of the tent.

She stumbles after me, wearing a sleeveless smock that reaches her knees. We go to the edge of camp and I spin Nari around until her back is to the wall.

"What—"

I brace my hands on either side of her head and stare down at her. Nari turns bright pink. "I need to know why you want to go to Sanoul so badly."

She squirms, her nose crinkling. "I—I—" her gaze darts away from my face. "Tetsu, I can't speak to you when you're standing this close to me."

I step away quickly. "S—sorry."

Nari clears her throat. "Well, um, I want to go to Sanoul because I want to see it for myself. I know it's dangerous but I want to see what we're up against."

"I can already tell you we have a very slight chance of even making a *dent* in the demon population."

"Oh?"

"You saw how many were spawned. But, I want to go to Sanoul on a surveillance mission and I don't want to go alone...will you come with me?"

Nari blinks, her eyebrows lifting. "Really?"

I nod. "It would just be me and you, though. Kyung would never approve such a thing so no one should know."

"Oh, of course." Nari leans her head back on the wall, staring at the sky above. "To Sanoul we go, then."

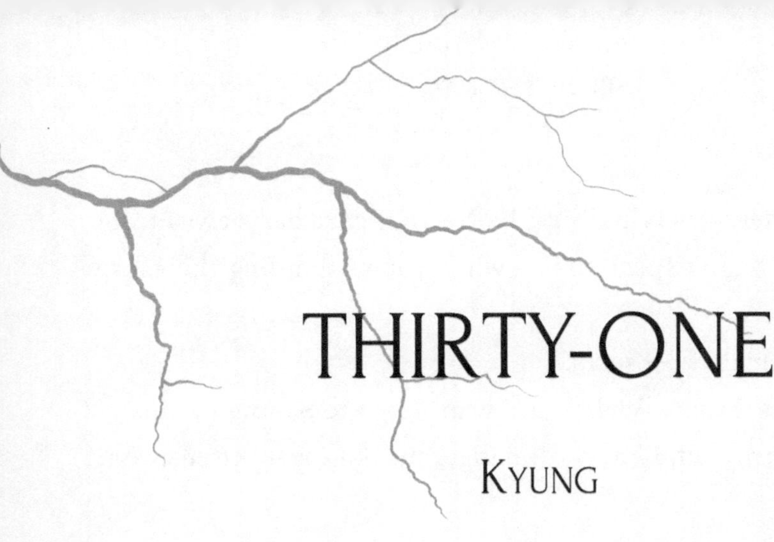

THIRTY-ONE

KYUNG

KYUNG KEPT A CLOSE eye on Nari as she walked through the camp toward the mess tent. He pushed off the pole he was leaning against and approached her. It had been a few weeks now since they'd taken her in and she'd grown to be civil. Kyung still didn't trust her. The girl was strange, not just in her behavior but in her looks as well. With eyes so dark they appeared to be black and bright orange hair, he'd never seen anyone around with such a color. Maybe it was an exclusively inherited trait. Maybe her birth parents were from a different part of the kingdom where the people had richer hair and fairer skin.

Nari's gaze drifted to him and she came to a stop, turning as she stiffened. Her mouth opened to speak but Kyung got to it first and said, "Come with me."

"But...food," Nari's hand twitched at her side and she looked at the mess tent.

Kyung walked past and beckoned her to follow. "It won't take long."

With a heavy sigh, she followed, her feet striking the ground and almost dragging. Kyung glanced back at her. The girl had hung her head and was swaying side to side as if she'd had too much *ji'sori*, the rice-based beverage he enjoyed on warm summer nights.

"Hurry up," he said gruffly and Nari did, until she was walking beside him but still a step behind.

"Where are we going?" she asked and tucked her hands behind her back.

"I'm going to teach you about fox traps."

"F—fox traps?" Nari's head rose and her eyes widened. "Are there any out?"

"No," he retorted and shook his head. "It's the middle of the day, why would there be any?"

She fell quiet and he was grateful for it. They traversed through the forest, over fallen logs and dead leaves curling and fading to brown. Autumn would soon end and winter would sweep through the kingdom. The demons would focus their energy on hunting and foraging instead of collecting tithes. But the spawning would never cease. There was to be another one at the Hansu Temple in the northeastern part of the forest, closer to Sanoul and several miles from where Kyung once lived.

They soon came upon the first trap he had set and Kyung knelt, carefully sweeping away the branches and leaves that hid it from view.

"This is called the Jaw of Steel. Once a fox steps inside, it will snap closed over its leg and it won't be able to move." He pulled up a bit of chain attached to a pike that had been wrapped around the nearest trunk and driven deep into the ground. "And it can't just run off either."

Nari remained standing, arms limp at her sides, her face paling. But she didn't say anything so Kyung went on. "I know there are more 'humane' ways to catch them but I have no use for a live demon. And why shouldn't they suffer? They've made us suffer every single day," he spat.

Kyung pat the chain down and covered the trap again. He took a small pouch from his pocket and left shreds of last night's chicken on top of the leaves. A laugh rumbled through his chest as he said, "If it gets its snout caught, that'd be even better. The steel digging into its face," Kyung paused as he stood and brushed his hands on his trousers. He turned to Nari and grinned. "I'd like to see them get mangled and disfigured for once."

She swallowed hard and set her hand on her throat, her fingers trembling against her skin. Kyung took a step forward, tilting his head so he was looking down on her.

"Since you were raised by wild dogs, I thought you would have come across these things at some point. Are you feeling sympathetic, Nari?"

"N—no," she stammered out, her voice small.

"Good." He brushed past her, purposely bumping into her. "Let's check the others then."

Nari followed along and Kyung could hear her breathing grow shallow as they moved from trap to trap. *Empty, empty, empty.* Kyung cursed under his breath. He had hoped to show Nari a successful trap with a dead demon and observe her reaction to it.

As they were rounding the camp to check on the last trap, Kyung squinted as he looked toward where it was set and saw wisps of light gray fur protruding from behind a large stump. He held his arm up and slowly moved forward. It became quickly apparent that the creature wouldn't stir and Kyung reached back to grab Nari's arm and drag her along. They stopped by the trunk and looked down at the dead fox, its arm caught in the trap. With dried blood on its fur, a bloated body with maggots eating a hole in its stomach, and flies buzzing about, he knew it had been here for a few days.

Nari, however, let out an ear-splitting scream at his side. Kyung released her to rub his ear and glanced at the girl. She took quick steps back, her hands over her mouth as plump tears welled in her eyes. His nostrils flared and he stepped around the dead demon to stand on the other side and face her.

"I thought you said you weren't sympathetic."

Nari squeezed her eyes shut and a sob escaped her. She gasped for a breath, her knees knocking against one another. The girl looked like she was about to collapse. It made Kyung's lip curl. Her reaction was nothing like he expected—it was much worse.

He removed a pair of gloves from his belt and put them on. "Open your eyes. You ought to know how to release it from the trap and dispose of it."

She shook her head.

Kyung grunted. He wanted to shake her, force her eyes open, force her to see the cruel creature's demise and feel *nothing* for it.

"Fine. But don't go yet. I'll show you where we take the bodies to burn them."

Then Kyung knelt again and released the fox from the trap, swatting away the flies that buzzed around his face. Its arm hung at an awkward angle and he grabbed its back legs, lifting it from the ground. He whistled at Nari and didn't check to see if she came along. At this point, he had already confirmed that she couldn't be trusted.

They walked to a deep pit a fair distance from the camp and he tossed the demon body inside. It hit the ashy ground with a thud and sent up a plume of the gray matter. Kyung covered his mouth and nose until it settled. He took out a piece of flint and steel and crouched down on the loose patch of dry grass surrounding the pit. He struck the flint against the steel until it sparked and set the grass on fire. Carefully, he lifted it and dropped it on the fox's body.

Nari was there, but standing among the trees, not daring to come any closer. When Kyung turned to look at her as the fire caught and spread, she was staring at him with pure terror in her eyes. Then she turned and ran back into the forest. Kyung shrugged and watched the body burn, covering his nose again when the scent grew too much. He waited until the fox was nothing but ash.

THIRTY-TWO

NARI

I RUN ALL THE way back to camp, my heart pounding in my chest and the scent of burned fur and flesh still ripe in my nose. The dead fox flashes through my mind. A young tod with gray fur and his eyes wide open, his body grotesque. He was probably out playing where he shouldn't have been, too close to the camp. I could have heard him. I could have saved him if only I was a fox again.

I burst through the gate and my vision blurs as tears blind me. I hiccup, an uncomfortable feeling low in my chest. Around the bonfire sit a few of the trappers and Tetsu. He stands when he sees me, a question on his lips, but I hurry to my tent and slap the flaps shut, diving onto my bedroll. I curl up, holding the thin pillow against my chest as I sob. Why would Kyung show me such a thing? Why did I even stay? I should have left when I saw the fur around the trunk. I knew then that it was a fox.

"Hey, Nari...are you okay?" Tetsu asks from outside my tent.

I don't answer and he takes that as an invitation to come inside. I stuff my face into the material but my breathing is erratic and it doesn't help. Tetsu touches my shoulder and I flinch, rolling away from him.

"What happened?"

"G—go away," I whisper. My throat hurts from the scream I released earlier but I want to scream again. I want to howl into the night and let everyone hear my grief. The tod may not have been from my skulk, but he was a fox and we are fiercely protective of one another. He is not the first dead fox I've seen but it never gets easier either.

"I think it's better if I stay," he says softly and I feel him sit down, his knee pressing lightly against my back. His fingers glide through my hair, brushing the strands from my face. "You don't have to talk about it right now, but I'm going to stay until you're okay."

"Why?" I snap and push myself further. "I don't need you."

"That's probably true but...you're my friend, Nari—"

"We're not friends!" I turn on him and look into his eyes, scowling. His hand hovers just above my head and his eyebrows rise in surprise. I lift the pillow and hit him on the chest. "You're not my friend, you don't want to be and you never will be."

He grabs the pillow on the fifth hit and peeks past the side. "If I didn't want to be, why am I here right now?"

I growl deep in my throat and lunge at him. He catches me at the waist and lays me down across his lap. The pillow falls against my chest as I stare up at him. Tetsu dips his chin, his dark, walnut gaze soft and I feel my heart beat for a different reason. With a huff, I squirm until I'm on my side and I squeeze the pillow tight, my head resting on his thigh.

He is quiet and I let my thoughts revolve through my head again. I soak the pillow and his trousers with my tears and snot until there's nothing left in me. Then I lie there, my fingers wrapped around his knee, and I close my eyes.

After a long while, I whisper, "Kyung showed me the traps."

Tetsu doesn't say anything and instead runs his fingers over my arm and hums the song that was sung on the way to the river. I let myself focus on the deepness of his voice until I can't hear it anymore.

I wake to the sharp scent of ash and the tod's body being burned flashes through my mind. I shoot upright with a gasp and accidentally elbow Tetsu in the cheek. He lies next to me and groans as he wakes, rubbing his face. Beyond the tent, it's bright white…something isn't right. The bonfire usually burns all night long and casts dancing orange and yellow shadows on the tent flaps.

Leaping to my feet, I step on Tetsu's hand and he swears. "Nari, what are you—"

"Something's wrong," I breathe and creep forward, opening the flaps just a sliver to peek outside.

Blazes as high as the camp walls burn only a few feet away. I stumble back, right into Tetsu who is now on his feet. "There's a fire!"

He nudges me aside and bursts out of the tent. I follow behind and reach forward to grab his tunic so he doesn't run off without me. The walls of the camp, once wooden, are alight and standing like burnt twigs now, still somehow fueling the fire. And it seems that only Tetsu and I are awake.

"The others," he says and I know what he means. I begrudgingly let go of his tunic and run to one side of the camp while he goes to the other.

"There's a fire!" I yell over the roar as I pass and shake the canvas like a bear rummaging through for food. "Wake up!"

Ranmi stumbles out of one tent, followed by Shik and Yul, who I learned are the spies gathering intel on the foxes. Their eyes widen and they move into action. As the camp is woken up, there's yelling of orders from Kyung and Ranmi countering with her own that it's no use. We have to leave before the gates fall and block our path.

Kyung ignores her and keeps hauling pails of water against the flames. Ranmi grabs my arm and races for the gates. I twist my head around, looking for Tetsu only to catch a glimpse of him helping Kyung out.

"Tetsu!" I call but he doesn't turn. He doesn't hear me.

I try to break free of Ranmi's grip but she doesn't let go and hisses, "They'll come if they want to live or they'll die as fools."

"Tetsu..."

We flee into the forest, along with the other trappers, and I hear a single howl shatter the night. It's unfamiliar but melancholy and I wonder if it's the young tod's skulk. They must have tracked his scent here. I feel my stomach roll as we move further and further, the crackling and popping of the flames growing dimmer.

When Ranmi stops, I turn back to the camp, searching among the trees for Tetsu and I see him and Kyung dive onto the ground just as the gates break and crash, blocking the path. Tetsu clutches a wooden box in his hands. I run for him as he gets to his feet and hurries away from the fire with Kyung at his side. Before he can turn fully and see me coming, I ram into him and knock him to the ground with an *oof*.

"Tetsu!"

Curling my arms around his neck, I hold on to him, even as the box digs into my chest. His hands move over my back as he asks, "Are you okay?"

"I'm fine," I say and sit up. I realize then I'm straddling his waist and the heat of the fire hits me again, flushing my cheeks. Quickly, I scramble off and plop down next to him as he sits up, cracking his back.

"You really have to stop tackling me to the ground, Nari. It hurts."

"Sorry." My fingers flutter over his sleeve, wanting to check him for wounds, but I resist. "How about you? Are you okay?"

"Yeah, I'm good." He looks down at the box and sighs. "Just had to get this."

Before I can ask what it is, Kyung pulls us both up and drags us away. "Don't sit here and chit-chat, you two, we're vulnerable out here."

He releases us once we get our footing and follow him to where the other trappers stand huddled together. I stand by Ranmi's side and Tetsu stands by mine, my shoulder pressed to his arm. Kyung runs a soot-covered hand through his hair and sighs. "Well, we're left with no supplies or weapons and the night has just begun. Let's head to Juhto. We can stay in Lady Sunhi's tea house until sunrise."

"What then?" Tetsu asks.

Kyung lifts his chin, his eyes slitting. "Swift revenge."

The trappers grumble as we turn and head toward Juhto. I stay with Tetsu but Kyung pushes past me and I hear him say under his breath. "Watch out for the traps."

THIRTY-THREE

Tetsu

THE BAMNAI FOREST IS unnervingly quiet as we make our way through. I clutch the keepsake box in my hands and stick close to Nari, sweat beading on my brow as my eyes dart into the darkness. Moonlight shines through the trees but it's a crescent moon so it doesn't give us much sight.

We follow the old trade path to Juhto and Kyung managed to grab his sword, but it wouldn't be enough against an entire skulk. Because of course, a skulk must have set the camp on fire, somehow. I glance back at Yento, a frown tugging at my mouth as it grows further away.

My eye catches on a pair of bright red eyes that stare at us from the dark and I startle. Next to me, Nari places her hand on my arm and looks back. Behind us, foxes emerge onto the path, the hackles on their backs raised and their lips curling in silent snarls. I feel my heart drop to my toes and Nari's fingers curl into my skin.

"We have to run," she whispers.

"What was that?" Kyung asks loudly and turns. He lets out a strangled sound before yelling, "Demons!"

Most of the trappers ready themselves for a fight, while others take off running down the path. The foxes don't move and their leader, a large gray one with a nasty scar across its snout and a missing front leg sits down on its haunches. It lifts its head and howls. The same deep, long howl I heard Kyung and I were fleeing.

With that, the foxes leap forward and I am left blinking and frozen in place. Nari breaks from me and runs toward the foxes, who nip at her legs. She maneuvers around them and slides across the ground toward the leader, stopping a few feet away. One of the foxes pounces on her back and I jolt into action, swinging the box around and smashing it in the face of a demon that yelps and falls to the ground. I run toward Nari but a demon jumps and sinks its teeth into my bare arm.

I let out a cry and drop my box, reaching over to slip my fingers around its throat and squeeze tight. A sharp, bright scent strikes my nose and I feel my hair start to stand on end. I look up toward the churning red sky and shout, "Lightning!" A second before a bolt strikes behind me. Someone screams and burnt flesh and cotton permeates the air.

The fox drops my arm and skitters away before I can stomp on its paw. I turn around frantically, searching for Nari. Up ahead, she's bowing down before the leader like a mad woman and I sweep down, grabbing my keepsake box as I sprint toward her.

"Get up!" I rasp and the bite marks on my arm pulse with heat and pain. Blood dribbles down my skin and pools in my palm.

The fox leader sniffs Nari's head and I reach her, grabbing her arm as I pull her to her feet. The demon growls but abruptly stops as it stares at me. It tilts its head in curiosity and I take the opportunity to make our escape.

"Tetsu, wait!" Nari gasps and trips over a rock. Her arm slips from my grip and she crashes to the ground, skinning her knees.

I stumble to a stop and turn, my head growing dizzy as I breathe hard. Again, the energy shifts around us and Nari looks up. Time slows as I watch lightning reflected in her eyes descend from the sky in angry veins. Nari stands, lifting her hand with her feet firmly planted on the ground, and the lightning connects with her palm, singeing her skin. She grunts and clenches her jaw tight, her eyes closing for a brief second as it passes through her.

Then Nari crumbles to the ground and I run to her side, tears stinging my eyes. "Nari? Nari! Wake up!" I shake her shoulder. "Come on, Nari."

Her lips part and a sigh escapes her. I roll her onto her back and lean my ear to her chest, listening for her heartbeat. It thunks weakly but at least it's still there. I set a finger under her nose to make sure she's breathing and someone touches my shoulder. I startle, swinging my arm back.

Ranmi leaps out of the way. "It's just me." She comes around to kneel by Nari's side. "What happened?"

I glance around, blinking as I see the demons have made their departure and there's only scorched earth and a few dead trappers left in their wake.

"She was...struck by lightning," I tell Ranmi.

Ranmi lifts soot-covered fingers to her mouth in surprise. "And she's not dead?"

I shake my head.

"Well, we should get her to Juhto. Can you carry her?"

"Yes." I lift the keepsake box toward Ranmi. "Can you carry this?"

She nods and takes it. I lean down and slip my hands beneath Nari's back and knees, lifting her against my chest. Her head rolls into me and her eyes flutter open slowly, a weak smile lifting her lips.

THIRTY-FOUR

NARI

BY THE TIME WE make it to Juhto, I feel energized. While Tetsu carried me, my body was able to heal itself and I thank my fox spirit for making the searing pain of being struck by lightning go away so quickly. He still takes me to see a physician, who grumbles as he's woken up and then puzzled to find I'm not brain-dead. The rest of the trappers, or at least what's left of them, are waiting for us outside so we can go to the tea house together.

"Are you sure you're okay?" Tetsu asks as we walk through the sleeping village.

"Yes, I feel great, actually."

"You were literally struck by lightning a few hours ago," he snorts. "How in the world can you feel great?"

Because I have regenerative qualities.

"It passed right through me," I tell him. *I also heard human souls ringing in my ears, taking the brunt of the strike. I think they must have saved me from permanent damage.*

As we approach Lady Sunhi's tea house, it reminds me of the Forsaken Sisters' homestead with cranes and pretty paper walls. I hang back and look around for an escape when I feel Tetsu take my hand and tug me forward.

"I promise it's not the Forsaken Sisters," he tells me as if he can read my mind.

I squeeze his fingers tight and narrow my eyes on the tea house. It has a slanted, tiled roof and walls made of bamboo, painted a rosy pink. The tea house is located on the edge of Juhto, next to a stream that weaves around the back side of the structure. As we draw closer, I hear voices and music from inside and Kyung walks up the steps, gesturing for the rest of us to wait in the courtyard.

I turn to Tetsu and eye the box he holds. "What's that?"

"Oh, uh, a box of keepsakes." He says, his fingers fluttering against the carved wood and loosening some dirt packed on it.

"What are keepsakes?"

"Objects you remember people by."

I don't have to ask to know he must have things in there that remind him of his family. My mischievous fox spirit wants to tear open the box and see for myself but I will have to refrain from doing so. If I still want Tetsu to like me.

A woman appears at the entrance to the tea house. She wears a pink silk smock and taps a silver hairpin with a lily flower on top against her painted lips, her black hair loose and curling around her shoulders. For a long moment, no one says anything as the woman studies each of us. I glance at Tetsu but he seems to be in a trance, unblinking, his mouth parted slightly as he stares at the woman. I lift his hand and pinch his skin. He snaps back to himself and casts me a heated glare.

"Welcome to my tea house," the woman says, her voice traveling like a melody to our ears, soft and luscious. "You may remain in the backrooms for the evening as I am hosting quite a crowd tonight. I will have tea brought to you along with a small midnight meal."

Then the woman turns on her heel and strides back into the tea house. The trappers move as one, flooding the tea house and heading around the wraparound corridor for the backrooms. I see Tetsu glancing over his shoulder until the woman is out of sight and I feel my nose scrunch up. I pinch him again.

"Ow!" he rips his hand from my grip. "Stop pinching me, Nari."

I have nothing to say. I feel spite boiling up inside me, burning my heart. Why is Tetsu even acting like this? Why am *I* acting like this? Maybe, when the other trappers are sound asleep, I'll sneak out and steal the woman's hairpin. Maybe he'll like that.

No, no, it's obvious he found the woman attractive, as humans do. But I don't want him to.

⇛⇛ ⇚⇚

I lie on my side, listening to the breathy snores of the trappers. We've been given a few bedrolls but no blankets or pillows so most of us are sleeping on the floor. Ranmi insisted that the women separate from the men, for some reason, and it feels like I'm back in the Den. Except everyone smells like fire and ash and sweet tea, which I didn't drink.

I have my back to the bamboo wall and in the dark, I observe the room. It's rather small with a pitched roof and paper-thin and opaque front walls, also painted in a similar fashion as the Forsaken Sisters.

The music has not ceased since we arrived but it's nice to listen to. It doesn't help me sleep though.

Once I'm sure the entire room is asleep, I quietly get to my feet and step around the bodies littering the floor. Ranmi is sleeping by the sliding door, her head turned toward me. I hold my breath as I slowly pry it open. She sighs in her sleep, eyes flickering behind her eyelids, and turns over on her back. I slip out and close it again.

The corridor is empty and relatively dark. I take light steps as I walk past where the men are sleeping and around to the front of the tea house. I pass a room emitting a soft, yellow light and a familiar voice drifts to my ears. I pause and crouch by the paper wall where the light doesn't reach in case I can be seen with it.

"I have a hunch that the demons are searching for you, Sunhi," Kyung says, his voice not as gruff and rude as usual. "They must have seen you at the camp a few weeks ago and thought you were still there."

"I didn't even go there much."

"Only at night, when they were awake."

A breath of silence passes and I press my hands to the floor planks, desperate to hear more.

The woman, Sunhi, sighs deeply and I hear the splash of tea being poured. "What do you want me to say, Kyung? Sorry on behalf of the demons? I pay the trappers to *take care* of those beasts. You should have prepared for this when you had that camp built out in Yento, made of wood and canvas."

Kyung grunts and the floor creaks as he shifts. "I didn't think they would get close enough to attack. I set up traps."

My stomach twists at the word and I see in my mind's eye the young tod again. I lift a hand to my mouth as bile rises in my throat. Closing my eyes, I exhale through my nose and try to focus on the conversation again.

"Apparently not enough." Sunhi pauses. "Are you going to retaliate against the demons?"

"Of course I am," Kyung scoffs. "I'll go right to their Den and slaughter the whole lot. They can't get away with burning down my camp. But I'll need funds to build a new one."

"Yes, you'll have your funds. Try to find somewhere that isn't so vulnerable next time."

The two fall quiet and I hear one of them stand. I leap to my feet and flee back down the corridor. Tetsu is awake and rubbing his eyes as he shuffles toward the men's room again. I grab his arm, spin him around, and yank him after me until we're around the corner.

Tetsu stumbles and grumbles, "What's going on?"

"Shh," I press a hand over his mouth and peek into the corridor to see Kyung enter the men's room. The door closes softly behind him.

Tetsu grapples at my hand, knocking it away, and slumps down to the floor. I join him as he squints at me, "Nari?"

"Do you think the trappers will really attack one of the Dens?" I whisper quickly, eyes darting here and there to make sure we're not seen.

"Why would…" he trails off, a sleepy look pulling his face down and his eyes closed.

I shake him. "Yes or no, Tetsu?"

"Knowing Kyung…yes."

My brow furrows and I take my hands back, sticking my knuckles in my mouth as I gnaw on my skin nervously. I know what I heard and I know now just what kind of man Kyung is but…I wanted Tetsu to say no. To say that it would be too dangerous, too much of a risk. There are thousands of foxes compared to humans and at the Den, where we go to sleep and play and relax, no one's guard will be up. I should warn the skulk.

Tetsu slumps against me, his mouth gaping open and a glob of saliva gathering at the corner. I push him off and he goes the other way, hitting the ground.

"What are you doing awake?"

I whip my head up to see the woman, who I realize now is Sunhi, a benefactor of the fox trappers. She tilts her head at me, her dark eyes boring into the scene before her. I scramble to my feet, my back to the wall, and let out an awkward chuckle.

"Um, I had to tinkle."

"And what about him?" she points a slender finger toward Tetsu.

"Oh," I lean over and slip my hands beneath his armpits. I drag him around Sunhi, his body heavy and his hands scraping the floor. I grunt at his weight. "He had to go, too. Great tea, by the way."

Sunhi turns with us, her eyebrow arched. I pull Tetsu over to the men's room and drop him. He groans softly and his eyes open again. I leave him to crawl on his own while I go to the women's and feel Sunhi still watching me. I slide the door open and slip in.

THIRTY-FIVE

SOOK

"YOU WANT ME TO write a ransom letter?"

"Two, actually," Sook said as she pawed at the ground outside of Bojin's cabin, her nose picking up the scent of something buried beneath the soil. "For the humans Lady Tamra and Lady Sunhi."

Bojin paced, the fox medallion hanging around his thick neck reflecting the light of his bonfire. Sook gave up when she'd dug a big enough hole and sat on her haunches, watching the fire. The flames danced around one another and licked the air, singeing it with bright orange embers.

"What do you want it to say?"

"Something threatening." Sook replied and tilted her head toward him. "I'm sure you're capable of that. I don't know what would convince the trappers to come find them."

"Money," Bojin said. "If they don't have their grubby hands in the ladies' purses then they have no food, no shelter, no weapons."

"No, it needs to be something more."

Sook stood and stretched out her back, her eight tails rising stick-straight behind her. She shook out her shoulders and turned around. "Figure it out. I'll deliver the letter once you've kidnapped them."

Bojin let out an enthusiastic laugh and Sook glanced at him to see him rubbing his hands together. His eyes lit up, his grin missing most of his teeth. "I haven't kidnapped anyone in a long while. I'll bring them to the Pit of Keshin."

Sook nodded. The sinkhole that had developed a fair distance from her skulk's Den was now a common place for the fox worshipers in the area to hold prisoners or offer sacrifices to the Heavenly Fox.

"I don't want the humans anywhere near my Den."

"I'll leave instructions."

Though Sook felt a bit queasy of the humans lurking near the Den, she would let Bojin do what he had to. As a devout member of the Divine Tails, the cult obsessed with the demons, he would do anything for her.

THIRTY-SIX

TAMRA

PARANOIA WAS HER NEW nighttime companion. After hearing of what happened to the other benefactors of the fox trappers, Tamra was certain the demons would strike her village next. So she had reinforced the walls and set up a strict guard watch, along with rules for the people. They were not allowed to leave the village once the sun went down as the gates were sealed shut until dawn.

She stood in her personal garden, trying in vain to calm her pulsing heart as she listened to the soft trickle of her pebble waterfall. The scent of her orchids filled her nose, sweet yet rich. Tamra reached up to rub her forehead and let out a slow breath. It was night again and she could hear the demons move just beyond the wall, their movement snapping twigs and crunching leaves.

Tamra went down to her knees on the flagstone path beneath her and dropped her head until her chin dug into her chest. She offered a prayer asking for protection, in hopes that maybe her glorious ancestors and their animal counterparts would listen. It had been a long time since Tamra had felt their presence stir in her bosom.

"Protect me from the evils that plague our world," she whispered as she rocked back and forth on her knees. "Let me live to prove I am worthy to stay, to help the trappers fight against the demons."

When she finished, she stayed still for a moment, her eyes closed. Tamra waited for that warmth and love to overwhelm her, as it did when she was younger. Her shoulders dropped and she felt tears prick her eyes. It was useless. If they never answered before, why did she expect them to now? Why did she keep trying?

Hope. Foolish hope, Tamra thought.

A thud nearby drew her attention and her head whipped up as her eyes flew open. Tamra looked around the garden and pushed to her feet but something sharp struck her calf and she went down. Catching herself before her face could smash into the flagstone, Tamra's breathing grew heavy and her head grew hot and weary. She looked at her calf to see a thin, nine-pointed piece of metal sticking out of her flesh. A dribble of blood ran down and collected at her ankle.

Then Tamra heard the thud again but it quickly turned into heavy footsteps. Her vision blurred and her mouth fell open to scream when a hulking man appeared above her, crushing orchids in his wake. He wore a cloak, the hood lowered over his head, but he leaned down and plucked the metal from her calf. A medallion swung free of the cloak and in her delirium, all she could see were the colors silver and blood red.

"Come along now, Lady Tamra," the man said, his voice grating against her ears.

"No..." she whimpered and fell on her side, a paralyzing numbness passing through her.

The man swept her up and over his shoulder. Now the scent of orchids was replaced with the rank scent of sweat. Tamra's nose tried to crinkle but it couldn't and she soon felt nothing of her body. It was as if she were weightless. The man turned and dropped a piece of parchment on the flagstones where Tamra had been kneeling a moment before. Her eyes rolled and bounced in her head as she was lifted over the wall and out of the village.

THIRTY-SEVEN

SUNHI

THE TEA HOUSE WAS all she had left. Sunhi lay on her bedroll, hands folded over her stomach as she stared at the ceiling. It was difficult to sleep most nights, though she'd never admit that to Kyung. The leader of the trappers was not the sympathetic type, even when they were growing up together. She exhaled sharply and picked up the hairpin she had set aside.

Sunhi ran her finger along the smooth metal and carved the lily flower encrusted with tiny diamonds and topaz. It was a gift from her late love, a man not many knew. Sochin was the recluse lord of the Hansu region of Daion in the northeastern part of the kingdom. She had gone there with the trappers and Kyung to gather supplies from abandoned villages. A risky trip, but a necessary one. Sochin was still at his estate, however, and rather insistent that he'd kill them all before they could set foot on his property.

She had been sent in to console him and found that the man had been alone for years and didn't trust his own people anymore. Sunhi worked with him and fell in love with his quirky spirit and his impeccable attention to detail when he was smithing. He'd made the hairpin for her with a lily flower, though it didn't represent how Sunhi had lived her life, she loved it more than anything that had been given her. He wanted to open a tea house with a smithy so they could pursue their dreams together.

Then, one horrible night when they finally convinced Sochin to come live in Juhto, they were attacked by the demons. Sochin jumped in front of her as a demon pounced, protecting her as its canines sunk into his chest and its claws slashed his abdomen open. Sunhi relived the memory alone and at night when her mind made her suffer more. Now, the demons were after her for supporting the trappers and after Sochin, she wished they would take her, too.

Sunhi was so lost in her head that she didn't hear or see the man enter her room until it was too late. He stood over her, a brooding figure. She remained still, staring up at the man as she clutched the hairpin in her fingers. No matter what happened, she would never let it go.

"Hmm, I thought you'd put up a fight, Lady Sunhi," the man said.

She did not reply and simply closed her eyes. He picked her up and hauled her off into the night. Sunhi kept the hairpin close to her chest, her finger tapping against the pointed end. Sharp enough to stab through flesh.

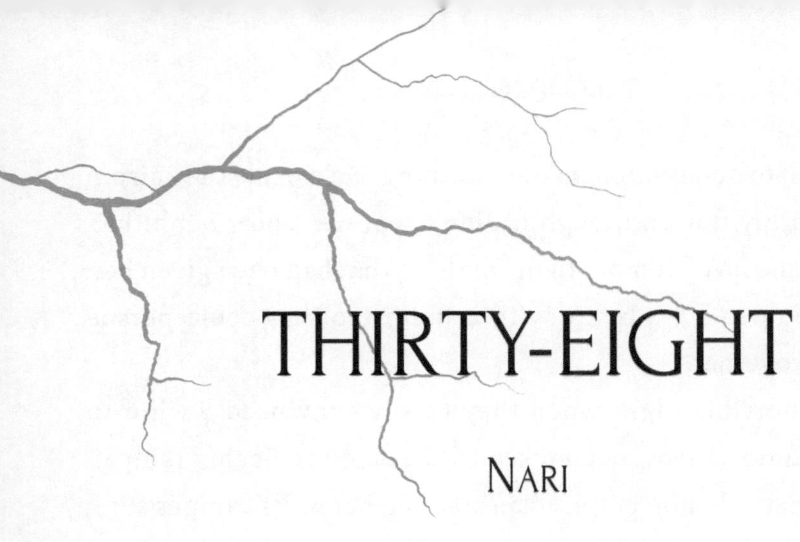

THIRTY-EIGHT

NARI

WHEN RANMI AND I step out of the tea house and into the courtyard, we see Kyung strutting around, cursing under his breath. I don't see Lady Sunhi anywhere and a young messenger girl with wide eyes glances at us before she runs off through the gate. Kyung pivots when he sees us and comes forward, clenching his hands at his sides so hard his arms tremble.

"The demons took Sunhi."

Kyung lifts his arm toward Ranmi and only then do I see the piece of parchment crumpled in his fingers. She tentatively takes it and unravels the message. I can tell the ink has been somewhat smeared and Kyung pushes me aside to stand by Ranmi. He blocks the message from me even though I can't read.

Ranmi hums. "This is not good...why would they take her to Keshin? That's a place for the Divine Tails, not the demons."

"It doesn't matter if it's the Tails or the demons' place. I received a message that Tamra was taken from her village last night as well." Kyung curses again and I step away as his shoulders tense and the muscles and veins in his arms bulge. "If Sunhi and Tamra are killed, we have no money for supplies."

"The ransom doesn't mention money."

"I don't care, Ranmi," he snaps. "We need to get them back."

"Of course," she says softly.

The other trappers emerge from the tea house then and I go to Tetsu's side as he runs his fingers through his hair and yawns. Quickly, I whisper, "Two ladies were taken."

It takes him a moment to register what I've said before his eyes widen and he goes to Kyung. "Lady Sunhi and Lady Tamra were taken?"

Kyung sighs as the trappers stop in their tracks and stare at their leader. I knot my fingers together as Kyung turns toward us and raises his voice for all to hear. "Yes, taken last night by what would appear to be a member of the Divine Tails." He pauses, his gaze sweeping over each of us. "To the Pit of Keshin."

An uncomfortable silence falls upon the trappers and I look at Tetsu. His skin pales and he sets a hand on his stomach. I've only heard of the Pit of Keshin once and that was from Sook, ordering us young kits to stay away from there. I don't know anything else about it, besides that now Ranmi said it's where the fox cult is.

"We can't go there," one of the trappers says.

"We can and we will—"

"They'll kill us and cut out our hearts to eat!" another cries.

Protests are raised against Kyung's decision and he lifts his hands, trying to calm the trappers down until he roars, "Quiet!" The protests turn to grumbles and Kyung's eyes narrow as he drops his arms. "If you want to be childish about it then I will go by myself. I will slaughter every last zealot and demon that I see until Lady Tamra and Lady Sunhi are safe."

I see Tetsu's chest puff up and his back straighten as he says, "I'll go."

"Me too," I second.

Tetsu glances at me, his brow furrowing but he says nothing. He's seen how I fight. Kyung asks, "Anyone else?"

Ranmi lifts a finger. "We have a better chance of making it out alive with more people *and* if we go during the day."

"Yes. So?"

Slowly, only ten trappers agree to go, including me and Tetsu. The ones that don't shake their heads and return to the tea house. Kyung watches them with a dark look on his face, rife with spite. Then he turns and we leave the tea house behind. I hurry to Tetsu's side and keep my voice low as we follow Kyung through the village.

"We have no weapons."

"I know," Tetsu says and shakes his hands out. "This isn't a good idea."

"Then why did you agree to go?"

"So Kyung doesn't get himself killed. Why did you?"

"So you don't die," I tell him.

Tetsu glances at me, his expression softening a little and I feel heat flare in my chest. Again, I have the urge to nuzzle his nose but I hold off. That would be too awkward to do right now, not because we're surrounded by the trappers, but because I don't know how Tetsu truly sees me.

We leave the village with nothing but the clothes on our backs and Kyung's fiery step leading the way to the Pit of Keshin. I look among the trees in the forest as we walk a path overgrown with vegetation but don't see any of my skulk nearby, which I am glad for. I feel Tetsu's knuckles brush mine and I jump.

"Sorry," he whispers.

I shake my head and slowly wrap my fingers around two of his. I cannot bear to see any foxes injured, not after the trap Kyung showed me. Gnawing on my lip, I squeeze Tetsu's fingers as we walk, trying to keep my racing heart from bursting.

THIRTY-NINE

TETSU

NEVER IN MY LIFE would I think I'd end up at the Pit of Keshin. As we approach on quiet feet, my chest constricts as I barely breathe. I'm trying to make as little noise as possible and next to me, I'm fairly certain that Nari is holding her breath. Her skin is purpling, her brow slick with sweat. I nudge her and she exhales, glancing at me with fear shining in her eyes.

The Pit is surrounded by thick vegetation that if someone wasn't paying attention, they would fall right in. It's a good thing we didn't encounter the Pit, or any zealots, on our way to and from the Itson Temple.

Up ahead, Kyung lifts a hand, motioning us to stop. Rough and worn voices drift to my ears and I strain to hear what the zealots are saying but it's garbled nonsense. Kyung said they had developed their own dialect and spoke to one another with random yips and the occasional high-pitched scream. They had become a blend of human and demon and it's eerie to listen to.

Nari drops low to the ground and scurries forward, where Kyung is crouched behind a fallen log. He startles when he notices her and his nostrils flare, lips curling back in a snarl. I focus on Nari, my mouth feeling as dry as cotton, and she curls her fingers on the log, peeking over. I'd like to see what the Pit looks like and how many zealots we're up against but my legs don't move. Nari looks back, notices I'm frozen in place, and drags me over.

I thud to the ground, wincing as my kneecaps strike hard. Kyung shoots me a heated glare, shaking his head at me. I inch forward and look into the Pit. It's much more structured than I imagined and its gaping maw is enormous, spanning across a fair bit of the forest floor. The Pit is broken up into tiers, with moss-grown slabs of stone creating makeshift stands, as if it were an arena instead of a sinkhole.

The sky above is clear of a tree canopy and tendrils of red energy move like smoke among the puffy, tinted clouds. Back in the Pit, one of the zealots lets out a loud howl of a laugh, causing me to jump. I stare with unease nestling in my belly. They sit among the stones, chatting like it's a normal day and time in our world. They wear makeshift fox ears and tails, some have sharpened their fingernails and teeth to fine points. Each has a weapon nearby and one woman chews on the end of a crossbow bolt, her teeth scraping the metal.

I roll up on my knees to see further down into the Pit and catch sight of Lady Sunhi and Lady Tamra. They lie flat on their backs at the bottom of the Pit on a slab of stone. Their wrists and ankles are tied with cord, and dirty cloths stuck in their mouths. Lady Tamra is visibly distressed as she thrashes against the restraints, her face stained with tears. Lady Sunhi, on the other hand, is completely still and pale, her eyes closed.

Around them lie thousands of spherical objects of varying sizes and colors, along with white lily blossoms. A woven tapestry depicting the sage of death lies across the bottom of the stone slab. The scene is set up for a sacrifice.

One of the zealots stops talking and looks up. I quickly duck behind the log and hold my breath. Agonizing silence passes before the chatter begins again. Slowly, I shift toward Kyung and murmur, "They're at the bottom of the Pit."

Kyung nods and crawls away. I follow after but look back to see Nari still crouching by the log. She turns her head this way and that, her ears twitching slightly. After a firm shake of her head, she joins us and we return to Juhto without a word until we're safe inside its gates again.

Kyung crosses his arms. "There's more zealots than I thought would be at the Pit today. We'll need weapons."

And so we follow the leader of the trappers to the village armory.

FORTY

CHUL

CHUL WAS SLEEPING SOUNDLY, all curled up in the Den, when Sook came in and nudged him with her snout. He grumbled and pawed at her face, knowing it was still the middle of the day. Sook nipped his ear and Chul's eyes slitted open as he rolled on his back and glared up at her.

"We're heading to the Pit of Keshin," she simply said.

That piqued Chul's interest and he got to his feet, his tails going stiff as he bowed and stretched. "What are we going there for?"

Sook had already moved on, waking the others. Chul yawned and blinked, his eyes adjusting to the dark. They followed Sook up one of the tunnels, soil breaking beneath their paws as they lumbered out of the small entrance one by one.

"Be ready for a battle," Sook told them and then took off toward the Pit of Keshin.

Chul kicked off the ground and ran to catch up with Sook, her eight tails whirling around so much they almost hit him right in the face. He ducked and asked as he came to her side, "Care to fill me in?"

Sook glanced sidelong at him and they split around a tree trunk before coming together again. "I had Bojin kidnap the last two benefactors of the trappers."

"Bojin?" Chul scoffed. The disgusting human that insisted on being Sook's servant. He had never trusted the man nor ever would. "And he took them to the Pit?"

"Yes. The trappers scoped the area out before they returned to the human village."

"How many were there?"

"Only ten."

Chul's brow lifted. There were at least fifty trappers at the camp the last time he and Sook went there. "Was Nari among them?"

Sook nodded. "And the boy."

He leapt over a bush full of sharp branches that grazed his underbelly and landed on the ground, the impact vibrating up through his paws and into his bones. So Nari was still human. Chul figured it'd be a difficult task to take a human to the Guardian at the Gate but he also figured that if Nari really wanted her body back, she wouldn't dally around with the humans—much less the trappers. Chul was beginning to wonder if Nari even wanted to be a fox again.

Before he could dwell more on the thought, they came to the Pit and he skidded to a halt, his paws hitting the edge. Chul glanced down into the Pit and saw two female humans bound at the bottom. His lip curled in a snarl. He could simply jump down there now and rip their throats out, no need for this fuss with the trappers.

Sook walked behind him and said to the others, "Nari is among the trappers so be careful not to hurt her."

"How will we know which one she is?" Gi, a vixen with four tails, asked between pants.

"You'll know," Chul said and his ears perked as he heard twigs snap afar off. "The trappers have returned."

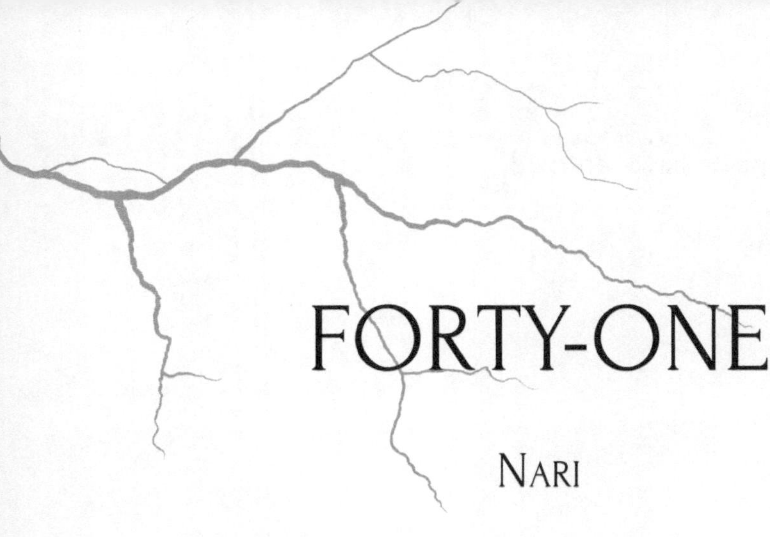

FORTY-ONE

NARI

I'VE BEEN GIVEN A bow and a quiver of arrows, though Ranmi gives me a pointed look and I promise her I won't try to shoot Tetsu again. My stomach feels like it's in knots and I keep my head down as we return to the Pit of Keshin. I know my Den is nearby, I can see the marks Sook etched into the trees with her claws, claiming the territory. I just hope Kyung doesn't know where the Den is.

Tetsu has been given a sword again, this time a shorter one with a wider blade. He stands aside and practices with it as we walk, his hanbok fluttering about his legs.

As we near the Pit, the silence of the forest makes the hair rise on my arms and I look up. My gaze narrows as I search among the trees for any sign of my skulk. For their sakes, I hope Sook hasn't organized this whole ordeal and it's just the cult's doing. I can take human life on a whim but not that of my own kind.

A flash of movement around the side of the Pit catches my attention—and Kyung's. He charges forward, a longsword gripped between his hands, and disappears behind a thicket. The rest of the trappers

188

spread out and suddenly I find myself alone. Frantically, I search for Tetsu and hear a low growl behind me. I whip around, holding the bow tightly against my chest, and I see Chul emerge. My chest deflates with relief but his hackles are still raised as he approaches, his black eyes cold.

"Chul, it's me," I whisper, shuffling back a step.

"I know," his gaze flickers over me and disgust curls his lip, "but you're still human."

"I'm trying, I swear."

Chul huffs and steps around me, his tails hitting my leg as he passes. "Stay out of the fight."

I turn as he bounds off in the direction that Kyung went and my heart leaps in my throat. I move. I chase after him like I did the night I turned. Chul is my mentor, my Den brother, the one who has always looked out for me and I have to look out for him.

A scream shatters the silence and is followed by the cult's yips and calls to one another. My skulk materializes from the bushes and jump down from high branches. I run past, following Chul's tails until I think we're no longer near the Pit. An ominous, opaque mist has emerged from the ground, slithering its way through every seam of the forest.

Then I hear Chul snarling and Kyung cursing the day and the sound of a sword arching through the air. But the mist and vegetation have grown rather dense and I've had to slow down to pick my way through. "Chul!" I cry when I hear a howl of pain.

"Nari!" Tetsu whispers fiercely from up above. I look up to find him in the tree and I hurry to the trunk, swinging the bow around to my back. He reaches down and helps me up as I anchor my feet and climb. Tetsu straddles a thick branch, sweat glistening on his brow, and a look of shame in his eyes.

"I was hiding," he admits, "but then I saw Kyung run this way, and you after him, so here I am."

"How'd you get here before me?" I ask as I step over him and almost fall from the branch, but I sit and straddle it myself.

"I think Kyung is running in circles."

I inch forward on the branch, fingers digging into the wood so I don't tip over. I feel Tetsu snatch the back of my tunic. "What are you doing?"

"Um, seeing where Kyung is," I say.

"Fighting a single demon, he'll be fine."

I shake my head and pull my tunic out of Tetsu's fingers. "Nari—"

"Shh."

More footsteps below and I look to see Sook and Gi appear beneath the tree. They glance up, right at me, and then Sook's gaze strays to Tetsu. Neither of us move and Sook's head tilts slightly, her mouth parting as she lets out a soft howl. A signal for me to follow.

I swing my leg over the other side of the branch and push off, striking the ground harder than I thought with an *oof*. Sharp pain echoes through my feet and I wince, hearing Tetsu fiercely whisper my name. But once the pain is gone, a split second later, I take off after Sook and Gi. I follow them to a clearing nearly free of the heavy mist where Chul is snapping his jaws and growling at Kyung. Both are injured but not gravely. Chul has a nasty, deep cut on his shoulder and half of his left ear is gone but Kyung hasn't driven his blade into his heart yet.

I run into the clearing as Sook and Gi prowl along the perimeter and Chul's head whips toward me. His hackles rise, back arching as he gets ready to pounce on me. Kyung, who has no time to tell me to get back, rushes forward and drops the sword low, swinging it up to lop off Chul's head. For a second, time slows as Chul notices the attack and tips his head back just in time. The blade takes off a tuft of his chin fur.

Chul is quick to counterattack and leaps up, sinking his canines into Kyung's hand. The man screams and drops the sword. It clatters to the ground and that's when Sook and Gi attack. They each latch onto Kyung's legs and he stomps as he swings Chul around, his other hand on Chul's throat.

"Kill them Nari!" he booms.

I remove my bow and nock an arrow, drawing the bowstring in one fluid movement. Chul releases Kyung to nip at his other hand and I exhale down the shaft of the arrow. They're all moving too much and I don't want to accidentally shoot Chul. But Kyung's fingers are closing tight around his throat and I release the arrow. Its fletching scrapes my bare forearm as it flies from the bow. Past Chul's throat, the head buries itself in Kyung's shoulder. He drops Chul, who thunks to the ground, and I resist the urge to run to his side.

Instead, Sook and Gi grab him and drag him away. I drop the bow, my eyes widening in mock shock. Tetsu comes up to my side, huffing and puffing. He glances at me and then runs to Kyung, who holds his injured arm against himself, his glare seething with every bit of hate that burns in his being.

"You," he hisses, "are done for."

FORTY-TWO

TETSU

"RETREAT!" KYUNG YELLS NEAR my ear as we make our way back to the Pit. Nari is walking behind us, no bounce in her step, and keeps muttering an apology to Kyung but he's not having it.

I gnaw on my lip, casting Nari a wary look. Clearly, she was pretty good with a bow when she had pinned a lock of my hair to a tree...so how did she miss the demon's throat at an even shorter distance? I had been too late to correct her aim and now Kyung is furious.

We give the Pit a wide berth and hurry back to Juhto. Evening crept in on us during the conflict and now shadows taunt us, waiting to swallow us whole.

Kyung rips his arm free of my grip and sits heavily on the steps of the tea house. I glance around at the trappers as they gather, silently tending to the wounded. Three are missing and a heavy feeling wells in my chest. We failed. My gaze shifts to Nari, who stands near the short wall surrounding the tea house, her shoulders hunched together.

"Get over here, Nari," Kyung snaps.

She hesitates before coming forward. I watch as Kyung beckons her closer and I move as he rises to his feet, lifting his hand. I rush forward and grab Kyung's wrist before he can strike Nari across the cheek. I've never seen Kyung hit anyone before and I definitely won't let the first be Nari.

"Let go of me."

"No," I choke out.

Kyung growls deep in his throat and rips his wrist free. He spits at Nari's feet and hisses, "You wretched thing. I should have never trusted you."

Nari winces and whispers in a hoarse voice, "I'm sorry—"

"No, you are not!" Kyung roars.

My pulse quickens as I step between him and Nari. Kyung pushes forward, spittle flying from his mouth as he curses at her over my shoulder. "You're no longer welcome among the trappers! You shot me on purpose to save those demons, didn't you. You're a fox sympathizer, one of those harebrained zealots, aren't you!"

"N—no."

Ranmi steps up then, clutching a blood-soaked cloth against her side. She's looking a little too pale in the face but her voice is firm as she says, "That's enough, Kyung, you're making a scene. Nari's just inexperienced, she's bound to make mistakes."

He ignores her and roughly grabs my shoulder, trying to shove me out of the way. With a grunt, I stumble back and hold my arms out, protecting Nari. His breath grows rapid and rancid, veins bulging from his forehead and neck. "Sit down, Kyung, please."

It takes a moment for Kyung to back off and drop down onto the steps again. "Get out of my sight," he tells Nari, his voice cold and detached.

I turn to Nari as she backs away. She looks at Ranmi, who shakes her head and refuses to make eye contact. I reach for Nari, my brow creasing with worry.

"If you go after her, Tetsu, you're done with us too."

My fingers curl into a fist, my jaw clenching tight. I can't be done and thrown out onto the street. Being part of the trappers is my only chance to help make things right in this world, even if it's a lost cause. Right enough to live a longer life, I suppose. And ever since Father perished, Kyung took me in and taught me so many things that Father should have. The trappers gave me a purpose, a way to deal out revenge for everything the demons took from me.

But Nari...

She bumps into the wall, silent tears streaking her cheeks, and I feel my heart pull toward her. But I stop myself and let out a deep sigh. Her expression crumbles into one I recognize—fear and uncertainty.

I'll find you, I mouth, wishing I could say the words aloud. *I'll find you.*

Nari stares at me for a moment longer before she slips away.

FORTY-THREE

NARI

I LEAVE THE VILLAGE and make my way to the Den. I don't know what Tetsu was saying but I feel like I've lost my chance to go to Sanoul. Though I can always find another human...I wanted Tetsu by my side. But not for the Guardian at the Gate—for myself.

A warm feeling flutters in my belly at the thought and then it is quickly overshadowed by fear. Am I falling for Tetsu? Bonding to him? I sigh and shove my fingers through my hair. Such feelings are forbidden and unnatural. We're enemies, I have to remember that, and maybe now that I've shot Kyung, he'll see it too. Finally.

I groan as I trudge through the forest and come up on the Den. Several tods and vixens are sitting on the ground, tending to each other's wounds. They stop and stare at me when I stumble into the clearing. The Den's entrance is filled with two kit heads who want to see what's going on. I drop down and sit, rubbing my eye as I ask, "Where's Chul and Sook? Are they okay?"

"We're fine," Sook says as she leaps down from the large tree that keeps the Den hidden. "Chul is resting inside." Sook comes toward me and her gaze wanders past, growing weary. "You weren't followed, were you?"

I shake my head.

"Everyone inside, just in case."

I crawl to the entrance and have to slide into the Den on my belly, the tunnel and cavern much more enclosed than it used to be. I sit with my knees to my chest, my head grazing the ceiling, and Sook digs into the ground a bit so I can sit comfortably. I look over at Chul, where Gi is licking his wounds.

I sniffle as the tears trail down my cheeks and I rest my chin on my knees. "I keep getting Chul hurt."

Sook sits next to me as the others disperse into other caverns of the Den at the wave of her paw.

"Chul is a fighter, Nari, and a risk-taker. I know you were just trying to protect him."

"Tried and failed."

Sook rubs her face against my arm. "If it wasn't for you, though, he wouldn't be alive. You saved his life by shooting that trapper. And before, when you pushed the other one in the pond."

"They kicked me out."

"The trappers?"

I nod.

"What about the boy?"

"Tetsu?" I sigh. "I can't bring him to Sanoul."

"Why not?"

My body flushes with heat and I glance at Sook, feeling incredibly foolish. Her brow lifts and she beckons me to follow her to another cavern. I do, squeezing through the tunnel and trying not to destroy the entire Den with my oversized human body.

Once alone, Sook says, "You have feelings for the human boy?"

"I don't know," I tell her and slide down to lie on my side. "Human emotions are different but I did experience a...estrous cycle—the human one."

"I see. Do you remember when I told you he may be half-fox? You may be reacting to him because of it."

"Yes," I say. "Have you found evidence that he is or isn't?"

"Not yet."

"And what if he is?"

Sook shrugs. "I doubt he'll accept it if he does not know already."

I remain quiet, thinking of Tetsu's possible fox blood. I would be overjoyed if he were half-fox and maybe then the Heavenly Fox can grant him the gift of shape-shifting, as I will receive once I turn over the soul beads. We are spawned with two spirits but cannot access the human soul until we turn. Then, when we turn over our beads, we can shape-shift between our two forms whenever we want.

If Tetsu is half-fox, I know what Sook says is true, that he won't accept it. Though, since I've been with the trappers, he hasn't shown much hatred toward the foxes, nothing like Kyung does. Still, when he finds out what I am...

A shudder racks through me at the thought. I don't know what will happen. He protected me from Kyung earlier...I don't think he'd do it again.

Sook drops down to the ground and rests her chin on her paws, looking at me. "You're in a complicated situation, Nari, but don't worry, I'll help you."

I nod and curl into myself, burying my face in my arms. I feel Sook's nose nudge against my elbow. "Sleep now, you're safe."

FORTY-FOUR

TETSU

THOUGH LADY SUNHI AND Lady Tamra are still in grave danger, all I can think about is Nari--alone in the forest with the demons and the cult. I sit on the steps of the tea house as the sun passes overhead, staring out past the village gate where Nari left yesterday. Kyung and the others are inside, resting and recuperating. We'll have to wait until tomorrow to try another rescue mission. But it feels hopeless. Eventually, the demons will get us all. They're too powerful, too sneaky, so why are we still fighting a war we'll never win?

Because hope lives on, even in the darkest of times.

The unwarranted words of Mother echo through my mind. I clasp my fingers together and rest my chin on my knuckles. Maybe it's time that I take my journey into my own hands, instead of relying on the trappers. Yes, the fight would be easier with more people, but as far as I can tell, we'll never make it to Sanoul.

I look down at my black hanbok and trousers, the copper breast-plate I wear, and the sheath at my hip. The breastplate is too small now, digging into my sides and throat. I unclasp the chains on either side and let it slide off me with a thud. I set the breastplate on the porch of the tea house and push to my feet.

If I'm going to Sanoul, the easiest way would be to pretend I'm a zealot and to do that, I need one of their medallions.

I head inside the tea house to collect my keepsake box so I can bury it again. But before I bury it, I open it one more time and dig around for Mother's compass. I tuck it into my pocket and bury the box.

I need answers about my family and without another look back, I walk into the forest.

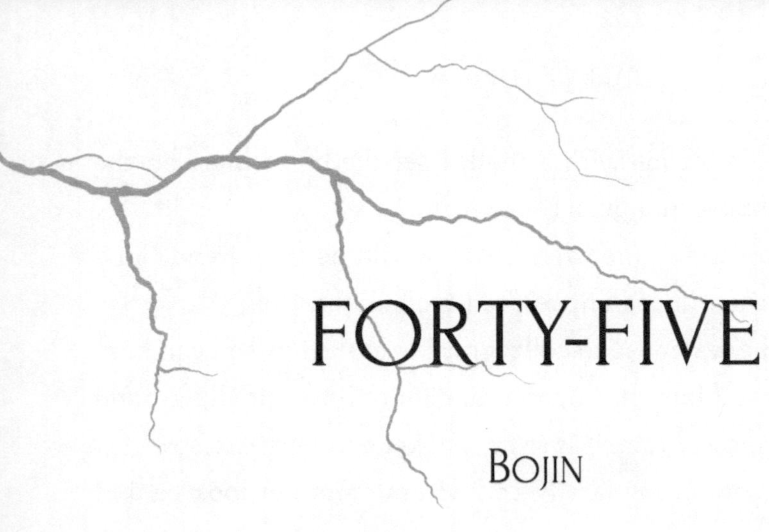

FORTY-FIVE

BOJIN

BOJIN SNUCK TOWARD THE Pit to pick at the remains of dead fox trappers after their unsuccessful attempt. Down below, he heard chanting and decided to peek over. The two women he had kidnapped were still alive but while one was writhing in terror, the other was completely still. He dropped down and rested his chin in his palms as he watched the sacrificial ritual take place. One of the Divine Tails' leaders, a man with long, tangled hair and wild eyes, stood in nothing but a loincloth by the stone slab. He had a staff carved of wood that was topped with a fox mask, the faux soul beads dangling from its ear.

"We have been tasked by the Heavenly Fox herself to kill anyone who denies her divinity!" the man shouted, spittle flying from his mouth. He pointed an accusing finger toward the women. "These two have been funding the fox trappers and therefore, are guilty of such treason! Pick up your arms and come forward so as one, we may purge the world of their wicked hearts."

Bojin thumbed the pendant around his neck and stood, wondering if he'd be allowed to join in. The Tails converged on the stone slab, yipping and howling as they snapped their jaws in spite.

Lady Tamra screamed against the cloth in her mouth and one of the Tails grabbed her leg, piercing her thigh with a dagger and pinning her to the slab. The spurt of blood made Bojin's stomach growl and he made his way down into the Pit, ready for a richer feast. As he got closer, something flashed in Lady Sunhi's bound hands and she reared up, stabbing the shoulder of the nearest Tail with a hairpin. The Tail yelped and she tore the hairpin free to ram it into their throat, cutting off their shriek of pain. Bojin paused, his jaw falling slack in surprise. She attacked again and again, blood splattering her pretty, pale face until the Tails swarmed the slab and the two women were hidden from his sight.

He felt their terror as his heart thunked in his chest and sounds grew distorted around him. Bojin stumbled back, clutching his chest as his throat constricted. For once in his life, he felt tears sting the back of his eyes and he closed them, taking in a startling breath. He sat near the edge of the Pit and kept his head down until there was nothing to be heard but the ravenous tearing of flesh and the crack of bones. His shoulders fell heavy and a foreign sense of remorse welled deep in his core.

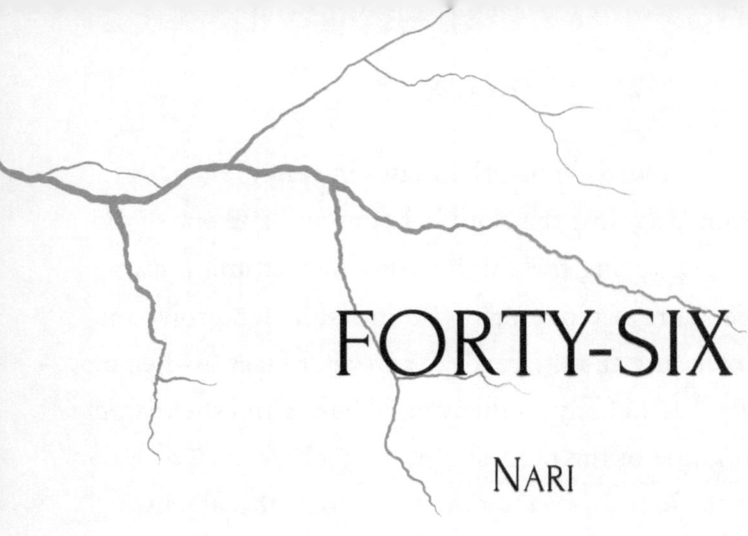

FORTY-SIX

NARI

I SIT IN A nearby spring with Chul, washing the soot and grime from my body and clothes. He moves slowly, keeping his neck above the water as he paddles around the spring. He hasn't spoken much to me since he woke up but insisted on following me to bathe.

"How are you feeling?" I ask.

"I could always be better," Chul responds gruffly. He turns and swims in the other direction.

"I'm sorry."

"Don't be, you're just trying to protect me, right?"

I wince at the way he says it, like he's mocking me.

"I truly am."

"Well," Chul grunts as he climbs out of the spring, having hardly been in it for a few minutes. He stands on the bank and shakes the water from his fur, droplets flying in all directions. "You don't need to worry about me, Nari, you need to get yourself to Sanoul."

"I know, I just—"

"You like that human boy."

I stare at him and close my mouth. My skin heats and I sink into the water, letting the steam obscure my view of him.

"Yeah, that's what I thought." Chul comes around to my side and glances sidelong at me. "Don't you want to be a fox again?"

My nostrils flare as anger boils up inside me and I turn to him, my voice rising, "Of course I do! But you left me alone when I turned, Chul; you gave me a simple instruction and *left*. Why couldn't you help me?" Tears brim in my eyes and my voice cracks, "I—I needed you and you ran away."

Chul stares at me and sits back on his haunches. His tails fall flat behind him and he dips his chin. "I don't know, it was just—shocking. Maybe I'm a little jealous too that you collected so many soul beads in such a short amount of time. I've always wanted to go to Sanoul, but you can't get in without the beads and a human who trusts you."

"I wish I could give them to you so I can just be a fox again," I mutter and rub away the tears on my cheeks. "I'm tired of being human, but I guess this is what I'll be forever now."

He is quiet for a long moment and I turn away. After a while, Chul heads back to the Den and I'm left alone. I absently scrub at my skin and then get out and dress in my damp clothes. I sit on the edge of the spring with my knees to my chest and stare at the water until my vision stops blurring with tears.

Then I hear the crunch of footsteps nearby but I don't move. If Chul has come back, I don't want to talk to him. The footsteps grow heavier and louder and my ears perk. I turn and look up as Tetsu emerges from the thick brush, swatting away stray branches. My heart leaps into my throat and I spring to my feet, pouncing on him. We tumble to the ground and I straddle his waist, leaning down as I curl my arms around his head. Without thinking, I start nuzzling his nose and then stop, my eyes widening.

Tetsu's skin is flushed a deep pink and his hands rest on my waist. "Um, hey, Nari."

I scramble off him and stand, sticking my knuckles in my mouth. Movement just beyond the trees draws my attention and I see Chul with a branch full of berries in his mouth. My eyebrows shoot up and I hastily look away, so I don't direct Tetsu's attention to Chul as he stands and brushes the dirt off his trousers.

Quickly, I grab Tetsu's arm and bring him toward the spring. He reels back, almost slipping and falling in. I let go and cross my arms, standing astride.

"Why are you here? How'd you find me?"

"I was worried about you," he says, his voice soft and kind. It makes my pulse quicken. "I tracked your path and then lost it and wandered around until I found you."

He was worried about me? Warmth spreads across my skin as a sense of hope stirs in my soul.

FORTY-SEVEN

Tetsu

NARI IS QUIET AND I rub the back of my neck, thinking about her knocking me to the ground, her lips so close to mine. I glance at her, my gaze wandering over her damp curls, with a stubborn piece sticking to her forehead. I can't say I *don't* want to kiss her but...then what would it mean? Would it be a form of comfort? A way to convince her to come with me? Do I want to kiss her because...because I want to? How would she react if I take her and pull her close?

Heat spreads across my face and down my neck. I clear my throat. "I've...decided to go to Sanoul. To see if my mother is really there."

She looks up at me, a line forming between her short eyebrows. "But the Guardian at the Gate...it will consume our souls."

"Well, I mean I don't exactly want to go anywhere near it but I think if we disguise ourselves as zealots, we may be let in."

Nari's dark eyes light up. "That's a good idea, Tetsu. How are we going to do that though?"

"Good question," I chuckle awkwardly. "I haven't thought that far, but the further north we go, the more Fox Dens and cult camps there will be. We have to be extremely careful but maybe we can convince some zealots we're friends, not foes."

Her head bobs in a nod. "I was listening to how they spoke to one another at the Pit, I think I can mimic it. I was raised by wild dogs, after all."

I shuffle closer to her. The darkness of night will soon be upon us and the forest will wake. We'll follow the pattern of the foxes as we did on our way to the Itson Temple. Though I'm tired and would rather sleep, I want to get a good head start north before Kyung finds out I'm gone.

"Are you ready to go?" I ask, more for myself than her.

"Yes," Nari answers and reaches down to take my hand.

The feel of her palm pressing against mine makes me happy that I met her. Alone no more, we trudge onward through the forest.

FORTY-EIGHT

CHUL

CHUL RAN BACK TO the Den once he heard the conversation between Nari and the boy. He slid down into the cavern, pain sparking in his neck and shoulder, but he found Sook talking with another vixen and was out of breath as he told her, "Nari's going to Sanoul. I have to follow her."

Sook blinked. "Oh?"

"The boy found her. He said he's going to find his mother."

"Are you sure you're capable of traveling by yourself?"

Chul snorted. "We can heal quicker than a normal fox, can't we?"

She rolled her eyes. "Yes, but you've been in quite the scuffle, Chul. Gi," she called out and the vixen emerged from another cavern, "you're going with Chul to follow Nari."

Gi bobbed her head and followed Chul from the Den. They tracked Nari and the boy easily and hung back at a fair distance where they couldn't be seen or heard. Chul's nose twitched when he saw Nari was holding the boy's hand. They could have simply walked side by side and would have been fine. The boy held a compass now, directing their path as he pulled Nari along.

"How long does it take to get to Sanoul?" he asked Gi.

"A few days," she told him and leaned over to sniff his muzzle. "Were you in a blackberry patch?"

"Yes, I was getting Nari some berries," Chul's jaw clenched, "then I saw her nuzzling the human."

Gi's brow lifted. "Oh. Do you think she's bonded to him?"

Chul nodded once. Unfortunately, it seemed to be so. He couldn't believe Nari would do such a thing and let herself be bonded to a human. That was another reason Chul was angry with her but also with himself. Yes, he had left her behind and he had no reason but that he was naive to how the whole process worked. He was shocked at her transformation and he was injured, his head rattled from the fight. Chul wasn't thinking straight and wanted to get as far away as possible. And she had saved the boy from the pond...he should have guessed then she might be at risk to bond with him.

Not only had Nari failed to protect him, but he had failed to protect her as well.

FORTY-NINE

Tetsu

AS THE FIRST NIGHT drags on, I feel something nestled in my soul begin to stir with vigor. The voice, that I've only heard when I was extremely sick or tired, emerges as a whisper in my ear. I bat at my head, though it doesn't go away, and when dawn breaks, Nari and I climb a tree to sleep in.

I sit against a thick, slanted branch and tuck Nari beneath my arm, my hand resting on her hip. She falls asleep quickly and I lean my head on hers, my eyes fluttering closed. Silence welcomes the voice to be louder but I'm too exhausted to listen and drift to sleep.

A fox demon with dark, reddish-brown fur and a white-tipped tail appears before my eyes and though I seize with fear, it doesn't pounce on me. It stands there, staring up at me with tawny-colored eyes and a wet snout.

"What do you want?" I snarl. "Are you the one in my head?"

When I accidentally hurt myself with Father's sword, he said that there were remnants of fox blood on it and that it had made me sick. Now, this demon haunts my mind but I don't know what it wants.

"Let me take the helm," the demon says, its voice slick like oil as it offers a sly smile. Its canines glisten with blood.

"Never," I spit.

The demon laughs, the ha-ha sound making gooseflesh rise on my arms. It has no right to invade my mind and torment me. I rush toward the demon but it leaps out of the way and chomps down on my hand. I cry out, trying to shake the fox off but it holds on, its eyes boring into me as it smiles around the bite.

"You can't get rid of me," the demon says when it releases me and I hold my bleeding hand to my chest. "I've been with you since the beginning. Two souls in one body—fox and human."

I gasp as I lurch upright and Nari grumbles at the movement. My vision is swimming with dark spots and my skin is slick with sweat. I swipe at my face, my chest heaving. Why did the fox say there was a fox and a human soul in my body? How is that even possible?

Next to me, Nari stirs and turns, her eyes cracking open as she looks up at me. "Is it night already?"

I look around, blinking away the spots. It's barely dusk but I don't feel like staying in the tree any longer. Nari stretches, her back arching, and I shimmy down the tree, thunking to the ground. I catch her in my arms as she jumps and set her down.

"Are you okay?" she asks, grabbing my hand before I can turn away.

"Yeah, just...had a strange dream."

Not a dream, the voice whispers, *but the truth of who you are.*

FIFTY

Nari

As we delve deeper into the Bamnai Forest, Tetsu and I come across small camps and makeshift dens for the Divine Tails. For his sake, we steer clear, though I'd like to interact with the zealots and see what they really believe.

I return to Tetsu after straying to relieve myself very much like a fox and he's turning to and fro, the compass in his hand. When I come up to his side, he startles a little and then his brow furrows. "It feels like we should be closer to Sanoul by now." He glances up at the forest. "But it's still as dense as ever. I imagined there would be more village ruins or roads to the imperial city."

Ever since we left the Den behind, I've felt a deep stirring in my soul, an invisible tether pulling from my belly as we move through the forest. I think it's leading me to Sanoul. But I don't tell Tetsu this. Instead, I shrug and continue onward.

"Let's just keep walking and see where we end up."

He grasps my shoulder and turns me in another direction. "Northwest is this way."

"Right."

Tetsu keeps staring at the compass as we walk and I focus on the pull in my belly. It's a strange feeling, like a string is actually tied to my innards. I pat my belly and in another step, my foot snags on something and I trip. Tetsu does too and before I know it, a trap made of ropes pulls tight around us and lifts us into the air. My leg is dangling through one of the holes, my other squeezed between me and Tetsu. I feel my pulse sputter in my veins before my heart begins to pound loudly in my ears. I scramble for Tetsu, winding my arms around his neck as I press closer.

"We're t—trapped," I stutter, fear sinking its heavy claws into me. Tears burst from my eyes and I try to yank my other leg free but the ropes tighten and tighten, suffocating us.

"Calm down," Tetsu says softly and grunts as he tries to get his arm out. "I'll just cut us free."

I stuff my face against his chest, taking in big gulping breaths. He smells like sweat and nature but I don't care. We're trapped and I don't know who set it, who is coming to get us. Tetsu hums softly, the sound vibrating in his chest and through my skull. I focus on it, hoping it will soothe my nerves. But then Tetsu falls quiet and a hand wraps around my ankle, tugging on it.

With a gasp, a young voice cries, "We caught two!"

Tetsu and I swing from the backs of two large humans from the cult, our hands and feet bound and sweat-riddled cloths stuck in our mouths. Tears stream down my forehead and hit the ground. This is it, our demise. If only I was strong enough to stop it. I twist my head to look up beyond the branches and leaves above. The sky churns a dark red tonight and I feel the energy in the air, stinging my nose.

We soon come to a well-established camp and are set down by the roaring bonfire. Two human-sized spits sit aside, their cooks ready to skewer us and haul us over the flames. Tetsu's chest rises and falls with heavy breaths and I spit out the cloth when a muscular woman wearing hand-sewn fox ears and a painted mask like the one I wore at the festival approaches us. She drops down into a crouch and pushes the mask up, smiling at me with sharpened canines. The rest of the zealots surround us, staring and salivating.

"You're a pretty one," she says and reaches forward, letting a strand of my hair run through her dirty fingers. "This color is remarkable. It looks like that of the holy foxes."

I lean my head away and let out a yip. The woman's eyebrow lifts before she responds in kind and I say, "We've traveled from the south, from the Pit of Keshin where those evil trappers raided our camp."

The woman's gaze glides over us, her eyes narrowing slightly. "Where are your medallions?"

"We lost them," I tell her, letting my brow crease. "Those trappers took whatever they could. We escaped by the skin of our teeth."

"Hmm," she doesn't look entirely convinced yet but unbinds my hands and feet. Then she stands back on all fours. "If you're really one of us then let us fight like foxes."

I get down on my hands and kick my legs back and am shocked to find how foreign it still feels. Behind me, Tetsu kicks my foot and I glance at him. His eyes are wide and frightened and his voice is muffled through the cloth before he spits it out.

"What are you doing?"

"Fighting like a fox."

I look at the woman again and stoop low to the ground, growling deep in my throat. She does the same and we prowl around each other.

The woman makes the first move, leaping toward me. I tumble aside and bring my fingers down in a sharp arc, my nails catching the flesh of her shoulder. She yowls and rears back. If I still had my tail, it would be sweeping the ground behind me. I miss my tail and my fur as the woman jumps again and catches her hand around my thigh, nearly ripping my trousers with her pointed fingernails. She drags me back and slams me to the ground.

I grab her wrist as her claws fly toward me and pull my legs back. With a bit of effort and strength, I kick her in the stomach, launching her in the air. The woman lands with a thud and as one of the other zealots stomps toward me, I run and jump, using him like a wall to leap from. The woman grunts as I land on her and open my jaws wide, ready to tear out her throat as I lean down.

"Nari," Tetsu's voice draws me back and I blink.

The adrenaline of the fight trickles away and I stand, brushing my hands on my trousers. The woman gets to her feet and lets out a hearty laugh. "That was quite a fight! I'd say you are a fox at heart."

My skin heats. The woman sets a heavy hand on my shoulder and then turns to Tetsu, her eyebrow lifting. "What about you? Care to fight me like a fox?"

He stares, panic rising in his face, and then looks at me. I step up. "He's pretty new to the Divine Tails and a terrible fighter."

Tetsu's eyes narrow. I lean down until our noses touch. "You know I'm right." He turns bright pink. I look over my shoulder at the woman. "We haven't had anything to eat in a while."

"Come along then." She waves us toward a larger tent as the zealots sigh and scatter. I hear murmurs about not getting to eat us. I take Tetsu's hand so he doesn't get snatched up and he stays close, almost stepping on my heels.

"My name is Dura, leader of this sect." She holds the flaps open and ushers us inside.

The freshly roasted scent of meat strikes my nose and I feel my tongue flop out of my mouth before I suck it back in. Dura's tent looks a bit like a fox den, with the canvas being a rusty brown color and the floor relatively bare. It's also incredibly dark in here, with iron lanterns hanging from the ceiling, offering little light. It takes a moment for my eyes to adjust and I feel the heat of the darkness, causing me to sweat in my tunic.

"Sit down," Dura says, directing us to the ground.

"It smells delicious." I sit down and Tetsu follows, kneeling beside me. He clutches my hand so tight it goes numb. I shake him off and scoot away just a tad.

In the dark, I can see Dura's white canines shine as she grins. "I hope you like heart and liver."

My stomach grumbles, offering the wrong response, and I gulp, smiling. "Oh, yes."

Next to me, Tetsu lifts the sleeve of his tunic to his nose, grimacing as Dura uncovers a hole in the ground with a whistling pot. She removes the lid and steam puffs out, coating us in a film of dry heat. With a large wooden ladle, she scoops out something and tosses it before us. I stare at the human heart, bright red and slimy. It even deflates when I poke it.

Tetsu sways and I catch him before he can fall back. To Dura, I say, "He hasn't acquired a taste for human hearts or liver yet."

"Why do you even eat it?" he asks, his cheeks puffing out.

Dura's chin tilts down, eyes gazing from beneath her brow. "We eat as the foxes do."

Never in my life have I eaten anything from a human.

"It looks...alive still," Tetsu whispers.

"Well, it was an hour ago." Dura lets out a sharp, unamused laugh and reaches forward to snatch the heart up. "If you won't eat it then I will."

Before we can respond, she sinks her teeth into the muscle and it spasms, bursting with sticky, hot blood that drips down her chin and onto the ground. Tetsu gags. I just can't believe this woman has no idea what foxes really eat.

I clear my throat as she wipes her mouth with the back of her hand. "Since my partner recently joined the Tails and things seem to be a bit different than what I learned at Keshin, would you mind enlightening us if we are to be proper worshipers of the foxes?"

Dura sits up straighter, her broad shoulders falling back and she rips off pieces of the heart, chewing as she talks. "Well, we hunt the sinful people who have rejected their chance at salvation. The Divine Tails believe that Daion was cursed long ago and the foxes were sent by our ancestors to deliver justice and execute us for our sins. The ancestors, nor their animal counterparts, have intervened so it must be by their order. To repent, the Tails were formed and all those who give up themselves in service of the Heavenly Fox are blessed. We live long, fulfilling lives and work in harmony with the foxes.

"Living and moving as they do draws us closer to them. We hunt for food each night and sleep during the day. We take the dead from the villages so souls aren't lost and boil their hearts and livers. We live by the rule of the forest, connecting ourselves with nature as the foxes are part of it. Worship the trees and the skies, and burn fires to mimic the foxes' power. Our young are kept in dens until they're old enough to learn the ways of the fox and then must pass through the flames like the foxes do to gain their power. Such is the life we are supposed to live."

Dura pauses, her breathing growing heavier as she stares at us and juts her chin forward. Her eyes gleam in the dark, a twisted smile curling her lips. "If you want to live this way, you must commit your whole self to it. Eat and fight and sleep as the foxes do. They know what is best for us. If you can't live this way, then there's a lovely bonfire outside for you to jump into. We won't let you leave this camp otherwise."

I want to shake my head and tell her that the foxes aren't here to be the executioner and we don't walk through flames to get our lightning. But I can't say that without Tetsu discovering my true nature. Still, I want to educate them about the foxes' past and why we do what we do. If I could read or write, I'd leave a detailed message behind.

Tetsu nods as he inhales deeply. "We understand."

Dura looks at me expectantly and I nod too. "Of course. I would give up my life for the foxes. Humans are a disgusting lot. We deserve this punishment."

"Yes, exactly." She reaches behind her and digs up a small metal box. Turning it toward us, she opens it and a couple of silver medallions clink together. A simple fox face and the crescent moon are engraved in the metal. "Take these. You are welcome to stay in our camp if you like."

"We want to go to Sanoul," I tell her. "It's been a dream of ours to see the imperial city and maybe catch a glimpse of the Heavenly Fox herself."

"Ah, yes, every young Tail should take a pilgrimage to Sanoul. I have been there myself and it was a life-changing experience." She reaches for another buried box, this one full of maps. "Here is the way to Sanoul from our camp. After, you can return here."

"Thank you, Dura." I take the map and look at it, pretending that I'm reading but it looks like a bunch of squiggly lines.

Tetsu says, "We would eat but..." he trails off, setting a hand on his stomach. "I'm not sure I'm ready yet."

Dura laughs. "Of course. Go out and ask for Minjun, he likes to hoard delicacies we salvage from the villages."

We stand and Dura fishes the liver from the pot as we leave.

FIFTY-ONE

TETSU

AFTER HAGGLING FOR CUTS of salted deer meat and a pouch of blackberries from Minjun, we leave the Tails' camp behind. I still feel sick to my stomach and keep having flashbacks of Dura biting into the human heart. Nari is holding a piece of meat between her fingers and trying to tear it apart with her teeth.

"Argh," she growls, her head thrashing like a wild animal. "Why is it so tough?"

I look away and open the map, angling it so the moonlight illuminates the thin and thick strokes of black ink. With Mother's compass in the other hand, I direct us on the right path toward Sanoul.

"Do you think the Kingdom of Daion really is cursed? That our ancestors have abandoned us?" I ask after a while.

I'm not sure I believe that the ancestors are in charge of the heavens, but I haven't learned anything else in all my years. There wasn't much talk of spirituality among my parents or village. I think the concept got tainted when the demons came.

"Nah," Nari says, her head going one way as her hands pull the other and she finally rips off a piece of meat. She starts to chew but winces and lifts a finger to her jaw. "It hurts."

I shake my head and snatch the meat from her, handing over the berries instead. Nari tears open the pouch and lifts it to her nose, inhaling deeply.

"If the kingdom isn't cursed then why are the fox demons here in the first place?"

She shovels a handful of berries into her mouth, chewing around them as she says, "If the kingdom *was* cursed, wouldn't the ancestors have made it known? Do you remember that portal the Heavenly Fox opened at the temple? Maybe the foxes are fleeing something."

"And so they came to make us miserable?" I grumble, nearly crumbling the map in my hand. "The demons have taken away enough from humanity...from—from me." My chest wells with grief and my throat constricts as tears prick my eyes. I come to a stop, my shoulders shuddering as I stare at the ground.

"What's wrong?" Nari asks softly.

"What's wrong? What's wrong is this entire kingdom, my entire life!" I roar. Nari jumps and shuffles back a step. I drop the map and pinch the bridge of my nose. "I'm sorry for yelling, Nari. It's just—what Dura said is getting to my head. Without a reason ever given for the demons' appearance, the idea that Daion might be cursed makes sense. But what have we ever done to our ancestors to deserve this?"

"I don't know," she whispers.

I sit on the ground, smoothing my thumb over the glass surface of the compass. "Me neither." Nari kneels across from me as she grips the pouch of berries. "My childhood was safe and innocent, our village was never raided by the demons. Then, my mother abandoned me and my father. A year later, we were raided and he was killed. I've been adrift since, not really feeling like I belonged with the trappers, but I had no other skill to offer, and nowhere else to go. It never made any sense, why fate would be so cruel to me when I did nothing to deserve it.

"Maybe...maybe we're being punished for the sins of the past. That makes sense, right?" I look up at her, wanting Nari to know everything so she can tell me why my life had turned out like this. "Maybe my parents did something or their parents did. Or maybe it's me." I pause and swallow hard. I've never told anyone else about the voice before but I feel safe with Nari and I need to get it off my chest.

"There's a voice in my head that gets louder as we come closer to Sanoul. It tells me to let it take control and the other night, when we were sleeping in the tree, I saw a fox demon in my dream. It said there were two souls in my body—fox and human.

"Years ago, I was sick and on the verge of death. I had...stabbed myself and gotten fox blood in my system—or so my father said. I know the demons like to trick us but...there's a lot I still don't understand about myself or my parents. Maybe they were protecting me from something else, you know?"

Nari is still, her dark eyes wide. My skin flushes and I rub the back of my neck. Maybe I shared too much. *What if she thinks I'm a fox demon?*

I open my mouth to object when Nari reaches forward and takes my hand. "It's okay to feel afraid and uncertain. I know there's a lot in this world to be learned and maybe there will be an answer for you in Sanoul."

"What do you mean by that?"

Nari gently squeezes my fingers and a little line appears between her brows. "Tetsu...I think you're half-fox."

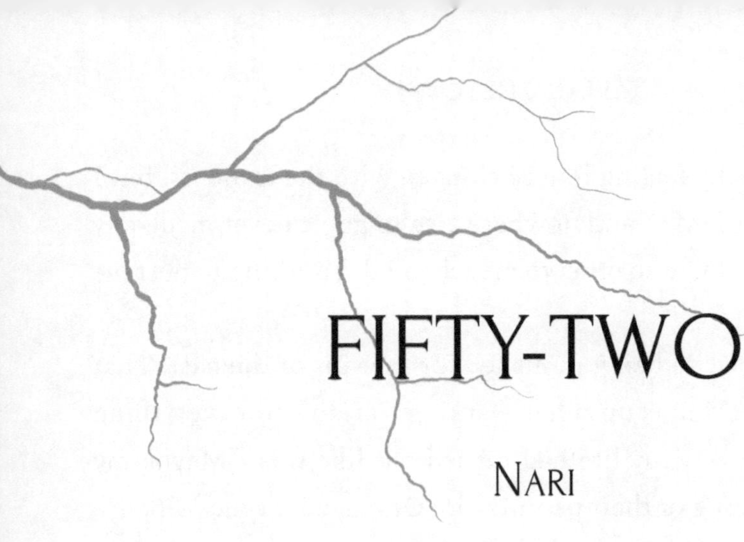

FIFTY-TWO

NARI

"HOW IS THAT POSSIBLE?" Tetsu asks, looking rather skeptical as his mouth presses together.

I feel like we've just wandered into a very dangerous conversation. I take my hand back and tug on my earlobe, trying to think of what to say. Should I tell him the truth about foxes turning into humans? But if he connects the dots, he could realize that *I'm* a fox and...I don't want him to know yet. He despises my kind so much that I fear he'll hate me too.

"It was something I heard Kyung say once," I tell him, "that some fox demons can shapeshift into humans."

If I blame someone else for such knowledge, Tetsu might not suspect me. And Kyung, he trusted him.

When Tetsu doesn't say anything, I look up at him. He stares past me, eyes shifting as he thinks. His eyebrows lift and clarity fills his expression, quickly followed by dread. Tetsu pales and sways slightly.

"Could my mother have been a demon?" he asks himself more than me. "Is that why she abandoned me?"

Yes and no, I want to say. But if anyone can tell Tetsu the truth, it's the Heavenly Fox. She is all-knowing when it comes to our kind and will be able to detect his fox soul.

I push to my feet and offer my hands to him. He takes them, his grip loose, and I help him up. Tetsu is unsteady and stumbles into me. I brace my hands on his chest to keep him upright and tilt my head back. He looks sad and lost.

His gaze flickers to me and Tetsu leans down, wrapping his arms around my waist and pulling me flush against him. I stiffen and everything in my mind has rushed out and left it blank. Now all I can do is feel him. I close my eyes and nestle my face against his neck as I slip my arms around him too.

This is too lovely for me to lose.

FIFTY-THREE

Tetsu

SANOUL RISES LIKE AN apparition from the land as dusk descends upon us. Nari and I stand still on a hill overlooking the imperial city, studying its layout. It's surrounded by a tall stone parapet with several guard towers dotting the perimeter. Human and fox guards alike march atop it, their gazes sweeping the land beyond. There are three gates, the largest at the forefront with heavy artillery stationed on the parapet from the time Sanoul belonged to the people.

The other two gates lead to the Itson region and the Hansu region. The city itself sparkles with glowing lanterns and busy streets. There are traditional homesteads with their slanted, tiled roofs and central courtyards. Up toward the palace, mounds of packed earth create large fox dens and the gardens surrounding them are well-kept with all sorts of fruit plants and trees.

Zealots and demons live in harmony here, though it's clear the demons have the upper hand as the zealots keep their heads down and to the side streets. I've never seen so many enemies concentrated in one place before and it makes me green in the face.

My gaze shifts to a pair of travelers on the road who approach the main gate. Something large and ominous falls from the shadows ahead and my jaw falls slack as the Guardian of the Gate appears. It's a hulking beast, much like a fox but more monstrous and grotesque. Its back is hunched and each tuft of fur stands on end like spikes. Its massive claws dig into the ground as it approaches the travelers. One unsheathes a sword that is more comparable to a twig than anything. The Guardian's long tail drags behind it and its lips curl back into a snarl, revealing several rows of sharp teeth and fangs.

I drop down to the ground, brushing a trembling hand over my head. How in the world are we going to get past *that*?

The other traveler steps forward and drops down to a knee. I squint as the Guardian pauses its advance and stands over the kneeling traveler, its nostrils flaring as it inhales deeply. Next to me, Nari slowly sits as the beast leaps over the traveler and attacks the other one, knocking the person to the ground. The traveler's high-pitched scream echoes in the air and with it, a white, glowing mist escapes their mouth. The beast breathes the mist in and tilts its head back, letting out an earth-shattering howl. The ground shakes beneath us, knocking us onto our bellies. The beast retreats to the shadows and the gate opens.

The unharmed traveler passes through without looking back and guards rush out to collect the body of the other, dragging it inside.

My pulse pounds sporadically in my ears and I clutch my chest as my heart burns. We can't get any closer to Sanoul or the Guardian will consume our souls. I squeeze my eyes shut and tumble onto my back. Nari's fingers flit across my chest and to my cheek as she leans down.

"Tetsu, are you okay?"

"No," I croak.

"What is it?"

I shake my head, unable to answer. I knew that it would be difficult to get into the imperial city but I didn't realize just how difficult it would be. How am I supposed to save Mother now?

Above me, Nari gasps. "Tetsu, look. A few zealots are approaching the gate."

"I don't want to see it."

She's quiet as she watches and then pulls my hanbok open, tapping her finger against the medallion. My eyes fly open at the contact of her hand on my bare chest and I quickly sit up, knocking foreheads with Nari. I groan and Nari leans back, still holding the medallion.

"We can use these to get past the Guardian. The zealots just did."

"You want to go *near* that thing?"

"It's the only way into the city."

"What if it knows we're lying?" I counter.

Nari gnaws on her lip, thinking. I rest my forehead on my knees and sigh.

"I think we should sleep before we try approaching the city," she says.

Nari stands, brushing her hands on her trousers before helping me to my feet. We retreat into the forest and I watch Nari's feet dance over fallen branches and knotted roots. Soon, boisterous laughter catches my attention and I look up, squinting through the dark. Further down the road to the main gate is a makeshift campsite with a carriage and several people sitting around a small fire. They pass around a bottle of *ji'sori* and chat amongst themselves, dressed in fine silk clothes.

Nari and I share a glance and decide to creep a little closer. A series of yips break out among the group and as their chests rise with each laugh, the silver medallions bounce. Zealots. My nose scrunches and I stop behind a tree trunk, gripping the bark. They look better dressed and well-fed compared to Dura's group—and less menacing.

The carriage even has a canvas sheet pulled over its frame and their horses look strong and groomed, grazing in a nearby grove.

Nari stands next to me, peeking around the other side of the trunk. I turn and lean back on the trees, crossing my arms as she looks at me. Her dark eyes are bright with a mischievous gleam and she smiles.

"I have an idea," she whispers.

"And what's that?"

"How do you feel about hijacking a carriage?"

I grunt. "From them? We're outnumbered, Nari."

"Oh, leave the fighting to me. I think you'd make a great distraction."

I cut her a sharp look. "Hey, it's not my fault I'm not great at fighting."

"It is if you never applied yourself." Nari covers her mouth with her hand as she snickers. "But I think they're settling down for the day so let's make a plan and come back tomorrow."

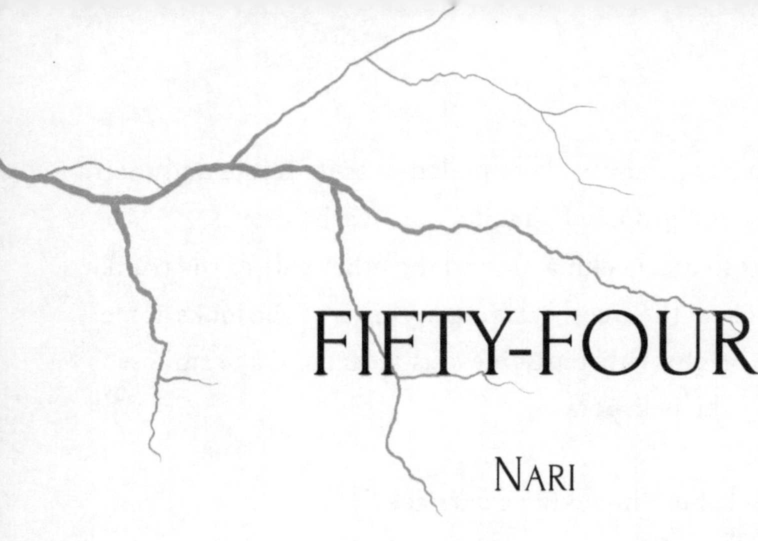

FIFTY-FOUR

NARI

IT TAKES AN HOUR for Tetsu and me to find a tree for us to sleep in that isn't infested with termites, ants, or spiders. The creepy little crawlers make him shudder but I'm used to them. The Den was underground anyway and I once woke up with a trail of ants surrounding me. Apparently, I still had a few chunks of deer meat stuck in my muzzle fur.

When we find one, I roll up on my tiptoes to reach for a higher branch when I feel Tetsu's hand rest on my hip. I go still and slowly turn around, shuffling until my back bumps into the trunk. His eyes are droopy with sleepiness and the rising sun trickles in through the canopy above, casting a luminous glow around him. It makes his hair look more reddish-brown in the light and the freckles and moles on his cheeks like stars in the sky.

Tetsu gulps, his hand heavy on my hip, and he studies my face, his expression softening. I feel my whole body flush with heat and I squirm. I don't know what he's thinking. Maybe I need to help haul him into the tree so he can get some rest. We've been awake for a while.

"Nari," he starts, his voice so soft and deep. "In case we don't survive tomorrow, there's something I have to tell you."

I feel my chest rise and fall with quick breaths and my heart pounds. What is he talking about? We'll be just fine...I hope.

Tetsu steps closer until there's hardly any space between us and I have to tilt my head back just to meet his eyes. He looks down at me and blinks slowly, warmth in his gaze.

"From the beginning, you were a pain to deal with—" he pauses and winces. "I mean...that doesn't sound nice."

"No, it doesn't," I whisper.

"Let me try again." He closes his eyes and inhales deeply. "I don't know how to say this but...I really like you, Nari. A lot. Like, an amount that you can't even fathom—" he gazes at me again and gnaws on his bottom lip, his skin turning bright pink. "You're an epic fighter and you're clever. You always seem to get us out of horrible situations alive, which I'm grateful for. And these past few months with you have been the most interesting months of my life."

His fingers slip behind my hair to the nape of my neck and he draws my face closer to his. "I don't want to go into tomorrow without doing this."

Tetsu leans down and gently presses his mouth to mine. My eyes go wide and I remember the first time he covered my mouth with his to shut me up. But this...feels different as warmth spreads through my belly and my limbs feel tingly. I have absolutely no idea what to do. When I'm not reciprocating, he leans back, looking at me.

Quickly, he jumps away. "Ah! Why are your eyes open?" his skin turns from pink to a deep red, almost the same color as lightning. "I...sorry for kissing you."

"Kissing me?" I ask. "I don't...am I supposed to do that to you?"

Tetsu stares for a long moment and then turns around, running his fingers through his hair. I lift my knuckles to my mouth and suck on my skin. *This is another human thing I don't know about. Is it like nuzzling?*

He rolls his shoulders back and faces me again. "I just realized that you probably don't know what kissing is considering your...upbringing."

"Can you show me?"

Tetsu nods and we ease together again. "Pucker up like this," he shows me and I try not to laugh—he looks like a duck. "And then you just...move your lips. Close your eyes too."

I do as he says and his lips fall on mine again. I reach out to grasp his waist so I don't slip under his weight as he presses me into the tree. The tingling sensation turns into a spark of energy, zipping through my body like lightning and I relax a little, following his lead.

Tetsu's mouth parts slightly, his hands on the small of my back as he brings me into him. It feels like we're molding together, becoming a singular being and my head starts to feel fuzzy and light as I wrap my arms around him. His teeth catch my bottom lip and gently tug up. My fox spirit rouses and rampages, feverish for more but when Tetsu pulls away, I breathe in a gulp of air and then nuzzle his nose before he can drift too far away.

"Wow," he exclaims.

"I think I like kissing," I say as I reach up and thumb his bottom lip. "And you, Tetsu. I really like you, too."

With a smile, he pulls me in and kisses me again.

FIFTY-FIVE

CHUL

CHUL SAT ON HIS haunches, staring in disbelief as his blood ran cold. Nari and the boy were standing very close together against a tree and he was nuzzling her...with his mouth. Chul had expected feelings to develop but, in his heart, he hoped that Nari would never give in. Of course, when human, foxes had an alluring nature. They needed to so they could gain the trust of a human but most had sacrificed the human to be a fox again. Chul was certain Nari wasn't going to do that now. Or maybe she was. Maybe this act was a ruse on her part so the boy would follow her anywhere.

His lip curled in a snarl and he fought the urge to run over and tear the boy to shreds. He couldn't reveal Nari now, not when she was so close to Sanoul. Anger flared in his belly and he wondered what Sook would do. Nari needed the boy to satiate the hunger of the Guardian at the Gate. It was simply required to gain access to Sanoul. The only foxes living within its parapet had already achieved their nine-tails and gained the ability to shapeshift on their own.

When he heard Nari's laugh, he looked at them again. She was smiling brightly at the boy, trailing her fingers through his hair and he nuzzled her nose. Chul's stomach dropped. What if they were bonded to one another? If the boy was really half-fox then it was possible.

He pawed at the ground and huffed before getting up. Sook would leave them be and let fate decide what would happen. They had made it to Sanoul, now all Nari needed to do was get in. Chul couldn't help with that so he turned and ran into the forest. He needed to find the Den Gi had snuck into before the sun shone too brightly.

FIFTY-SIX

TETSU

AS THE DAY PASSES into the evening, we crouch in the brush near the zealot's campsite. They're lost in a hazy sleep and I pray to Hoji that they don't wake up. I also hope I don't keep getting distracted by the thought of Nari's lips on mine. So short I had to crane my neck to meet her soft, plump lips. I blush and set a cold hand on my neck. *Focus.* But Nari fit so well in my arms as if she belonged there. Maybe fate had brought us together for this. I sigh and gaze at her, my chest filling with warmth.

Nari glances at me. She gnaws on her knuckles, a nervous habit. "What is it?" I ask softly, shuffling closer so I can slip an arm around her waist.

"How good do you think you are?"

My eyebrow lifts and unwarranted thoughts flood my mind with a thousand possibilities of what that could mean. I clear my throat, trying to hide my blush with my hand. "What do you mean?"

"Morally, how good do you think you are?"

"Oh, um...I don't think I've ever done anything to claim myself the embodiment of evil. I'd say I'm a good person."

"And...are you willing to bend that a little if things don't go according to plan?"

"Just spill it, Nari. What's your idea?"

She drops her hand from her mouth and rolls up on her knees, glancing over the brush. I do the same, my hands hovering over the branches. "If the Guardian knows we're lying about being zealots then we can pretend to be something else. Take a few of the zealots, tie them up, and offer...offer them as sacrifices to the Guardian if it comes to that."

My stomach churns at the idea and bile threatens to rise in my throat. Though I don't care for the zealots' beliefs and have no idea why they would *worship* the demons, they're still people. I should be absolutely appalled by Nari's suggestion but...if I want to learn anything about Mother or even find her, we have to get into Sanoul. It'll be us or the zealots.

Still, I hesitate. "I don't know, Nari."

"It's only a suggestion," she says quickly, her voice cracking. "I know it's horrible, but it is an option..."

I nod, hoping it won't come to that. Now, we need to focus on getting ahold of the carriage. Slowly, Nari rises to her feet and tiptoes around the brush. She's in charge of securing the carriage and, I assume, selecting the unlucky potential sacrifices. I have to gather the horses and soothe them, earn their trust.

I skirt around the campsite toward the meadow where the horses are sleeping and kneel next to one, gently petting its head. The horse exhales through its nose and its eyes flutter open as it lifts its head. The other horse is standing up and as still as a statue. I speak softly as I reach into my pocket and offer the horse some leftover berries. It sniffs my palm and gets to its feet, its lips drawing back as its wide, large teeth snatch the berries. The bite nearly takes my skin with it and the horse nickers. The other wakes.

"Come along now," I whisper, shaking the rest of the berries into my hand for them to see.

I walk backward as I lead the horses to the carriage and brush my hand along their coats as I harness them to it. Nari comes around, creating a wide berth between herself and the horses with a questionable look in her eyes. To me, she says, "I need your help putting them in."

We walk around to the back, where the canvas flaps are held open by pins and two squirming zealots lay at our feet. I gulp. The zealots' hands and ankles are bound tight and separate cloths cover their eyes and mouths, leaving their noses free to breathe. My gaze strays to the other three who are still asleep, unbeknownst of what's happening to their fellow zealots. One turns on her side, letting out a deep breath.

I haul the zealots into the carriage and help Nari up before jumping in myself. The back is full of trinkets, trunks, and supplies. Maybe the zealots were on a pilgrimage, like Dura said. *No,* I shake my head, *don't think of what they were up to. That only makes things more difficult.*

Nari rummages through the trunks, pulling out a long-sleeved floral dress and a coat with gold stitching. She hands me the coat and I slip my arms into it, gasping at how soft and light the material is. I've never worn something so expensive before, it feels forbidden. Nari shimmies into the dress, getting stuck for a moment with her hands straight above her head. Her muffled voice comes through the fabric. "It's tight around my shoulders."

I pull on the hem of the dress until it's past her thighs and we hear the fabric splitting in the back as Nari drops her arms. She turns and I see that the seams around her armpits have come loose. Stifling a laugh with my hand, I use the other to arrange her hair so it covers the tears. She looks through the trunks again and pulls out two cloaks.

While the dress is small on her and looks odd with her regular clothes beneath, the cloak is too big and swallows her whole. The hood comes to the top of her mouth, covering most of her face. Nari rolls it back a little so it comes to her eyebrows instead and takes the pins from the flaps, securing the hood.

We climb onto the carriage perch and I take the reins. With a snap, the horses huff and we're off. When I was younger, I drove a much smaller carriage than this with the family mule, running errands for the whole homestead. If Father needed wood, I'd go out and cut it down. If Mother needed certain herbs or spices for her medicinal treatments, I'd travel to the market and buy what I could find.

But this is nothing like that. The horses are much stronger, the carriage larger, and we're heading to the one place I'm absolutely terrified of. I feel sweat beading on my skin as we ride down the road, jostling back and forth on the perch. I don't notice Nari clutching my thigh until her fingers dig in and I wince. She's staring ahead intently, her jaw set as we draw near to the main gate of Sanoul.

I want to say something but my mouth is as dry as cotton. I sit stiffly as the horses snort and ease to a stop on their own. They stamp the ground with their front hooves and even though we're not near the gate, the Guardian slithers from the shadows.

My heart pounds erratically in my ears, drowning out any other noise, and I stare at the Guardian as it approaches. It moves like smoke across the ground, its body now looking less tangible than it had the night before. Its eyes are blazing white and the hackles along its back shift and shudder with each movement.

Nari slowly stands and presses her hands together as she bows to the beast. A moment of silence passes and I see her trembling slightly but when she speaks, her voice comes out strong and confident. "Great Guardian of Sanoul, we are but humble travelers on a journey to devout ourselves to Her Divine Majesty, Khana the Heavenly Fox." Nari reaches beneath the collar of her dress and shows the Guardian the medallion. The beast's eyes drift over her and it steps forward as if to get a closer look. Then it looks at me and its mouth pulls back in a snarl, revealing its teeth that could tear me limb from limb.

I scramble for the medallion in my pocket, nearly fainting with fright, as I present it to the Guardian. The beast comes closer still and I shut my eyes as it inhales deeply. *This is how I die...pretending to be something I'm not.*

"Great Guardian," Nari says, "if you wish for a sacrifice—" she cuts herself off and I dare to crack an eye open. The Guardian stretches a large paw toward her, its incredibly long and sharp claw lifting Nari's chin. I leap to my feet, ready to save her, but Nari stops me. She stares into the Guardian's eyes, her mouth parted and a strange, billowing wind surrounds us, ruffling our clothes.

"You may enter," the Guardian says, its voice soft. I blink. I didn't even know the beast could speak.

Then it slinks away and vanishes into the shadows once more. Ahead, the gates to Sanoul crank open. I drop onto the perch, my chest heaving with each breath I take and my head starts to feel fuzzy and warm. Nari points toward the imperial city, grinning from ear to ear.

FIFTY-SEVEN

Nari

EITHER WE WERE CONVINCING enough with our zealot medallions or Tetsu really is half-fox. Either way, I'm astounded that the Guardian let us into the city. I sit down next to Tetsu as the carriage lurches forward but when I look at him, he's pale and sweating. I take the reins, though I don't know how to control the beasts who drag us forward. I let Tetsu lean on my shoulder and we approach the gate. It's made of silver iron with round locks and tiny details of foxes at play.

"Are you okay?" I ask Tetsu.

He grumbles something I can't make out and I tell him to get in the back of the carriage. He falls as he does but when I peek back, he's lying down and rubbing his head.

As we enter the city, I feel my heart soar in my chest as I look around in wonder. The roads are made of perfectly placed stone, a smoother ride than the path to the city. It takes us along the edge of the parapet where I have a view of the human homesteads with their terracotta roofs and pristine, white structures. Humans and foxes wander about, living in peace and harmony and I can even see a fox shapeshift into a human as they enter a market.

I take in the city with delight and feel a warmth in my belly when I see lanterns rising toward the sky from the western part of the city. It reminds me of the Salaisna festival and my smile broadens with the memory of the Heart Quest. I check on Tetsu and he's removed the cloak and the coat, his tunic rolled up over his belly and his boots kicked off. I blink, staring at his forehead where something glows white beneath the locks of his hair.

I stop the beasts with a pull on the reins and then drop into the back of the carriage again. The zealots have stopped squirming and shifted toward the back. If the road inclines, they may just tumble out. But I go to Tetsu's side and kneel, brushing away his hair.

My eyes widen when I see the crescent moon resting on its back with three raindrops beneath and two dots above.

He *is* a fox.

But his skin is incredibly warm and Tetsu groans, his eyes fluttering. Fear pits itself in my stomach and I turn to the trunks, searching for something to cool him off.

Tetsu's hand grasps the cloak and tugs slightly. I whirl back to him and ask, "What's happening to you?"

"I'm...sick," he says, his voice hoarse, and his fingers move to his belly. I look at the glowing scar, which I had completely forgotten about, and now it's hot to the touch as well. His skin ripples, as if there's something beneath, and I shudder. I leap up and return to the front. If anyone can heal him, it will be the Heavenly Fox.

I snap the reins and the beasts take off with a loud sound. As I thought, the road inclines as we go along the parapet and I hear the items shifting in the back. Something thuds on the ground and a muffled, high-pitched scream follows, telling me one of the zealots has fallen.

The palace soon appears and I admire it as we approach. It has jade-tiled roofs with a silver structure and a wide courtyard blooming with nature. There is no gate or guards so we ride right into the courtyard and I stop the carriage. I hop down as a pair of large foxes run toward us and a thought occurs to me. If Tetsu's forehead is showing the fox symbol, then mine must be too. I yank off the cloak and touch my skin. It's not as warm as Tetsu but it's there and glowing, casting my fingers in a white light.

The foxes slow, their armor reflecting in the evening light. I tear the dress off and see the beads have tumbled out of the pouch I kept them in and looped themselves around my arms and at my waist. I straighten and say, "I'm here to see the Heavenly Fox."

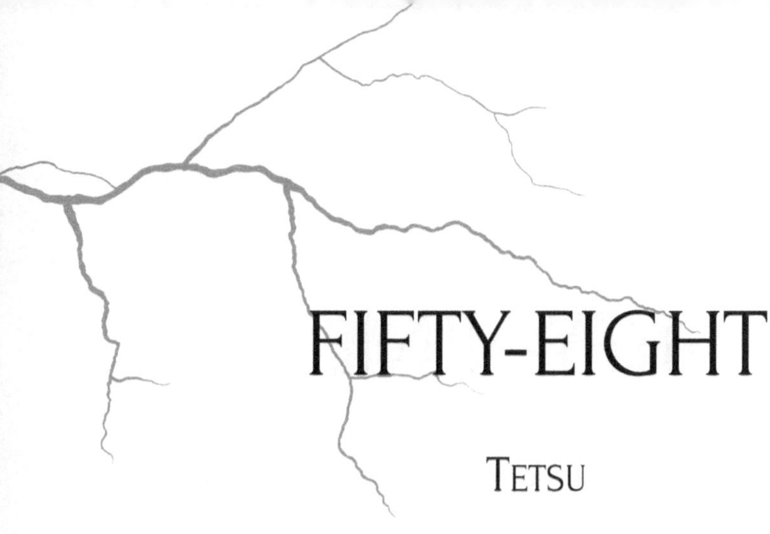

FIFTY-EIGHT

Tetsu

MY HEAD IS ON fire and I can't understand what anyone is saying. Or see. Sweat drips into my eyes and blinds me but I know I'm being carried by a large person, probably a zealot. I don't know where Nari is and I can't help but think I've been taken to be slaughtered. With a groan, I wish the demon in my head would just leave me be. The heat drowned out its voice but it's still there, begging to be released.

My body sways back and forth until I'm set on a plush surface and my weak fingers curl against it. My brow furrows and I cry out, gasping as the heat ticks up a notch. The demon's voice rings loud and clear in my ears, screaming, "Let me out! Let me out!"

"No," I murmur, "never."

FIFTY-NINE

Nari

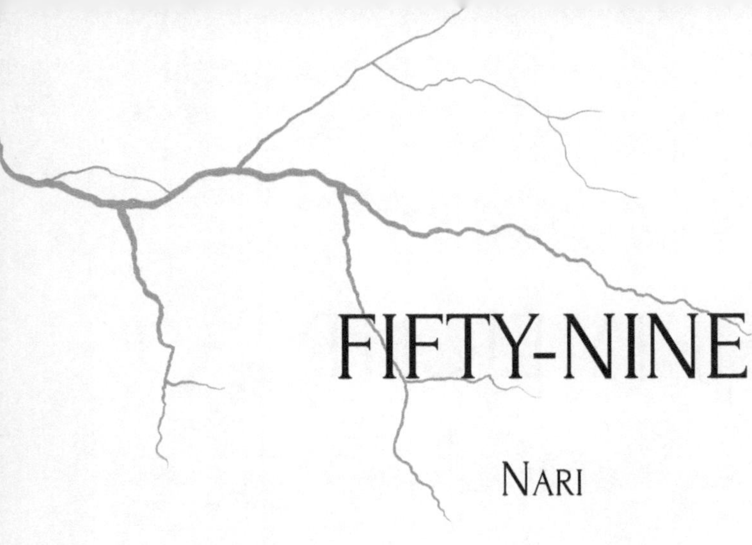

THE HEAVENLY FOX IS as glorious up close as she was at the Itson Temple. We have been brought to her throne room and Tetsu has been laid out on the blood-red carpet. Her Divine Majesty sits beneath an arbor laced with moonflowers and thin skeins of lightning cast a display on the tall wall behind her. On either side are heavy curtains and from behind one comes the vixen that chased us away from the temple. Her mahogany fur with white ringed around her neck and ankles is smoothed out and her eyes clear. She has a few strings of soul beads looped around her head and her ears twitch.

I drop to my knees, clutching my hands as I stare in awe and tears burst from my eyes. I've been waiting for so long to be here and finally, *finally*, I can be a fox again. The Heavenly Fox stands and comes forward. I gasp and bow to the ground, my body trembling with excitement.

"Nari," she says, her voice silvery and light. "I see you have brought your soul beads to me. Straighten and come forward."

Though I'm excited, I sit up and glance at Tetsu, my brow creasing.

He's flushed red, his face twisted in pain. I glance at Khana. "Can you help him?"

Her gaze shifts to him and she beckons the other vixen. The two of them go to Tetsu's side and I sit at his feet. "He's been like this since we met the Guardian at the Gate," I tell them. "I thought he was just frightened but now I don't know."

"He's sick," the vixen says, her mouth drawn in a frown. She looks at me, her eyes matching the color of her fur. "My name is Yona and Tetsu is my son."

My jaw falls slack, though I can clearly see what Tetsu is. Yona lays her paw on his exposed stomach. "Years ago, I turned and met a human named Dal. I chose him to be my sacrifice to the Guardian but fate had something else in mind. We fell in love and I bore Tetsu; his fox spirit is what's ailing him. With his pure human soul, it has been a constant battle in his body for control. Tetsu held it off well enough as a child until the fox slipped and nearly killed him. Tetsu was as sick as this when I transferred the one thousand souls I had collected in hopes that it would be enough to save him. His fox is unstable and destructive as it knows he's human. They are not meant to hold such power as we do."

"But we have human souls," I say softly, "when we are spawned."

"Correct," the Heavenly Fox says, "but it does not rule our bodies. It provides us with the ability to communicate with humans and shapeshift, but we are foxes through and through."

Yona drops her nose down to Tetsu's face and nudges his cheek, her shoulders falling slack. "I didn't know this would happen to him. He was safe with the souls."

I gasp, slapping a hand over my mouth as I recall our first meeting. Yona and Khana look at me and I say, "When we first met, I saved him from drowning...I think I stole all the souls."

Yona's gaze narrows slightly but then she nods and looks to the Heavenly Fox. "What can we do?"

"I can ease his suffering for now, but it won't last long," she says. "His fox spirit is a part of him and he must learn to accept it."

"I have over two hundred souls now, maybe—"

"No, Yona. Tetsu cannot live without knowing his true self. He has to accept it." Khana sets her paw on Tetsu's forehead and hums softly, a light emanating from her.

I feel my hair lift and shift and watch Tetsu's face closely as the pain dissipates. His body relaxes and the heat washes away. Yona tugs his tunic down over his stomach again and steps back, her head hanging as she looks at her son. I gnaw on my knuckles because I know what Tetsu thinks about the foxes and it worries me. If he can't accept it, will it really kill him?

Slowly, his eyes flutter open as the Heavenly Fox retreats to her throne and I'm left sitting at his feet. Tetsu's chest rises and falls in steady breaths and he pushes himself up, rubbing his head. He stops when his gaze focuses on me and his eyes travel to the symbol on my skin. I feel my body droop as dread fills his expression and he scrambles back with a gasp. His eyes grow watery but he spits with as much hate as he can muster, "You're a *demon*."

SIXTY

YONA

"YONA," KHANA CALLED AND she moved to her side again. "You have to tell him."

Yona glanced at her son, who stumbled to his feet and tried to flee until the guards caught him. She sighed and lumbered forward as he was brought back and forced to his knees. The young vixen, Nari, who had brought him here was crying, her face buried in her hands as she sat there. Tetsu's jaw was clenched tight and his nostrils flared as she came closer.

"Get away from me, demon," he spat, spittle flying from his mouth.

Though he tried to keep his wits and his strength about him, Yona could tell his mind was running. There was confusion behind his teary eyes as his gaze darted between her and Nari. Yona sighed and shifted into her human form, standing tall as her body lengthened and her fur rose to sit on top of her head in long, mahogany curls.

Tetsu's gaze flickered and the tears broke forth, trailing down his cheeks as he whispered, "Mother?"

Yona knelt before him and reached out to touch his chin but he jerked away. She dropped her hand to the carpet and dug her fingers into the material, her heart ticking in her chest.

"Yes, Tetsu, it's me." She told him and paused, swallowing hard. She had never wanted it to come to this—to tell him the truth. Tetsu was raised in the human world and would live in it, she knew, and it was dangerous for him to be half-fox. But she had done this to him. Yona had ached for love, affection, and attention and Dal had given that to her. She wasn't just another vixen in the skulk, another demon.

Dal hadn't been obsessed with or afraid of her. And Tetsu, her beautiful miracle of a child, had loved her unconditionally. Now he looked at her like all the other humans did, full of terror and hate.

"I need to tell you what's happening to you—"

"No, you're just trying to manipulate me," he countered. "My mother wasn't a demon!"

Yona sighed and took a moment to recall the lullaby she had sung Tetsu when he was a baby. It wasn't a human song, it had come from her own mother when she was a young kit.

Softly, her voice tumbled out of her, a bit rough as she hadn't sung in years but surely Tetsu would still know it.

"Young and bright may you grow, my love,

quick and sly may you be.

As the light that flows above, my love,

fills your heart with glee.

Kit-le-dee-la-lu-my love,

forever shall you be free."

When she looked at him, his skin had paled and Yona told him what he was.

SIXTY-ONE

NARI

I LIFT MY HEAD when someone starts singing a lullaby I've heard before and watch with trepidation as Yona sings to Tetsu. His expression opens and his skin pales, mouth parting in shock. As they speak, I turn to the Heavenly Fox who beckons me forward. I crawl over, my legs too weak to stand, and sit at her feet, looking up into her face.

"Now, Nari, are you ready?"

"Yes, Your Majesty."

"Call me Khana, sweet one."

"Oh, I couldn't."

She smiles and drops her head down, touching her forehead with mine. After a moment, Khana hums. "That's interesting."

"What is?" I ask.

"You've lost one hundred souls."

I lean back, glancing up at her as I try to think, my eyes squinting. Then, I remember the night in the forest when we left the trapper camp. I tell her, "I got struck by lightning once. Could that have done it?"

Khana chuckles lightly. "Yes, that is possible. They must have saved you the brunt of the energy and heat. Now, let's turn you back."

I nod and stay still as I tilt my forehead against hers. I close my eyes as the beads slip off my arms and waist, clinking together. The swirling power of the Heavenly Fox surrounds me and I feel myself being lifted up. I gasp as my eyes fly open and I stretch my arms out. Power dances around me in red and white light, sparkling with celestial dust. I feel my body grow shorter and my hands flesh out into paws. My hair races over me, my orange fur returning with black around my paws and ears, and white along my muzzle and chest.

Sounds become sharper, my eyesight dims colors to the pastel shades I'm familiar with, and my nose elongates into a snout, my whiskers sprouting. My senses have improved and I am set gently on the floor. I feel the excitement trickle back into me and I leap around, yipping with joy. I'm a fox once again. I glance back to find I have nine tails, tipped with white, and I flare them out, admiring them. Then I bound over to Tetsu to show him but skid to a halt.

His eyes are shadowed over as he leans away, his shoulders hunched in defeat. He looks at me for only a moment before staring at the carpet. Yona shifts back into a fox and says to the guards, "Bring him to a holding cell for now. I'd like to monitor him until we release him."

The guards clip their heels and pull Tetsu to his feet. His legs bow and his feet drag as they carry him but I run after, my stomach twisting.

"Tetsu—"

"Go away," he retorts, his voice distant and cold. "You lured me here for your own gain, demon, and now you've sentenced me to my death.""You're not going to die," I say and paw at his foot.

He kicks my arm away. "Leave me alone!"

I stop and lie on the ground, resting my face on my paws. It feels so wonderful to have my fur back as it engulfs and hides me away. But I watch Tetsu as he's taken from the throne room, feeling my heart ache in my chest.

SIXTY-TWO

TETSU

I FEEL LIKE AN imbecile.

Nari is a fox demon.

It's obvious now as I reflect on her past behavior and how she seemed to be so confident against the Guardian and the zealots. I close my eyes and shake my head, my heartbeat growing weaker as it contorts with uncertainty. Now I'm chained up in a cell beneath the palace, awaiting whatever twist fate will bring me next.

I set my head against the wall and wish I could forget every moment I spent with her, everything I've felt. It was foolish to kiss her the night before; I practically opened up my heart and soul for the taking. My trust didn't falter and that's where I was betrayed.

The words of the fox who claims to be my mother come to mind, that I'm half-fox and need to accept the demon spirit within instead of fighting it. That I'm too weak as is without a thousand souls to protect me. Two warring souls. My mother a fox demon, my father a human. The flaring pain and heat in my body as I got closer to Sanoul. It's an overwhelming amount of information that I'm not sure I believe yet.

But it makes sense and that's the worst part.

SIXTY-THREE

NARI

WRETCHED GUILT RAKES THROUGH me as I sit in the throne room, feeling too weak once more to get up. Yona comes to my side and sits with a sigh.

"You're bonded to him," she says matter-of-factly.

My head lifts and I look at her, my tails fluttering with nerves. "I—I like him, I don't know if I...bonded with him."

"Darling Nari." Her head tilts, her gaze softening. "I can tell your feelings run deeper than that. If not, you wouldn't care what happens to him."

But what is a bond between two foxes like? I want to ask. Most of the time, I still feel like a kit that doesn't know much about being a vixen. I didn't even acquire one thousand souls by myself, it was an accident.

Yona sets her paw on mine. "He's bonded to you too, but he's hurting right now and feeling betrayed. Someday, maybe you two can reunite."

I drop my head. "But I don't want to be away from him."

"He'll need time to heal and think about who he is, grow up a little.

You both are young, there's no use rushing it and if it's meant to be, it will be."

"I want to visit him at least...tomorrow maybe?"

Yona glances toward the Heavenly Fox and then nods. "You have Her Divine Majesty's permission." She nudges my shoulder for me to stand up. "Come, you can rest in my Den. You're home now, Nari."

I follow Yona from the throne room and out to the palace courtyard again, where she takes a turn around the surrounding wall. A series of Dens dug into the hill the palace rests on come into view and foxes meander about, some simply sitting by and chatting.

"Every fox has a different routine here," Yona tells me. "So you can sleep or go out at whatever time you want."

We slide down into the Den and the warmth of the soil surrounding me brings me a sense of comfort, along with the pitch-black darkness that fills my gaze. But now with my eyes back to normal, I can see just fine. A few foxes are fast asleep, all curled up with their tails tucked around them. Yona and I settle near the back of the Den and she stretches out, her tails flaring.

"What skulk are you from?" she asks softly as we lie down.

I rest my chin on my paws and glance at her. "Sook's skulk."

"Sook?" Yona's brow lifts and she blinks once. "We grew up as young kits together but weren't close."

"Really?"

She nods.

My mouth droops into a frown. "I miss her--and my Den brother, Chul." I pause and swallow hard. "Do I have to stay in Sanoul now that I've achieved my nine-tails?"

Yona shakes her head and gnaws on her wrist. "Not at all. You're free to travel the kingdom and are always welcome back to Sanoul. I chose to come here and serve Khana because I thought being around

Tetsu would put him in danger if anyone ever discovered what I was. But now...I feel regretful of that decision."

"He thought you abandoned him," I tell her.

Her shoulders fall and she rests her head on the ground. "I shouldn't have left."

"He still wanted to know what happened to you, though," I add. "Since it was his idea to come to Sanoul."

That does little to alleviate the gloomy expression on her face but she nods. Yona closes her eyes and I follow suit, feeling conflicted about what I'll do next.

SIXTY-FOUR

TETSU

MY ARMS WENT NUMB long ago, strung up against the cold stone wall by heavy chains. I keep my eyes closed as I hang my head, my chin digging into my chest. There's not much to see in the cell anyway and I drown out the cries and groans of pain of the other prisoners. All humans, all doomed to a fate worse than death.

When I'm on the brink of unconsciousness, I hear the scraping sound of fox feet on the ground. My whole body tenses and my lip curls as my brow furrows. *Would Nari really visit me after her betrayal?* I don't want to see her as a demon or hear what she has to say...that she probably manipulated me into bringing her to Sanoul. Like she wanted in the beginning.

Along with the footsteps comes the clanking of the keyring dangling from the zealot jailer's belt. The sounds draw near then scrape to a halt. I don't look up. The jailer unlocks my cell and I pull my knees to my chest, resting my forehead so they can't see my face. The fox footsteps are light and a pungent odor streaks my nose, making my stomach turn. I release a slow breath through my mouth, not wanting to breathe in again.

The jailer leaves, clambering down the corridor until nothing but heavy silence follows. A moment later, a quiet whooshing sound draws my attention and I see Nari shapeshift back into her human form. She sits near the cell door, her legs tucked beneath her. The pungent smell evaporates and I glance away.

"I understand if you don't want to speak to me, but I only ask that you listen," Nari says with a sigh. She sounds tired and afraid, her voice frail and hoarse. "I need you to know that I didn't save you from the pond just to bring you to Sanoul."

So why did you? I want to ask but am too stubborn to voice the question. I shake my head instead. I would have rather drowned.

"And, at first, I did choose you to be my offering to the Guardian at the Gate. Then I learned of your heritage—that you might be half-fox. I knew we would be okay if you were."

"What's your point?" I grumble. "That you gambled with my life?"

"I don't…I don't know," she says softly. "I know I've betrayed your trust but if I told you what I was, you would have killed me."

My nostrils flare at the thought of that. If I'm being honest, after spending this much time with Nari, I can't kill her. I can't trap her or hand her over to Kyung. It wouldn't feel right.

"That night when my skulk was raiding Pangul, it was my first raid. I'd been training for the last few months but I wasn't ready. It was nothing like I imagined and then I saw Chul chasing after you and I thought maybe I could help if there was just one human against the two of us.

"Your mother's souls are what turned me into a human. I didn't mean to take them, I didn't even know they were with you."

I say nothing. I know she's telling the truth but it doesn't excuse all she's done. And what has she done?

She lied and kept her true form a secret, even joined the fox trappers to maintain the human facade.

But...she also saved me so many times. From the pond, the bandits, at the Itson Temple, and from my demonic self. Nari made me feel happy for once since Father passed. She had ignited something deep in my soul, waking it from its long slumber.

Am I...in love with her?

"Yona said I've bonded to you," Nari whispers. She sits with her chin in her hands, her hair falling in messy curls that frame her face. Hunching her shoulders, her mouth pulls down into a frown.

"I think it's true. I thought I would be happier to have my body back, but I know it disgusts you. Being human was tough and strange. I've grown to like it, though."

"You can shapeshift," I remind her.

"Yes, but you know what I am now."

I shrug. "Better for me to know now than never."

We fall quiet then, the silence between us a deep, dark chasm that neither can cross alone. I feel myself aching, but grind my teeth and vow to stay away from her. Nothing is tethering us together now. She's a fox again and I learned what happened to Mother. If I'm released from this prison, I'll go back to Juhto and never speak of this trip to Sanoul to anyone.

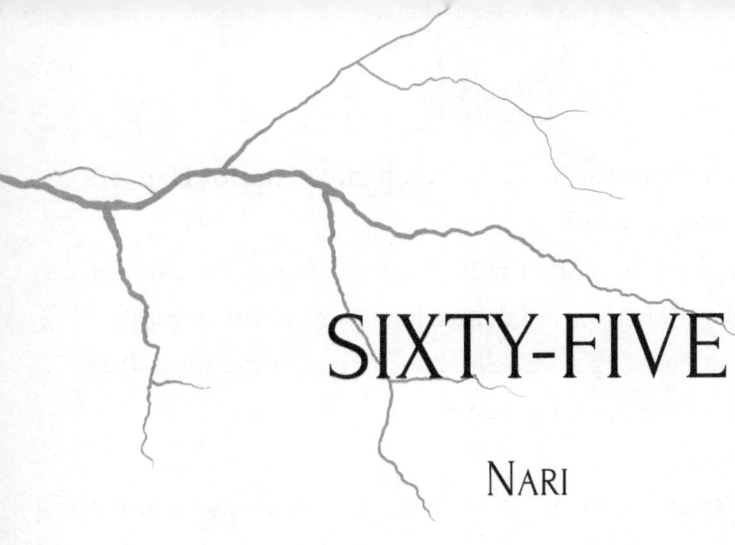

SIXTY-FIVE

NARI

I LEAVE THE CELL after a while and shapeshift in the corridor, fleeing the palace prison. A winding, stone staircase wrapped around a guard tower leads me to the pristine palace floors above. I slip on the marble before the rough pads on my paws catch hold and I hear not-so-discreet voices drifting down from the tower.

Glancing up, I see a small window has been cut out and I scamper to the side and hide beneath. Thankfully, I don't have to strain my ears to listen to what the guards are saying.

"That boy that was brought in today, I heard from Kunja that he's half-fox," a man with a husky voice says.

"What do you mean he's half-fox?" a younger, less experienced guard asks.

"That he was born of a vixen and a man. A filthy abomination."

The young guard gasps. "Why would a holy fox ever taint her kin with human blood?"

"Mhm, my thoughts exactly. Kunja said Lady Yona wanted to monitor him and then release him—that he was her son."

"Lady Yona with a human?"

The older guard drops his voice to a whisper. "She lost her path before, maybe she's straying again."

"But Her Divine Majesty surely wouldn't let the abomination be released? No human not of the Divine Tails has ever left Sanoul with their life."

"I know." A pause and a sharp intake of breath. "If the Heavenly Fox does release him, I say we hire a sword to take care of him once outside the city. If the boy tells anyone about his heritage, faith may waver and fuel may be added to the fire of the heretics. They'll have a reason to wage war if foxes and humans are mixing."

Hire a sword? Wage war? My eyes widen and I lift my paw to my cheek. Besides the obvious fact that his fox spirit is making him sick, I see no problem with Tetsu's heritage. It has happened before, I'm sure. Even now, I am bonded to him and he's more human than fox.

The guard continues, "Seeing a heretic granted grace by Her Divine Majesty or knowing a fox spirit has been weakened and trapped by a human will do neither side any good."

"Do you know any swords?"

"Plenty."

I push off the tower and race down the corridor, my tails whipping behind me as I go. I must warn Yona of the guards' intentions. If there's anything left I can do for Tetsu, it's to save his life one final time.

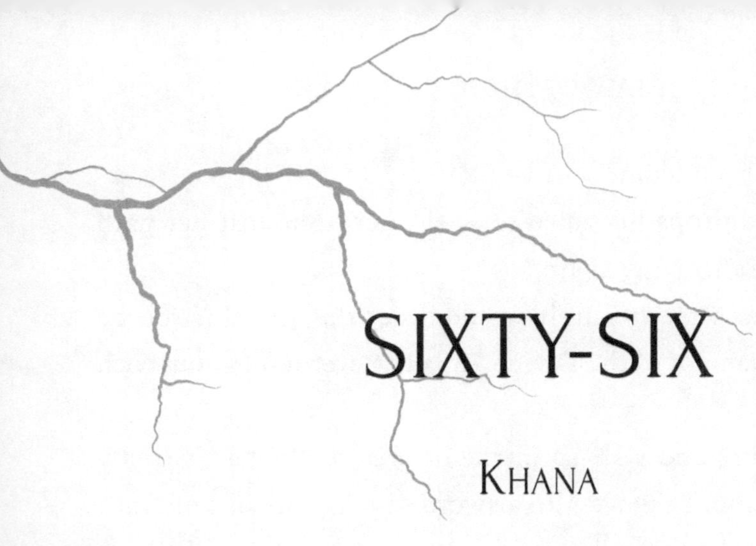

SIXTY-SIX

KHANA

KHANA ROLLED HER SHOULDERS back, stretching her neck out as she yawned behind her paw. She hopped off the throne and let her feet sink into the plush rug that had been rolled out before her. A long night beget a warm feast and the comfort of her personal Den. As the foxes by the glass doors of the room stood to escort her out, Khana's ears began to tingle.

She paused and lifted her head, letting her senses wash over her. As a being from the stars, though fallen and disgraced for stealing the dragon's lightning, Khana was omniscient and mischief was amuck in the palace. She closed her eyes and listened, her mind unfurling a map of the palace as she searched for the mischief.

Being in a city full of foxes and members of the Divine Tails, there was bound to be trouble but nothing felt like this. The tingling in her ears grew in strength and she clenched her jaw as it cascaded down through her skull, leaving an icy and numb trail behind. Images flickered before her eyes, rippling like a stone in water until they cleared and she saw Yona and Nari racing through the palace. Their voices filled her ears like a puddle and Khana watched.

"What will we do about the guards?" Nari asked, the inflection of her voice rising as her tails remained high on alert.

"They won't leave their post—" Yona paused and looked ahead, right into Khana's eyes. She slowed a bit, the fur on her back relaxing with ease. "Your Majesty, the guards—"

"Have a plan to hire a sword against your son, I know," Khana said softly in her mind. The information came to her in an instant and left her mouth before she could even process it. Such was the way of the Celestials. "I will distract the guards. Get him as far away from Sanoul as you can."

"Thank you," Yona dipped her head and the image disappeared as she and Nari passed right through Khana.

Her eyes opened and she felt her fur ruffle as the essence of the stars living inside her settled down. The foxes stood guard, ears perked and ready for her next command.

Khana cleared her throat and turned as she walked back to her throne. "Call a mandatory meeting for all guards in the palace, including the human ones." She sat on the throne with a sigh as the foxes left and thought about Tetsu.

He wasn't the first half-human, half-fox she had ever encountered but they were rare. Khana had no desire to kill him, to think him an abomination. It simply wasn't her way, no matter what the humans had come to believe. Khana had been born of the stars and tasked with the safety of the fox demons—her kith and kin.

Soon, all would be free of the Eternal Darkness and would gain their bodies here—vessels only available on this planet. Then, they would find another realm to make their home and she would protect them from whatever lay ahead. Whatever vengeful plot would follow them next.

SIXTY-SEVEN

TETSU

THE SOUND OF FOX feet haunts me as I drift in and out of conscious-ness. I don't know how long I've been chained up, but the guards have refused to offer me food or water, despite Mother's request. The prison has been warm and humid the last few nights and I'm slick with sweat. If I did care about the smell emanating from my armpits, I'd try to hide it, but now, I smell like the beasts that hold me prisoner.

"Tetsu," Mother's voice calls from afar.

I lift my head and squint, heat flaring as the cell tilts and wobbles. I squeeze my eyes shut, pressing my lips together to keep the bile rising in my throat from spewing past my lips. At least when I was brought here, I had relief from the demon raging inside me but now, the relief has worn off. How can I ever learn to accept something that's been trying to kill me all my life?

"Tetsu," comes the call again, this time much closer.

The cell door jangles and squeaks open, slamming into the one next door. I hear a whoosh and then cold, clammy hands wrangle my wrists from the chains. My arms drop like heavy sacks of rice, my knuckles striking the ground and sending a sharp sensation up my limbs.

Slumping against someone solid, fingers brush the greasy locks from my forehead. "Tetsu, I need you to fight back for a little longer, okay?"

I don't reply. Fighting is no use if the demon makes me this sick. I can't stand or see, let alone fight.

"I'll take his other side."

Nari.

I jerk away when she touches my arm but she snatches me and pulls me close. The whisper of her breath against my ear makes me flinch. "Stop fighting me, we're trying to save you, Tetsu." Her voice breaks on my name and I feel my pulse skip a beat.

"Get away," I want to snap but my mouth falls open and I roll forward, dry heaving until my throat burns.

She lifts me, my feet dragging on the ground, and tucks her arm around my waist. Nari's fingers dig into the fleshy bit above my hip and my gaze flickers as we walk further into the prison. The further we go, the darker it gets. Maybe Nari is lying and she's bringing me to my death. Then the demons will feast on my heart and liver.

I struggle against her, groaning as I try to shove away but end up tripping. Mother catches me and I look up into her face, her hair creating a curtain around us.

"Stay with me, Tetsu, we haven't far to go," she says softly and helps me stand upright again.

I feel so pathetic and weak so I grit my teeth and dig my heels into the ground, trying to move my legs forward. I think of Father, a quiet and kind man who had few words in him, but when he did speak, I always thought it prophetic.

A phrase comes to mind now in Father's voice, strong and bright even before death claimed him.

The demons may win but show no fear; never lay down and die when you are capable of so much more.

SIXTY-EIGHT

Nari

THE HIDDEN TUNNEL WE sneak through to get Tetsu out of the palace is damp and musty. As we usher him along, my bare arm brushes the slimy stone walls and I squirm, wanting to shift so I can move faster through the tunnel. Yona leads the way, her eyes open and alert, her human ears twitching the slightest at any sound that reaches us.

As a bug leaps onto my shoulder and scampers down my arm, I focus on Tetsu. He's still burning up, his skin slick with sweat and his eyes unfocused. I never thought a fox spirit could ail him like this but we are strong, sly, and fierce. A fox gets what it wants.

I curl my fingers tight around him when he slips and slumps against me, pressing me into the slimy wall. Tetsu's head lifts, his gaze meeting mine for a split second. His eyes look glazed over and distant and I know that if we don't get him out of Sanoul soon, he'll succumb to the fox.

"We have to keep moving, Tetsu," Yona says gruffly, though she touches a gentle hand to his cheek.

He nods and we press onward. The passage narrows and declines until we have to shuffle single file and crane our necks. My breathing grows heavy as the walls press in on us and I stare forward, waiting to see something that indicates an exit.

"How much—how much further?" I rasp. My mouth is dry, my tongue the texture of bark, and I feel sweat roll down the crevice of my spine. *I need to get out of here.*

"We're almost there," Yona says.

I hold on to Tetsu's shoulders and press closer to his back. The walls move in on us, squishing us down until we're on our hands and knees before soft moonlight trickles from an opening above. Yona jumps and grabs the side of the opening, clumps of grass and dirt breaking free as she scrambles up. Then she holds her hands down and beckons Tetsu.

He stands there, now a bit more aware and stable on his feet, but he doesn't take his mother's hands. I push lightly on his shoulder. "Go."

When he still doesn't move, I scoot around him and lift his arms. Yona grasps his forearms and starts pulling, grunting at his weight. I lean down and scoop my arms around his hips, helping him up and Tetsu finally reacts.

"Let me go," he squeaks and when I look up at him, his face is bright red.

I ignore his plea and snap, "Help haul yourself up then. You're heavy."

Tetsu manages to scramble up the side and then it's my turn. But no hands hang down to help me and for a moment, I think that they're going to leave me in this cramped tunnel and my heart leaps into my throat. I jump, grasping nothing but loose dirt until I slip and fall flat on my rump. A quick pain shoots up my back, along with moisture that seeps into my trousers.

"Nari," Yona calls from above.

I glance up, relieved to see her arms outstretched. I stand and climb, leaving the suffocating tunnel behind. On the surface, I wobble on my feet but look around. We're in one of the forested parks of Sanoul, near the parapet, and Tetsu is leaning on a tree, looking rather grim.

"There!"

We whip around to find an unholy amount of humans standing among the trees, torches in hand. They're dressed in their finest silks and boots, the silver medallions glinting in the moonlight.

"That's the abomination!" one of the zealots roars and they charge forward.

"Nari!" Yona says and I glance at her. "I'll take care of the rest and lead you out. You help him."

I grab Tetsu's arm and pull him along, even as he stumbles. Yona shifts and fends off the rest of the zealots, snapping her jaws on their legs and knocking torches to the ground to set the moss and leaves on fire. She lifts her paw to call down a series of lightning strikes, that burn the zealots to a char. Most are scorched to oblivion, their howling cries echoing in the night.

We weave through the trees until we come to one of the roads—also littered with humans. The zealots turn as one toward us, eyes glossy and lips curled in a snarl as they point and rush us. We head for the gate as Yona blazes a trail. Running down the incline throws both Tetsu and me off balance and we end up tumbling down to the main gate. The Guardian emerges from the shadows, large and looming with a curious tilt to its head.

"Cover for us," Yona commands it.

I bolt to my feet and drag Tetsu along. He winces, resting a hand on his chest, but hurries the best he can. The Guardian moves in behind us and I hear squeals and wails of terror as it gnashes its teeth at the zealots. One glance back makes my stomach turn when I see a series of severed limbs and a head fly in different directions, spewing thick, red blood. I know we foxes never cared for the zealots or their worship—in fact, Sook always said she thought it was creepy and unnecessary.

I suppose now they will see that we never asked to be worshiped. Never asked them to be like us.

SIXTY-NINE

TETSU

MY LEGS ARE ACHING and trembling by the time we reach a run-down, empty cabin in the forest. I collapse on the dusty floor and slump forward, hiding my face in my folded arms. The heat and pain has slowly dissipated the further we got from Sanoul but I still feel weak. A faint, ringing sound racks through my brain and the whisper of the fox demon begins its torment again.

"I'm sorry," Mother says softly and the floorboards creak as she sits down next to me. "I'm sorry I kept your true nature a secret. I thought you would be better kept in the dark."

"Did Father know?" I ask.

"Yes, but you know he was never afraid of or obsessed with the foxes. He didn't think it was something abominable."

"Is that what you think of me?"

"Of course not." Yona sighs. "I have loved you as you are all my life, Tetsu, and I wish I could have stayed. But my duty called me to Sanoul and then I learned of the raid on Nagaseo and..." she trails off, her voice breaking. "And I thought you were taken as well. Then I saw you at the Itson Temple and I wanted nothing more than to speak with you...

"I am bound to serve the Heavenly Fox to the end of my days and can't go far without her at my side. That is my duty. But my heart and my love belong to you. It always will."

I sit up slowly and look at Mother in her human form. I remember her skin being smooth and unblemished, her cheeks always rosy, and a soft smile on her face. Now she bears brutal scars across her jaw and neck, dark circles beneath her eyes, deep lines creasing her skin that had not been there before. She hadn't been gone for long but time had caught up to her.

Mother had been by my side whenever I was sick or sad or happy. Except now, she has missed the last six years of my life. She missed the quiet, restless grieving period after Father was killed. Me growing up and joining the trappers who fueled the hate I feel for the fox demons. She had missed my clumsy attempts at being a man and falling in love for the first time—

I shake my head, refusing to let my thoughts go down *that* road. Mother's shoulders fall in defeat. "I understand—"

I lean forward and wrap my arms around her, giving her a brief hug as I mutter, "I wish you were there."

Tears well in her eyes as I draw back and she lets one cascade down her cheek. "Me too."

Mother cups my face, her gaze softening as she takes me in. Then she stands. I don't watch her leave, I can't bear to witness it while conscious. So I close my eyes and sit there, pulling my knees to my chest.

Though Mother is gone, Nari stays. She is quiet except for the short, quick breaths she releases. I focus on that for a long while, thankful that I'm not completely alone with the demon in my head.

SEVENTY

Nari

I STAY WITH TETSU in the barren cabin long after Yona has left and I don't know why. I should head back to my Den and be with my skulk again. Or, now that I can shapeshift, I could live in Sanoul. Flutters in my belly rise as I think of the beautiful imperial city but the feeling is soured by the thought of the zealots. They saw my face, they knew I helped Tetsu escape. They'll think I'm associated with an "abomination".

My gaze strays to Tetsu as my thoughts clear. I open my mouth to say something but no words come out and I feel my skin flush. Settling down on my hands and knees, I prepare to shift when Tetsu says, "Thank you for saving me, Nari."

I gulp, my heart thunking in my chest, and sit back on my legs. "I thought I could do it one last time before we...before we part."

He lifts his head and looks at me, his dark eyes all-consuming of my soul. "I truly enjoyed our time together, I want you to know that. But you broke my trust. Things will never be the same."

"I know and I'm sorry, Tetsu."

"And even though you're a demon," he winces, "you haven't taken my soul."

"You need it more than I do."

A hoarse chuckle escapes him and I feel warmth stirring in my belly. My fingers inch forward, reaching out for him, and Tetsu notices. He glances at my hand and I stop, curling my fingers against the creaky, wood floor. A breath of silence passes between us before Tetsu unfolds himself and crawls toward me. I forget to breathe as he draws near.

With heavy-lidded eyes, his gaze rakes over me and an inferno is set beneath my skin. The tip of his nose almost touches mine and I instinctively wet my lips, which pulls his attention. Tetsu blushes but he doesn't move away.

"I think I was falling in love with you, Nari," he whispers. "You challenged me and brightened my dark and dreary world. You were a lightning bolt strike straight to my heart and you've captured it. But," he leans back, gnawing on his lower lip, "I need time to figure things out and adjust to this new part of myself."

"Being half-fox isn't all bad," I tell him with a smile. "We may be a bit smellier and mischievous but we're cute and have each others' backs."

Tetsu nods, the corner of his mouth ticked up. The urge to nuzzle his nose burns through me but I resist. He lies down, his back to me as he tucks his arms beneath his head, and I shift. It feels like I'm walking through mud as I leave Tetsu in the cabin.

SEVENTY-ONE

Tetsu

AFTER NARI LEAVES, I feel my body sink into the wood of the floor and tears prick the back of my eyes. Alone now, it feels strange. Mother has gone back to her duty, leaving me once again. I sigh as I rub my eye and curl into myself. My stomach grumbles and I know I should get going but I don't want to move.

So I let myself fall asleep.

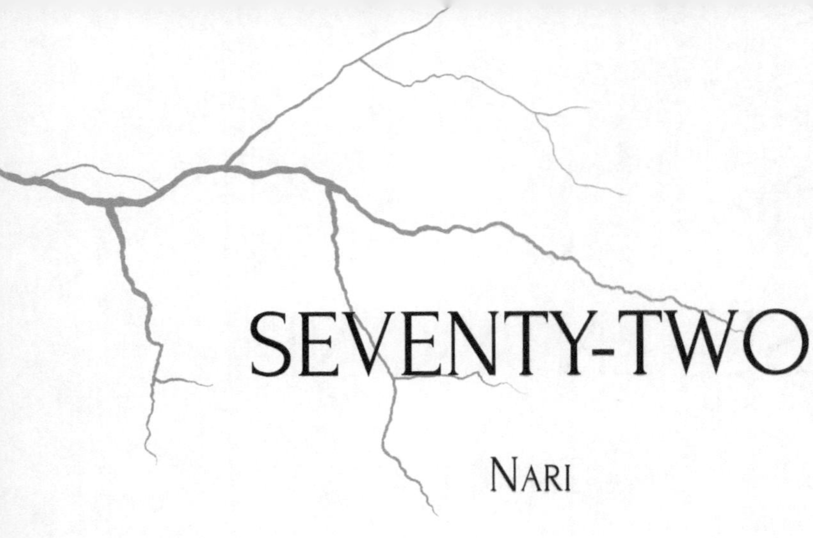

SEVENTY-TWO

Nari

MY EARS ITCH ONCE I reach the road to Sanoul and I pause to scratch at them with my hindleg. I itch and itch, my snout crinkling, until a hazy white light appears before my vision and I see a highly realistic image of the Heavenly Fox's face. I gasp and quickly bow low to the ground.

"Your Majesty."

"Nari, rise."

I do and sit on my haunches, my head level as I meet her glowing silver eyes. I know she isn't really here and this happened when Yona and I were on our way to the prison but it feels strange as I only hear her voice in my ears and see her with my eyes.

"I saw that Tetsu safely made it out of Sanoul."

I nod and dip my chin slightly. "Thank you for all you did for him, Your Majesty."

"It was my pleasure. But I wanted to tell you that I was moved by your tenacity, Nari, during your entire journey to reach Sanoul. Now that you are a *kumisune* with your nine-tails and shifting abilities, you are eligible to be a part of my court, if you wish."

My eyes widen and my tails flutter in excitement. Me? Being part of the Heavenly Fox's court? I salivate at the thought of rich foods and servants tending to my every need. I could be a warrior like Yona or one of the vixens at court who lazes about all day and gossips.

But...Chul, Sook, my skulk. I can't leave them for a life in Sanoul. And the forest is where I belong. The soil I learned to walk on, the trees I learned to navigate, and the life I lived as both human and fox have been in this forest.

Slowly, I shake my head. "I can't."

She nods, offering me a warm smile, her canines slipping past her mouth. "Well, the offer is always open. Have a safe trip back to your Den, Nari, and thank you for bringing the soul beads. You have granted another nine hundred of our kin the opportunity to join us here so we may all be together again and free from the Eternal Darkness."

Then she slips away, her image scattering like smoke on the wind.

I run to the Den when it's in sight as the day ends and shimmy down through the entrance. It feels wonderful to be the right size again and I leap on top of a still sleeping Chul. He startles awake and grunts, bucking me off of him. A high-pitched laugh escapes me and when Chul blinks enough to realize it's me, he pounces forward and we roll together across the ground, trapped in a playful embrace.

"Nari! You're back!" Chul yips and stands astride, his gaze lingering on my tails. "You've gotten an upgrade too."

"I can shift whenever I want," I tell him.

"Nari?"

I turn to Sook and though I don't attack her like I did with Chul, I still lumber forward and rub my cheek against hers in greeting. Sook grins at me. "I'm happy to have you back."

The rest of my skulk crowd around me but I don't feel compacted. I feel loved and appreciated as I tumble around with other vixens and tods until Sook has us settle down. She stands near the entrance of the Den and I watch a spider caught on a thin web dangle just above her head.

"Now that Nari is back, our skulk is whole again. As per Her Divine Majesty's request, we have been asked to move further west to the Itson region. In the next few years, all foxes will be united with a vessel and she would like us all to be at the Itson Temple to witness it." Sook tells us.

Chul and I share a surprised glance.

Soon, the foxes will leave Earth and we will have a home to call our own.

But far, far away from Tetsu.

SEVENTY-THREE

Tetsu

EXHAUSTED AND DISTRAUGHT OVER my journey to Sanoul, I manage to make it to Juhto and into an inn before my legs give out. I stretch out on the bedroll and contemplate what my next step in life is. I can't go back to the trappers. Kyung will never accept my apology and I can't trap foxes knowing how I feel about Nari.

My fingers twitch at my sides. I still need to pick up my box of keepsakes outside the tea house. Father's tools are inside and though I haven't carved anything spectacular in the last six years, I still remember everything Father taught me. Maybe I'll be a woodcarver like him. Live a quiet life in a small village and never think about foxes again.

ONE MONTH LATER

SEVENTY-FOUR

Nari

NOW THAT TETSU AND I aren't fleeing from bandits or on a mission for the fox trappers, I can appreciate the Itson Region in all its glory. It's denser with a lot more springs and thicket to get caught up in. Autumn is upon us now, with vibrant orange, yellow, and red colors that I can only see when I am human. As we head further west past the Temple, the air grows humid and warm until we reach the end of the forest. Our new Den is near the sandy shores but still hidden in the forest. Every night, I like to walk along the shore and dip my paws in the glistening, golden water. Sook said all rivers in the forest flow into the sea. What lies beyond? We don't know.

I stand and watch the moon rise over the horizon. It's much larger and brighter out here but still cast in a red glow from the sky above. I haven't had a chance to call down lightning yet. Sook said the magic inside me had to get used to my *kumisune* form but now, I lift my paw and splay my toes out, head tilted up. Energy slowly builds inside me, trickling down into my core and warming my belly. A spark flashes among the clouds and I hold on, my teeth gritting as the heat increases.

Crack.

I look behind me to see a small tree split in two, charred and smoking already with bright red embers falling to the grass beneath.

I run toward the tree, kicking up white sand and smooth pebbles in my wake. The embers catch on the grass and I quickly stamp it out before a fire can start.

"Nari," Chul says, startling me. I glance up to see him approach, his brow lifting as he observes the tree. "Did you do that?"

"Yeah," I stomp on the grass one more time for good measure and then take off running with him back to the Den. "Is the royal envoy almost here?"

"Yes," he says, leaping over a thick branch that has fallen in our path.

"What do you think the message will be?" I ask.

"Maybe we'll start collecting tithes again and raiding human villages."

My stomach twists at that. Since we've been out here, we were told to lay low and not interact with any humans. I don't know why Khana would order such when there are so many more fox spirits waiting to gain their vessel. I've seen Sook take messages with a grim look on her face but she hasn't made any sort of announcement to the entire skulk.

Back at the Den, the skulk is gathered outside and the messenger fox with his shining silver breastplate and a ringlet about his pointed ears is almost as big as the Heavenly Fox herself. His ear twitches as he leans down to listen to whatever Sook is whispering to him. Chul and I settle in the back and a hush falls upon us as the messenger straightens.

He clears his throat and says in a husky voice, "As you can tell, I've been sent by Her Divine Majesty to deliver a message to your skulk. It is time for you to know what has been going on in Sanoul for the last month." He pauses. His honey-colored eyes, rimmed with a mask of black fur, glance over us. "The humans, that claim themselves devout worshipers of our kith and kin, became bitter after a half-fox, half-human boy escaped Sanoul. They believed him to be an abomination and when Her Divine Majesty did nothing about it, the Divine Tails plotted a coup and sealed the gates.

"Thankfully, Her Divine Majesty is unharmed and the gates of Sanoul are no longer sealed. The zealots living inside the city have been taken care of but the Heavenly Fox knows the intentions of the rest of the Tails and so now it is time to collect their tithes. From now on, this skulk and all other collectors will focus on the Tails. Their numbers have swarmed in recent years but these humans are more prevalent in the Itson and Hansu Regions of Daion.

"I must warn you that the zealots will likely know we're coming and will be more violent. Watch out for traps, listen closely, and never leave anyone behind." A small smirk curls the corner of his mouth. "They have asked for their sins to be forgiven, what better way than to collect their tithes?"

A series of yips and howls follow and the messenger stands, leaning down to Sook once more. She looks so tiny compared to him and Chul nudges my shoulder. I glance at him and he smiles so wide his canines slip over his bottom lip and his eyes nearly disappear into his fur.

"This is the best news we've had in a while." Chul drops low to the ground, his tails swishing behind him. "I'm ready to pounce on those zealots and maybe when they're all gone, I'll finally become a *kumisune* like you." His gaze trails to my tails. "I'll admit I'm a bit jealous."

I snort. "I know you're jealous. I find you hugging my tails every evening when I wake."

"No you don't," he claims and pounces on me. We roll across the ground, laughing and nipping each other's ears. Then we bump into a pair of sturdy legs and look up at the messenger fox.

His head tilts as he stares down at us and Chul and I scramble to our feet. "I know you," he says to me.

"Zuma, this is Nari," Sook says, gnawing on her lip as she sits on her haunches.

"Hmph." He studies me for a moment and I squirm, feeling awkward under his scrutiny until I decide to study him as well. I've never seen fur as red as his or the black mask of fur around his eyes in another fox before. "Are you ready to help usher in the rest of our kin, Nari?"

I nod. "Yes, of course."

"Good. I expect nothing less. Her Divine Majesty sends her regards. She liked you quite a bit while you were in Sanoul."

I lift a paw to my cheek. "Oh."

Zuma nods to Chul, to Sook, and then turns. He disappears into the forest beyond and Sook looks after him.

SEVENTY-FIVE

TETSU

I STARE AT THE small hunk of wood in my palm, trying to figure out what I should carve first for my newly built woodworking shop in Juhto.

Father's carving knife sits by my thigh on the log and I pick it up, tapping the blade against my mouth. If I keep waiting for an idea, I'll be dead before I know it so I get to work. It takes a bit to get the rhythm right and I manage not to cut any of my fingers off. I let my mind run on a stream of thoughts, thinking about everything and anything and not paying attention to whatever I'm carving.

When a bird shrieks high in the branches just above my head, I startle and blink away my daydream. Looking down at the figure in my hand, I brush away the curly shavings and my shoulders stiffen. The carving is rough but decent and I squint until a line forms between my brow.

I've carved a fox.

"I know who you are now," I say to the darkness. "And who I am."

The fox demon emerges from the thick, suffocating darkness that surrounds us and I swallow hard. I haven't confronted the demon in a long while and have successfully kept it under control but now, I'm ready to talk. The demon looks mangy, tufts of its dark fur are missing on its sides and around its paws. Its tawny eyes are bloodshot and its lips curl back in a snarl. Once strong, now weak. I wonder how it came to look like this but before I can ask, the fox speaks.

"Why won't you let me go, human?"

"Well, in my experience when you've tried to take control, you nearly killed me," I spit.

The fox growls deep in its throat. "I wasn't trying to kill you, I was trying to escape your mortal vessel. I wanted a body of my own."

I blink. I hadn't thought of that. Slowly, I ease myself down to my knees in a thin layer of black water, but the moisture doesn't seep through my trousers. With a swipe of my hand, it feels like air but ripples like water. I shake my head and focus on the fox again.

"Look, I'm not going anywhere and neither are you so we might as well work together. Why do you look so frail?"

The fox sits down and tilts its chin, glaring at me. "You haven't been listening to me so I've been starving without your attention."

"It's been nice to have a sense of peace in my head," I say and rub the back of my neck. "But I know now you're a part of me and I've come to accept that. I grew up hating the fox demons but when I got to know one...she wasn't evil."

"Nari," the fox whispers and its face softens slightly.

I blush. "Right...I suppose you know her too...in some way."

It nods. "But we are only doing what we must to survive. You humans don't know what the foxes have gone through and though I was created by half of your mother's fox spirit, some of her memories reside within me." The fox glances away, its eyes glazing over as it reminisces. "We come from a place called the Eternal Darkness where we were banished long ago. It is cold, quiet, and lonely. We were all separated from one another and forced to relive the pain and torture that we endured in past lives on other worlds. The fox demons have existed for millennia and Earth is not the only place we've come to but it is the first we've escaped to. The ancestors cannot see or feel us here, the Heavenly Fox guarantees that with her divine power. We have been safe here but we cannot remain forever.

"All we want is a home to call our own where we are not forced to carry out anyone's dirty deeds or inflict terror and brew hatred. By nature, we are mischievous but in our hearts, we are loyal and fiercely protective of one another. Our spiritual connection that thrives in each fox spirit runs deep."

The fox tips its head toward my hand, its tawny gaze meeting mine again. "That ring was forged in the fires of the Eternal Darkness. It will help you shift into me when you let it and protect your human soul from the fire that burns in my core."

I look at Father's ring and twist it around my finger. "I thought it was meant to show the true nature of something."

"I am part of your true nature, am I not?"

An inkling of doubt wells in my mind as my jaw clenches tight. What if the demon is lying? How can I be sure that once I give it control, it won't take off running and shove me into a corner of my mind?

"I promise to work with you," the fox says.

I look up at it, my eyes narrowing. "I've only just accepted you; I don't think I'm going to trust you with my body just yet."

Its nose twitches and it shakes its head.

"Do you have a name?" I ask as I stand and feel myself being pulled from the dream.

"The same as yours," the fox replies and fades away.

TWO YEARS LATER

SEVENTY-SIX

TETSU

I GROAN AS I stand from the bench, stretching my arms above my head as my spine pops.

"You know," Tetsu, now Teeto the fox, says in my head, *"we foxes live for a long time and don't have to deal with that human aging problem."*

I chuckle and roll my eyes, brushing the wood shavings from my apron. "I'm not giving you control, Teeto. Not yet, at least. Besides, I'm still in my youth."

"For now." Teeto's laugh is a minor annoyance now rather than something that struck fear in my heart.

I wander out into the night and walk around the back of my workshop where a rickety ladder stands. It's a bit wobbly but sturdy enough to endure my weight. I pull myself up onto the roof and lay back on the thatched material.

"The stars are always there as they were last night and the night before."

"I know that, I just like coming up here to think."

The clouds and ribbons of energy are still blood red but beyond that, the sky bears its usual deep azure with twinkling stars. I tuck my arms beneath my head and let myself relax. The foxes haven't raided any of the villages in nearly two years. For months, I wondered if I should reach out and find out why, but now we're just glad we have our peace. There have hardly been any sightings of foxes in the surrounding forest.

"Are you truly at peace?" Teeto asks. *"Over her?"*

With a deep sigh, I cross my ankles and swallow hard. *Nari.* Of course I haven't forgotten about her but the thoughts are still poignant, though less so as time passes. I still wonder what she's up to. Teeto informed me that foxes who receive their nine-tails would live lavish lives at the palace or head top-secret missions for the Heavenly Fox.

"I don't think so," I tell him.

"We're bonded, you know."

I nod. Teeto also told me about bonding between foxes. It means we chose each other to love and protect and our souls are now forever intertwined. A blush heats my skin and I shake my head. I doubt I'll ever see her again.

"Oh, don't doubt so soon, Tetsu."

My pulse quickens. "What do you mean?"

Teeto tsks. *"Only that fate will have her way."*

SEVENTY-SEVEN

NARI

THE PIT OF KESHIN looks vastly different than it had before. Now, a tight-knit community with a reinforced wall and turrets surrounds the Pit. The turrets are housed by archers who will try to strike us down when we approach. Keshin is the last stronghold of the Divine Tails and my skulk's final raid, if successful.

I run alongside Chul but this time, I'm not fluttering with nerves. My tails flow with the movement of my body as we bound forward, following a well-worn path through the forest. A horn blast signals that we've been spotted and I lift my head, eyes narrowing as I scan the turrets above. The walls of the fortress are slightly slanted so we'll be able to climb up if we can dodge the arrows and bolts and fireballs being launched at us. But we have our lightning and nothing can survive that.

Chul and I share a glance and sly smirks before we part and I leap onto one of the walls, shifting my focus toward the heat building in my core. Sizzling energy burns bright in my nose and within a second, a loud crack and flash strike the turret near me. Gut-curdling screams fill the night air, along with the stench of scorched flesh and hot blood.

My ears perk as I hear a volley of arrows whistling toward me and I look, dodging just in time before they pierce me. Another bolt of lightning strikes the offenders, spraying shattered rock and body parts everywhere. I hurry up the wall, the pads on my paws gripping the stone and I launch myself up and over.

Careful not to tumble into the Pit, where two sets of skeletons sit on the slab draped in flower wreaths, I skid to a halt and whirl into action as the rest of my skulk joins me. I catch sight of Sook's dark silver fur glinting in the moonlight before she pounces on a pair of zealots and sinks her claws into their chests, ripping them open. She absorbs their souls and moves on. I have to keep an eye on Sook because I know she's close to turning and we can't have that in the middle of our raid.

I feel a chunk of my fur get cut off and I turn, ducking to avoid getting slashed across the throat. The zealot has wide, terrified eyes and blood dribbling from her mouth. Her teeth have been shaved down to points and though the mask and ears she once wore are gone, the white ink of our fox symbol remains on her skin.

"How could you turn against us?" Dura shrieks, spittle flying from her mouth. She slashes at me again and I drop low. "We devoted *everything* to you and you decide to slaughter us!"

Without an answer, I ram into her legs and she stumbles back, the dagger waving wildly above. When she falls on her back, I take the blade between my teeth and yank it out of her hand. The woman scrambles but I hop on and hold her down, pressing my paw over her mouth. Her sharpened nails scratch at me and though she's rather small and frail-looking now, she's still fierce and keeps on fighting until the heat within me is too much for her to bear. I bring the dagger down across her throat and gurgling blood fills her mouth before she goes still.

I absorb her soul and move on.

It's time.

I sit with my skulk at the Itson Temple, my heart pounding in my chest as the entirety of our fox kin are gathered. We've just witnessed the last spawning ceremony and now it is time for us to leave Earth.

Khana, the Heavenly Fox, stands by her statue alone and addresses us with a loud voice. "My kith and kin, you are the reason I was granted the power I hold and now, you have all been freed from the Eternal Darkness." She pauses and stands, walking among us in her glorious magnificence, her eyes glowing and her fur shining beneath the full moon. "No longer will we be pawns to those who would never respect us. No longer will we be the face of terror and wickedness."

She comes to the symbol in the middle of the temple as the crowd parts. I lean closer to Chul, who rises on his back legs to see better.

Khana continues, "It is time we find a place to call our home. A true one."

She tilts her head back and lets out a long bay and soon, the rest of the foxes join. A chorus that fills my ears and rattles my bones. I love it. When all falls quiet again, Khana rises on her back legs and opens a portal, this one is not to the Eternal Darkness. On the other side, I can see a field of green, swaying grass and bright flowers under a clear night. Moonlight and dew grace the blades of grass and beyond, a line of tall, sturdy trees.

"One by one," she instructs and the crowd starts to move forward.

I'm pushed on but stumble and my brow knits as I search for Sook. She's standing near Zuma, their tails once interlocked now coming undone as they stand. I weave my way toward them and feel Chul nip at my tails but follow along. Sook glances at me, her eyes softening as a smile brightens her face.

"Nari—"

"I can't go," I say before I even process the thought. With a gasp, I lift a paw to my mouth and my eyes widen.

"Why not?" Zuma asks.

"Yeah, what are you talking about?" Chul counters, setting a paw on my shoulder.

"I—I—" I look around at the three of them, my throat constricting with everything I want to say but am unable to. I swallow hard and drop my chin, shaking my head.

Sook steps forward and rubs her cheek against mine, saying quietly in my ear, "I know a way you can stay. Let's speak with Khana."

"Stay?" Chul's voice cracks on the word and I turn to him. His mouth turns down and his shoulders drop. "Why would you stay here?"

"It's...complicated."

For a moment, Chul is quiet, studying me with a distant look in his gaze before it dawns on him. His lip curls and he growls, "For the human?"

I reach for him. "Chul—"

He steps back and out of my reach, his tails flaring behind him as his eyes narrow. "You do realize the humans will never accept you, right? You're a *demon*, you always will be."

"Chul," Sook warns, her voice taking on a sharp edge. "Nari is allowed to make her own decisions. Let's not be harsh before we hear what Khana has to say."

He huffs and turns, refusing to look at me any longer. My heart sinks into the pit of my stomach and Sook nudges me forward. We shuffle along and I drag myself up until we reach the Heavenly Fox.

The portal remains open as she drops down and lifts my chin with a slender claw. "Nari, dear, what can I do for you?"

I look up into her silver eyes but then glance sidelong at Chul as he sits aside, not budging as foxes move around him to the portal. "I—I want to stay." My gaze shifts to her again. "Sook said you can do that?"

She drops her paw and nods, sitting back on her haunches. "There is one way but once I am gone from this Earth, you won't have lightning anymore."

My pulse spikes as my mouth drops open. "Will I still be a fox?"

"Oh, yes, you'll still be able to shapeshift. But you won't be a demon. You'll be a regular fox and a regular human."

I hop on my feet, grinning at her. "I want that!"

Khana chuckles softly and dips her head toward me. "Shift into your human form and take a gem from my crown."

I do as she says and now stand nearly face-to-face with her. The gems are glittering red and I notice that two are missing. Before I can ask, she says, "Yona had the same idea."

I glance around, blinking and just realizing I haven't seen Tetsu's mother here. Khana folds her paws over my hands with the gem nestled in my palms and closes her eyes. Bright, warm light emits from her and the breeze ruffles my hair and the loose smock I wear. When she drops her arms and I open my hands, the gem has formed into a crescent pendant and I drop it over my head. I rub the smooth stone with my thumb as it pulses with power.

"This will keep us connected through realms so I know how you're doing and you'll be able to contact me."

"Really?" I stare at her, my eyes wide and brimming with tears.

Khana nods and leans closer, dropping her voice even though we're among foxes. "And if ever you want to see our new home, let me know.

You won't be separated from us forever, Nari, you—and Tetsu if he wishes—can visit us whenever. All you have to do is reach out through the gem while standing on this symbol."

The tears spill forward and without reserve, I leap and wrap my arms around Khana's neck. She lets out a sound of surprise and then rubs her cheek against mine. I let go and turn to Sook, Zuma, and Chul. I drop down to my knees.

"I'm sure you heard all that," I say to Chul.

He grunts and doesn't reply. A knot forms in my stomach and I sniffle, wiping my tears on my arm. "Please, Chul, this isn't goodbye."

"Regardless, you're staying behind," he whispers.

"I'll visit." I lift my hand to the back of his ear and though he stiffens at first, he relaxes as I scratch. "I promise we'll see each other again."

Chul moves into my embrace and it's odd that his soft fur feels so coarse on my human skin. I squeeze him lightly. "You'll always be my best friend and my big brother."

"How am I supposed to protect you now?" he grumbles.

"I'll be okay."

"I love you."

I hold him closer, burying my face in his fur. "I love you, too."

I release him and move on to Sook, pulling her close. "Thank you for always being my guide and help."

"Of course. Be safe, Nari."

With farewells in order for my skulk, I make my way to the edge of the temple until I'm by the fallen pillar Tetsu and I once hid behind. I sit on it now and watch all the foxes go through the portal. It takes nearly all night and I almost doze off before I pinch my arm to stay awake. Khana is the last to go, lifting her paw in farewell before she leaps through the portal. Quiet befalls the night as the portal disappears and I feel very alone. I stand, lifting my knuckles to my mouth as I look at the sky.

The red begins to fade, along with the energy dominating it and I feel my core darken and extinguish deep within my belly. It makes me choke up and claw at myself for a moment until the gem glows again and I hear Khana's voice in my head.

"It's okay, Nari, I'm still here."

"Can you stay with me until I reach Juhto?"

"Yes."

I take in a deep breath of cool, fresh air as the sky opens and thin droplets of rain strike my face. I hop over the pillar, my ears twitching at the stillness of the forest. It makes my skin crawl so I pump my legs and run.

SEVENTY-EIGHT

TETSU

"TETSU, I NEED YOU to trust me," the urgency in Teeto's voice startles me from my slumber.

With a groan, I push myself upright and scrub a hand through my messy hair. "Huh?"

"I know you heard me. I think it's time you learn what it's like to be a fox."

My eyes widen as my whole body stiffens. "Teeto..." I warn.

"I'm serious. I...feel her. She's near."

That gets me off my bedroll and into a pair of trousers. I pause, blinking when I'm halfway into a tunic, and ask, "Should I even wear clothes?"

Teeto snorts. *"You still want to be decent, don't you?"*

"Yeah." I wiggle into the tunic and strap on a belt. At the door, I sit to pull on my boots and lace them up. "What's this bit about trusting you? I can see her just fine as is."

"Ugh, you're so stubborn!" Teeto groans. *"I promise I won't stuff you away, Tetsu, we're in this together, remember?"*

Sure, I've gotten used to Teeto in my head and I haven't been severely sick in a long while now. Teeto is no longer fighting to get out and I'm not trying to shove him away. We've come to be completely intertwined and it's like I have a twin, but only one I can hear, feel, and see in my dreams.

Inhaling deeply, I step out into the crisp night and the smell of petrichor from the evening rain is still ripe in the air, along with the earthy scents of fresh soil and pine. I breathe it in, letting the scent soothe my soul.

In my head, Teeto gasps and I jerk my chin upright. The sky is clear and azure like I've seen glimpses of before. But, it's unfamiliar without the skeins of energy and blood-red clouds. I rub my eyes and look again, my mouth slowly falling open as my knees grow weak. What does this mean? Did the foxes...leave?

"They're...gone," Teeto whispers. I can feel Teeto's spirit stirring in my belly. Heat flares across my scar and I wince, placing a hand on my abdomen. *"They're gone,"* he growls now. *"Without me."*

"The foxes?"

"Yes, and I—" Teeto is cut off by a sharp cough that rings in my ears. *"I have no power here—I'm dying, Tetsu."*

The fox lets out a melancholy howl and I fall to my knees, reaching into my mind as my vision blurs. My heart thunks hard in my chest. I don't want to lose Teeto but I don't know how to save him either if the Heavenly Fox has taken all her power with her.

A clammy hand clamps down on my shoulder and a thin string pulls against my throat. I gasp and dig my fingers into my neck, trying to free myself of the string only to find it's a strap of leather. At the base of my throat rests a crescent-shaped gem. I whip around, squinting as my sight begins to clear and the gem glows, pulsing with a soothing, ethereal melody.

Above me stands a woman wearing a long hooded cape. She pulls back the hood and a smile lifts the corner of her mouth. I scramble to my feet. "M—Mother?"

"Hello, Tetsu."

SEVENTY-NINE

YONA

HE LOOKED SO GROWN up now...and so much like Dal with his soft eyes and scruffy hair.

Yona swat away the tears that came to her eyes before they could fall and stepped forward. Tetsu remained still and looked to the sky again. His brow furrowed in confusion.

"How are you here?"

She gestured to the pendant looped around her neck and the one at his. "These pendants are the last of the Heavenly Fox's power on Earth. It keeps our fox spirits connected with her but when we shift, we will simply be foxes, not demons any longer."

Tetsu blinked and glanced over his shoulder into the forest. "Does that mean...could she..."

"Maybe," Yona leaned aside to catch his attention again. "What does your fox say?"

He was quiet for a moment, his expression shifting from confusion and surprise to peace. Tetsu closed his eyes and nodded. Yona took a step back and sat on the steps to the workshop as Tetsu shifted into a fox for the first time. It was a glorious sight to behold.

He gasped as his body shortened, his nose and mouth lengthened, and fur spread all over his body, obscuring the human clothes he wore. His fur was the same reddish-brown as his hair and as his tail sprouted, it was tipped with white. Tetsu wobbled on his four legs, his rump high in the air as he stood there stunned.

Yona laughed lightly and beckoned him forward. Tetsu walked awkwardly as if he were wearing boots on all his paws and Yona took his face in her hands, resting her forehead against his.

"Calm down," she instructed. "Breathe in slowly, hold it, and release."

"This is—I don't—"

"Shh, just breathe."

His ears flickered but he did as she said. Yona sat back and released him, her eyebrow lifting. "Now, I think there may be someone you want to see?"

Tetsu's dark eyes met hers, hope wavering as if he didn't want to get it too high. "Do you think she stayed?"

Yona shrugged. "There's only one way to find out. Follow your fox."

Tetsu nodded and turned around, facing the forest. He gulped and marched into the brush. Yona waited until he was out of sight before she went into the workshop and made herself cozy by the blazing fire in the hearth.

EIGHTY

Nari

I SHIFT INTO MY fox form after a while and already feel the difference in my body. No core warming my belly with heat anymore, no nine-tails, and my stomach growls. I don't know the last time I ate but I can't think of food right now when I hear something crashing through the forest. My pulse ticks up a notch and I follow the noise.

I break into a clearing the same time another fox does and we both come to a halt, staring at each other. My singular tail stands up straight in alarm until I get a better look at the fox. He pants, his tongue lolling out of his mouth, and a whimper escapes him.

"Tetsu?"

"Nari," he breathes.

I want to race forward and knock him to the ground, ready to nuzzle his nose, but I don't. Instead, I shift back and he does too. We stare at each other and my eyes widen as I take him in. Tetsu has grown taller and his shoulders are broader. He has a light beard growing in and wears a pair of trousers and a tunic. His hair, once always loose or tied at the nape of his neck, is just curling past his ears now and shaggy locks hang above his eyes. There's a string of black beads around his biceps and I know in an instant they were once soul beads. They must have been Yona's.

Slowly, I approach him, holding my hands at my sides to show I mean no harm. His gaze takes me in anyway and makes me blush.

"You accepted your fox spirit," I say softly.

Tetsu nods and opens his mouth. When no sound comes out, he clears his throat and tries again, "His name is Teeto."

"And how do you feel?"

"More alive than I've ever been," he whispers. "I haven't gotten sick in a while."

"Did you see the sky? Did Teeto—" My gaze catches on the pendant around his neck. "Oh, did Yona find you?"

"Yes, she's back at my workshop."

I stop a few feet from him. "Workshop?"

"I'm a woodcarver. Nari, you...you look different."

"So do you."

Tetsu gulps, the lump in his throat bobbing, and he steps toward me now. I hold my hands up and feel nerves bundle up in my chest. "Wait, wait. I, uh, I need to say something before...before anything happens."

His head tilts in curiosity and I inhale deeply. I look into Tetsu's eyes, trying to feel fearless, but my voice trembles as I tell him, "I never got the chance to tell you how much you mean to me, Tetsu. Not just then but now as well. When I turned, it was a terrifying experience and though you were a bit annoyed with me, you were patient as I learned how to be a human. I'm grateful for that, for your kindness and care from the beginning." I rub my foot against the ground and wrap my arms around myself, chuckling lightly. "I know I was a nightmare to deal with and you wanted nothing to do with me, but I clung to you. I felt comfortable with you and after a while, I think you felt comfortable with me too.

"But that doesn't excuse what I did and I'm sorry I dragged you to Sanoul with me." I pause and exhale shakily. "You made being a human tolerable and I thank you for that. And I—I think I know what love is now." I shuffle back as my blush deepens. "I understand though if you still want nothing to do with me. Just...I had to say my piece."

Tetsu remains quiet for a painstakingly long moment, staring at me with something stirring in his eyes that I can't decipher. I lift a cold hand to my cheek and turn, accepting my defeat.

"Hey," he says softly. I go still but stay turned away. Tetsu comes up and I feel the warmth his body emits at my back. His fingers graze my bare arms and my breath escapes me as he leans down to my ear. "Despite everything, I'm glad I met you. I wouldn't have it any other way."

His arms fold around me and I turn, resting my hands against his chest. Tetsu smiles and drops his face down to mine. "I found you and I don't ever want to let you go again. Stay with me, Nari."

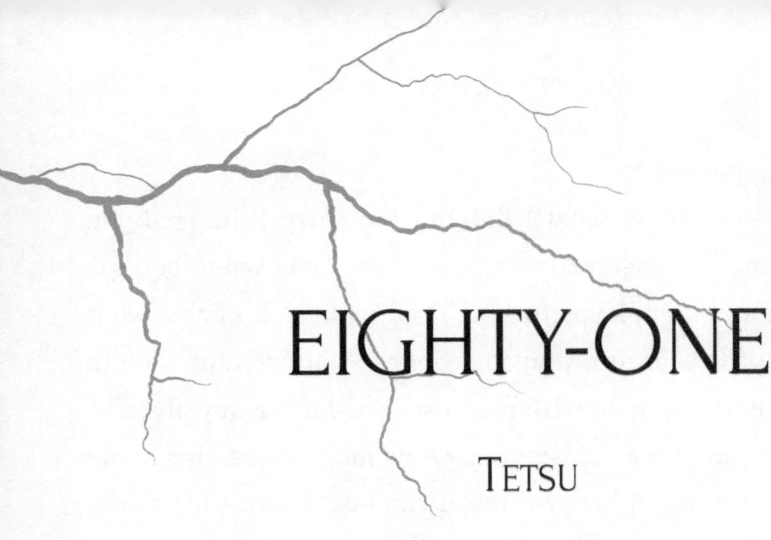

EIGHTY-ONE

TETSU

"STAY WITH ME, NARI," the words echo in my head after they leave my mouth.

Her dark eyes are wide and beautiful and I brush my nose against hers. Nari startles slightly and tears well in my eyes. She nods. I reach up and slip my fingers into her shoulder-length orange locks, drawing her head closer to mine. Our lips meet, soft and slow as my pulse beats rapidly in my ears. Nari presses closer, her body now hardened with muscle and the beads strung around her arms clink together as she hugs my hips. She still fits so, so perfectly against me.

I deepen the kiss as my fingers stray to the small of her back. Though I would never admit it, I've been longing for this moment for a while now. For Nari to be mine again. We've been apart for two years and have had our time to reflect on the past. I realize now that Nari truly helped me. Teeto and I would still be at odds if she hadn't wormed her way into my life.

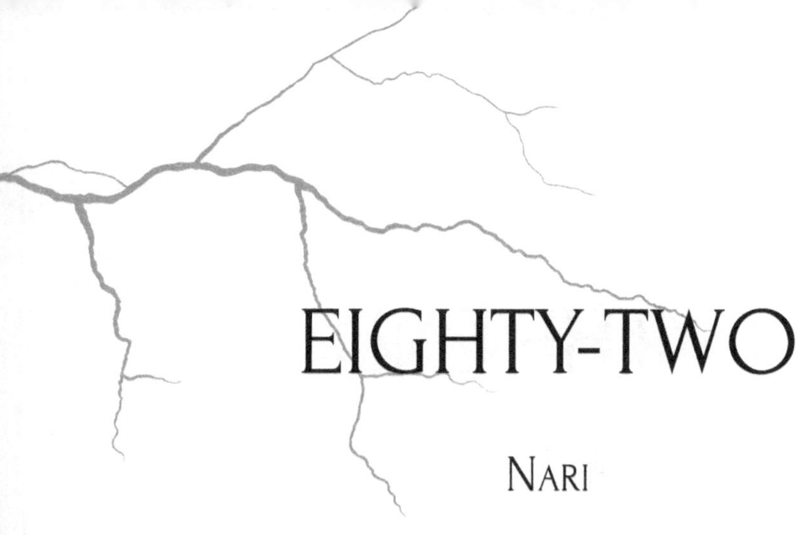

EIGHTY-TWO

NARI

TETSU PULLS BACK, TAKING my bottom lip between his teeth. But I don't want him so far quite yet so I grab his face and kiss him again. A chuckle rumbles from his chest through mine, deep and full of joy. I feel safe and secure in his arms and incredibly happy. There is nowhere else I want to be. I made the right choice.

When we break, I say, "I'm staying, Tetsu, staying forever."

He lifts a thumb to the scar on my cheek and then slips his hand into mine, tugging me after him. "I've got just the place then."

"And where's that? The Forsaken Sisters Guild?" I joke.

He shakes his head. "Somewhere better. Home."

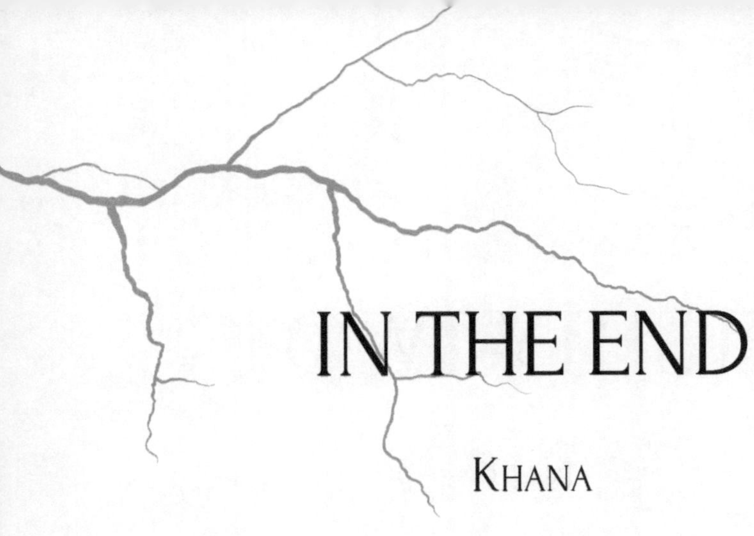

IN THE END

KHANA

A SMILE GRACED HER mouth as she watched Nari, Tetsu, and Yona live the lives they were meant to on Earth. They were happy, full of love and hope. The other humans seemed to get on well, establishing their new lives in a once fallen world.

She settled down in the grass of the meadow, letting the warm sun graze her back as she sighed. Young tods and vixens were playing before her, tumbling around with laughter. Their new realm, which she called Pax, was full of peace and light, a place where the dragons couldn't reach them and Khana felt like she had finally fulfilled her duty.

Her kith and kin were safe.

They were free.

They were home.

THE END

ABOUT THE AUTHOR

LOREN S. OLSEN HAS been writing intriguing young adult and new adult fiction since she was twelve years old. She enjoys writing fantasy, space operas, and urban fiction with lovable characters and unique stories. Loren graduated with a degree in English, and an emphasis in Creative Writing, from BYU-Idaho in 2023 and is excited to continue exploring her passion. She is an avid reader and spends her time "studying" other YA and NA books, scribbling a couple of lines in her current works, and drawing art of her characters. Tale of the Fox is her debut Young Adult novel.

Connect with Loren:
Instagram: @lsolsen.author
Website: lorensolsen.com